Praise for

This Eternal Darkness

"This book terrified me. It'll make a hell of a movie" –
Jeff Wilkes, Valley Daily News

*"Masterfully done – we enter the world of terror and
are trapped in its logic" – Paul Connors, free lance critic*

*"A master of the genre has arrived"- Steve Keller,
Contributing Editor*

Books by George Poncy
Published by Grey Knight Press

Strait of Hormuz

All-American Boy

Blackjack to Win:
A Layman's Guide to Beating the Game

This Eternal Darkness

THIS ETERNAL DARKNESS

By
George Poncy

"The cradle rocks above an abyss, and common sense tells us that our existence is but a brief crack of light between two eternities of darkness." – Vladimir Nabokov, 1947

"If there is a Hell, sir, surely the entrance is at 316 Primrose Lane. If you doubt me, go and see for yourself. It will not take but an evening." – Rev. Upton Black, 1907

ISBN-13# 978-0615555713 ISBN-10# 0615555713
Library of Congress Catalog # applied for

Grey Knight Press
mail@capitol-pictures.com

To George, Scotty, Jack
Johnny, Will and Tory
Grace
And Susan
Those brief cracks of light

Cover design by George Poncy with Bryce Adkins

Prologue

St. Augustine, Florida

Emily Wilkes looked at her watch, took off her glasses and rubbed her eyes. It was just after three o'clock. Outside the Proctor Library window, there were the usual afternoon clouds, but it didn't look like rain. She was supposed to meet Mary Ellen Whitten, fellow American History major in the Liberal Studies Department, at 3:30. The Student Tennis Center was just a short walk up Valencia Street. If Emily looked at the material for another fifteen minutes, she'd either have a raging headache or see two tennis balls. It wouldn't do to lose to Mary Ellen; she'd never hear the end of it.

Still, she didn't want to stop working just yet. Looking at the digital photos of the journal pages was easier than trying to read the actual text, and besides, she would have had to work under restrictive conditions at the nearby Mission of Nombre de Dios. This particular journal was well over four hundred years old and the original could only be viewed in semi-darkness and with cotton gloves. It was much easier reading pictures of the ancient documents in good light, where she could spread things out on the long library table.

Emily, a West Palm Beach native, had wanted to attend Flagler College in St. Augustine from the moment she'd set eyes on the campus three years ago. She found the college breathtakingly beautiful, a redolent flower of Florida history, gilded with Henry Flagler's fortune and care. Early Florida history was Emily's fascination, and she was in the perfect location in the state's oldest city. She hoped to do her paper on the early journeys of the priests and missionaries from the nearby mission.

Emily had read all the letters sent by Father Francisco Negron to his superiors at Mission of Nombre de Dios. They began in the spring of 1568 when the priest left the outpost and traveled down the east coast of the Florida peninsula; Emily had relived the fascinating journey through his writings. When Father Negron had been discovered near death, she'd pieced the story together with the aid of subsequent missives sent back to Spain by the mission. Emily had to submit a draft of an outreach to Professor Frank for project approval, and she'd chosen Father Negron's ill-fated trip. Her goal was to become a historical writer, and she'd won a few local prizes in high school for her stories and historical accounts. Her article on Seminole Indian settlements had even been printed in the Palm Beach Post.

She'd rewritten her composition several times. It needed to be turned in tomorrow. True, it was a bit dramatic, and of course she'd had to fill in dialogue, but Emily was confident she'd captured the essence of what had occurred almost four hundred and fifty years earlier.

She read her paper one last time:

*   *   *   *

In 1568, a Spanish Roman Catholic priest named Father Francisco Negron traveled south from the Mission of Nombre de Dios in St. Augustine, Florida to make contact with the Tequesta Indians and introduce them to Jesus Christ. The journey of two hundred and forty miles through pine scrub, palmetto and swamp was difficult and uncertain. There were encounters with snakes, alligators and wild boar. The afternoon rain showers shrouded the priest in steamy fog and mosquitoes. Progress was slow. He kept on.

After three weeks, he located the tribe in an area that would eventually become West Palm Beach. The Tequestas spoke the same language as the Calusas and the Mayaimas, and Father Negron was able to communicate. The young priest had a passion for his Christian outreach and, unlike many of his contemporaries, a sincere desire to respect the traditions and practices of the native people. He worked side by side with the Tequestas, harvesting palmetto, hunting panther, fishing the ocean and the Loxahatchee North Fork. He ate lobster, octopus, trunkfish, snails and the occasional sea turtle egg. A patient man, Father Negron did not overtly hawk Christianity. Over many months, his letters to the mission indicated a confidence that the priest was earning the trust and friendship of the tribe. Eventually his perseverance was rewarded.

It was still daylight in late July after a supper of turtle eggs and red snapper. Father Negron sat with the tribesmen around the fire, just outside the circle of stones in a clearing near the huts. The chief leaned over to the priest and fingered the cross around his neck.

"What is this?"

It was the moment Father Negron had been hoping for. Over the next several hours, he told the Tequestas the story of Jesus Christ. He described the Immaculate Conception, Jesus' life and his preaching. He explained about the trials of his Savior, the crucifixion and resurrection. The Tequestas were very interested in the death of Jesus and asked many questions. Father Negron was excited and encouraged. Later that evening, he wrote a detailed account of the event in his journal.

The next night, after a meal of hogfish and palmetto, the braves sipped tiswin from coconut shells as they sat around the stones. The fire had ebbed and insects began to drone beyond the clearing. Again, the chief touched the cross around the priest's neck. The sky had softened to twilight, with streaks of orange and blue to the west. More wood was placed on the embers.

"If this Jesus was a god, why did he allow himself to be nailed to the wood?" the chief asked. "What kind of a thing is this?"

Father Negron smiled, perhaps patronizingly. "He sacrificed himself for us."

"What does this mean? Sacrificed to whom?"

"To His Father, our Lord. Jesus carried away the sins of the world."

"You are father," the chief said. "Father Negron. Did he sacrifice to you?"

"No, no. I am only a priest, a servant of the Lord."

"And he came down from the wood?" .

Father Negron nodded. "Three days later he arose." It was going well, he thought. He believed he was getting through.

The chief looked on with skepticism. "And you have this Jesus as your friend?"

"He is my Savior."

"And would he save you?"

The missionary frowned. "I don't understand."

"Let us see if this magic is true or just a story."

Earlier, while Father Negron harvested the palmetto, the tribe had decided they might want to see a crucifixion. They also felt, as a true test of faith, the missionary should experience one firsthand. The chief made a gesture. Two braves came forth and grabbed Father Negron. Startled, he attempted to break free without success. Others appeared with the wood.

The priest was lashed to a cross barely twelve inches off the ground and directly above a giant red ant hill. A brave sliced him open with small cuts as he cried out. Father Negron hollered and sputtered as another poured sweat bee honey on his head. The dark golden liquid oozed down his body and into the cuts. A brave poked the anthill with a stick and immediately the ants began to swarm from the mound and up Father Negron.

"Priest!" the chief called out. "Come down from there and we will believe! We will wait three days!"

Laughter as the missionary struggled. The Tequesta Indians sat down in a semi-circle around the fire and waited for the priest to come down from the cross. They laughed and talked and drank large quantities of tiswin for several hours. Father Negron, through his agonized haze, thought he might have seen a strange figure around the stones, an ancient cleric in black vestment whose cataract-clouded eyes reflected the firelight: a specter surrounded by darkness. The hallucination faded along with his vision. Father Negron gradually ceased struggling and became silent. Later, he moved his head and moaned as a raccoon nibbled on his testicles.

The Indians looked at him in the flickering firelight. Blood was streaked down his legs. The chief decided Catholicism was not a working religion.

"Enough! The Jesus magic is untrue. This man was crazy."

As they got up to leave, one threw his coconut shell and hit Father Negron in the torso. Another followed with a stone. There was no reaction, except the raccoon scampered off. The black figure threw a cross, which landed upside down as it pierced the anthill.

Father Negron was found not quite dead a day later, eyeless and swollen with ant bites. The raccoon had returned.

The Tequestas remained unconverted.

*   *   *   *

Emily put the paper down, satisfied. Excited, really. She thought Professor Frank might challenge her on the bit about the dark figure around the fire, but she'd put it in anyway. It added an element of the unknown, heightened the drama. The thing was, other missionary journals – three, to be specific – had alluded to the same dark figure appearing from time to time, in strange and usually life-threatening situations. Emily felt justified including the eerie specter. What the hey, he could only tell her to take it out. She gathered the papers and stood up. She'd have to hurry not to be late for her tennis match.

Unbeknownst to Emily, her intuition had been remarkably accurate. Had she known the crucifixion of Father Negron occurred on the site where the altar of Westminster Congregational Church would be built some three hundred and thirty years later, at 316 Primrose Lane, her paper might have been different indeed.

1

Las Vegas, Nevada

They looked to be in their early twenties, dressed well enough to attend a good school, perhaps as graduate students, and they wore baseball caps, one red and one blue. The pair had been tracked from the moment they walked through the double doors of the Oasis Hotel and Casino and down the steps to the gaming floor. Behavior profiles, gathered and refined over decades of casino operation, were responsible for flagging the men as accomplices from the get go. The subjects hadn't realized surveillance extended to other areas of the hotel and out to Las Vegas Boulevard. After a conversation on the sidewalk, they had split up before entering the Oasis. One walked in almost a full minute before his partner, and so the cameras and security people tracked their progress. The special intel used by the Oasis was not shared with Griffin Investigations or with the other casinos in town. Unlike other hotels, staff turnover at the Oasis was very low – actually none – and so neither Griffin nor the other casino operations was aware of the system's existence, simply because there was no one to tell them.

The two players were clearly novices. They didn't realize the baseball caps worn low were red flags, an obvious attempt to thwart the cameras, nor did their plan take into account that a third base seat at the blackjack table was additional confirmation. Perhaps they had read about facial recognition software, which had thus far proven an illusory weapon for the gaming industry. Its main benefit had been deterrence. The software had not worked well in a casino setting and some hotels had quietly given up on it.

In the casino operations center, a trim forty seven year old gaming executive named Jack Richards sat in a leather swivel chair and watched Red Cap's play on a split screen monitor, one of a series mounted across the wall in front of him. The subject was at table BJ 22A, currently operating as a twenty five dollar minimum, six deck shoe game, and had bought in at the shuffle for three hundred dollars. Richards' partner, a heavyset man in his late thirties named Frank Rizzo, tracked Blue Cap as he wandered the casino floor, occasionally stopping to place a five dollar wager on a roulette wheel or craps table.

"What's Blue Cap doing?" Richards asked, eye on Red Cap as he bet a single quarter check.

"He's at roulette 3. Minimum bettor."

Richards, who could count cards as well as any of the patrons, continued to watch Red Cap as the decks played out towards the cut card. A slew of small cards came out on a particular hand. Red Cap took off his hat and placed it in his lap. Richards had to laugh.

"You think these assholes could be more obvious?" He leaned over and looked at the monitor Rizzo was watching. Blue Cap was peering over at blackjack table 22A. He collected on his small roulette wager and walked straight to the table, where he took a seat as far from Red Cap as possible. Red Cap scratched his head and put his hat back on. As he did so, Richards dialed the floor man, standing at the podium in the middle of the blackjack "A" tables.

"Carmine," came the voice.

"Carmine, this is Jack Richards. Twenty two A, red and blue hats."

"I'm on it."

Frank Rizzo moved over and watched the monitor over Richards' shoulder. Richards fiddled with the toggles and trained five cameras on 22A, getting shots from above, to the rear, the sides and head on. It was hard to tell with the baseball caps, but as expected it didn't appear the two subjects acknowledged each other's presence. Blue Cap bought in for two thousand dollars. The security men watched the monitors for the invariable tell that would inform Blue Cap the condition of the decks. Sure enough, Red Cap rearranged his checks. With a quarter check and two reds stacked to his right, he was signaling Blue Cap as to the count, which Jack Richards knew was plus seven. It was a simple system, and almost childlike to the men in the security station, but the two students apparently thought they were a sophisticated and undetectable team.

The game resumed. Sure enough, Red Cap continued to bet the table minimum while Blue Cap put up a three hundred dollar wager. The high cards came out as anticipated by the math. Blue Cap stood with a pair of kings as did Red Cap with a ten and a nine. The dealer, whose up card was a seven, turned over his hole card to reveal a nine. He drew a queen and busted.

Richards let the game continue until the shuffle. Blue Cap was up twelve hundred dollars over that short period. As expected, he stood up and gathered his checks while Red Cap remained and waited for the next shoe. Blue Cap was steps from the roulette wheel when he was intercepted by two uniformed, armed Oasis security guards. At almost the same instant Red Cap was startled by a tap on his shoulder and turned to face another pair of officers.

2

Bernie Goldman, Ph.D. candidate in Religious Studies at Arizona State University in Tempe (Blue Cap), tried the authoritative tack as the two guards whisked him down a corridor leading from the Oasis gaming area. They passed through a door and down a narrow hallway. Beyond the casino, plush carpet and flocked wallpaper gave way to linoleum tile and cinder block. A definite mood breaker, Bernie thought.

"What are you doing? I know my rights! Take your hands off me!"

The words had no effect. Bernie was aware how ridiculous he sounded. The confidence and bravado he and his partner, fellow Arizona State University grad student Wesley James (Clinical Psychology, Red Cap) had felt before flinging themselves across the state line to Nevada was rapidly evaporating. They'd practiced counting cards an entire semester, both in the library and an unused office in Payne Education Hall. They had read the experts: Professor Thorp, Lawrence Revere, The Grey Knight. Bernie subscribed to all the important blackjack newsletters. They studied Stanford Wong, believing he was really an Oriental, and thought they were going to be successful. The pair had accumulated a five thousand dollar nest egg for their grand assault on the gaming establishment, including twelve hundred dollars from fellow students. It had all seemed so perfect, so intelligent, so exciting, except they had the bad luck to choose the wrong casino in which to begin their quest.

The guards held his forearms firmly. The feeling of being in custody was new to Bernie and it rattled him. He was taken to a small room with bare block walls and a pair of metal folding chairs around a scarred, wooden table. The floor was industrial tile, marred with rubber marks and scratches. A large mirror took up most of the left wall. An overhead florescent fixture with an annoying buzz was the only other object present. The room looked like one of those little cubicles seen on black and white cop interrogation videos. Bernie realized with a slight shock it was indeed an interrogation room. The two guards, who hadn't spoken a word, took his blue baseball cap and lifted his wallet from his back pocket.

"Hey—!!"

He was shoved into a folding chair. The guard flipped through his wallet and took out the driver's license, then dropped the billfold on the table. He hadn't touched the money or credit cards. The two abruptly left with Bernie's baseball cap and his license. He heard the click of the lock and footsteps that faded away.

The room was freezing. Frigid air poured on him like ice water from the ceiling vent directly overhead. He stood up and tried the door, which of course did not open. He moved to the other chair but that was just as cold. He could almost see his breath. Bernie began to think his fingers would stick to the metal if he touched the chair. The buzz from the florescent fixture was incredibly loud and, he noticed, the light had an annoying flicker.

Without his baseball cap, Bernie reached into his pocket and withdrew a folded yarmulke and placed it on his head. He sat for maybe ten minutes, cooling his heels. Actually, he thought, freezing his heels. Hey, they hadn't taken his winnings. They weren't allowed to do that, he was pretty sure. He fingered the checks in his pocket as he looked around. He had read about these rooms – cells, really – and knew that they couldn't actually do anything except hassle him and let him go. Still, the sound of the lock turning was unsettling. It was one thing to read about these places, and quite another to be in one. He was being *detained*. Anyway, he was pretty sure they were going to kick him out after maybe threatening to rough him up. The mirror was obviously one-way glass. Bernie figured he would be under observation for the interrogation, if they weren't watching him already. He used the time to gather his thoughts and regain his confidence, although it wasn't working very well. The only thoughts he could manage were to wonder why it was freezing and where his partner was. Had Wesley gotten away, or had he been whisked to another room or what? Were they even aware he had a partner? Probably not, he realized. So why was he in here? He reassured himself they had to let him go but somehow all the stories about shallow desert graves and broken fingers or worse crept into his brain. He would have quite a story for his classmates when he returned to ASU. He hoped.

There were other sounds that penetrated the room, strange and unnerving sounds. Once or twice he was startled by a loud, deep boom as though a heavy object had been dropped down the hall somewhere, and there was a persistent sound of groaning metal. Underneath that, he detected something that sounded like a shovel trailing on cobblestones. Were they trying to creep him out? If so, they—

The door opened and Jack Richards came in. He sat down opposite Bernie Goldman.

"What's this all about?" Bernie said. Richards said nothing for a time, then looked up at the mirror. Bernie followed his eyes. Who was watching?

"Take that stupid hat off," Richards said.

Bernie Goldman was agog. He couldn't have heard right.

"What?"

"That goddamn skull cap. Off."

"I won't!"

Richards shrugged with a trace of a smile. "It'll go worse for you."

What?

"What are you talking about?"

"Your partner. He's not a Jew, is he?"

Bernie Goldman was again dumbfounded. He couldn't be hearing right. He realized, then, he'd better get past the disbelief part because this all could go very badly.

"What partner?"

Jack Richards took a deep breath. He turned to the mirror, smiled and slowly shook his head. He stood up.

"It's your funeral."

And then, without another word, he left the room.

3

In the small back room of the Oasis casino, Bernie Goldman trembled uncontrollably. He couldn't believe the debilitating cold. He looked at his Rolex replica. He'd been alone in the tiny cell for fifteen minutes after that strange - what? interrogation? That crap about his yarmulke? – but it seemed like two hours. He had gotten up and walked around the tiny cubicle, rubbing his arms and chest briskly. The arctic air from the vent blew directly down on him at gale force, no matter where he stood. The light flickered more than ever and the buzz from the defective fixture was nerve-wracking. They must be doing that on purpose, he thought.

Before today, Bernie had always thought *Goodfellas* was a great movie. Someone had put that guy Frankie Carbone in a frozen food truck, he remembered, and the hoodlum froze solid hanging on a meat hook. Bernie was beginning to identify with the poor bastard. He decided to exercise. That should warm him up and distract him from the situation. He had just gotten down on the floor for some push-ups when the door lock turned and the two guards came in.

They looked down on him as though he were crazy.

"Come with us, please," said the guard who had removed his wallet.

Bernie was about to protest again when he thought the better of it. 'Please' somehow made the request more ominous. At least they would be taking him someplace warmer, unless they really were going to put him in a meat locker. The grad student shivered as he left the room.

The men kept their hands on his arms as the trio proceeded down the hall. They walked down a carpeted hallway, past people working in offices who didn't look up. The guards stopped in front of a pair of mahogany doors – the décor had improved as they traveled – and opened one. They gestured Bernie through and closed the door behind him.

Bernie Goldman found himself in a small conference room, paneled and wainscoted, with light blue carpeting. A single painting graced one wall, perhaps too small for the space. It was a strange scene. A river ran through a bleak landscape; the whole thing was tinted towards the red spectrum. There was a smudge in the river that might have been a boatman standing in a craft; there was something in his hand. A pole, maybe, or maybe there wasn't a boatman in a boat at all. It was a jarring sight in an otherwise pleasant room and gave Bernie the creeps. There was a pitcher of water on a large table and glasses alongside. The glasses looked like crystal and the table might be pecan, Bernie judged. The young Ph.D. candidate wandered the room, found nothing special, and sat. The temperature was comfortable. Now that his physical surroundings had improved, he was beginning to get impatient as he thawed out. Perhaps his card counting system was so sophisticated they wanted to talk to him about it. Maybe they were going to apologize. And who was that jerk and where did he get off threatening him? He—

The door opened to a strange sight. An ancient – what, priest? – in black cassock stood in the doorway. His eyes were clouded with cataracts. What was an old priest doing in the back rooms of a casino, Bernie wondered? Could the guy even see him?

"Are you the one that wanted Communion?" he asked.

Bernie realized his mouth was hanging open. "Uh, no, that's not me."

The priest seemed to peer at the grad student. "You sure?" Evidently he couldn't see Bernie's yarmulke.

"Aah— yes. I'm positive."

"Wouldn't hurt, you know. You could be wrong." He waved towards Bernie's covered head.

What?! For the second time that afternoon, Bernie was agog.

"Anyway, I'm sure you're not in a state of grace," the priest said. "I can tell by looking at you, kind of. Got a toothbrush?" He opened his mouth wide and removed his dentures. He held them up close to his left eye, the one with the smaller cataract. A strand of drool extended, oozed to the floor.

"What about a toothpick? Dental floss?"

Bernie was immobile, jaw slack. The priest shoved his teeth back in, worked his jaw.

Then he turned and left.

Bernie sat for a few minutes, trying to make sense out of his latest visitor. Trying to makes sense out of anything that had happened so far, actually. He'd fallen down the rabbit hole, that was for sure. It suddenly became warm, dank. What the hell? Bernie found, incredibly, he was getting sleepy. He leaned back in the chair and was just closing his eyes when—

- the door opened again. Bernie looked up and saw a man of modest height and slender build, perhaps fifty years old. From midnight tuxedo to pure white shirt, jet black hair to the dusting at the temples, he was a study in black and white. Even his pupils seemed black, and the whites shone as if illuminated from inside. Bernie Goldman felt something when he looked at the man, a feeling he couldn't place. It wasn't a thing that put him at ease. The tuxedo was immaculate, not a wrinkle, not a crease; it fit him perfectly.

Suddenly the man was in the room, standing on the other side of the table. Had he blurred for an instant? Bernie blinked. He was no longer sleepy. There was an energy, a tension in the room.

Bernard Goldman had come face to face with John Roselli, the owner of the Oasis Hotel and Casino.

4

John Roselli looked down at Bernie with a penetrating gaze. He spoke as he poured himself a glass of water.

"Do Jews go to Heaven?"

What!?

"What!?"

"Do you believe Jews go to Heaven? You are about to graduate with a Ph.D. in Religious Affairs. It's a simple question."

Bernie Goldman was staggered. How could this man know about him?

He managed a question. "What – what are you talking about?"

Roselli's expression was as if talking to an annoying four year old.

"Answer the question," he commanded.

The man's shirt was as snow, Bernie thought, almost glowing. He realized the entire experience was beyond any realm of understanding, any frame of reference he had ever had.

Roselli sat opposite. As he moved, Bernie thought of rustling silk.

"I – I don't know what most Jews believe."

"Of course you do," Roselli said as he sipped his water, "although that wasn't the question. Pay attention. Christians cite things like John 1:10-12. You studied the Christian Bible."

"I studied a lot of religious books."

"Even the Bible allows Jews to go to Heaven. Revelation 20. The so-called second Resurrection. Do you understand what I am talking about?"

"Yeah, sure. I know what it says. It doesn't specifically say Jews, though."

"Of course it doesn't. It's an obvious inference. Follow along here." Roselli shook his head slightly, as if he expected more. He continued.

"Revelation is a fanciful group of fables, is it not? Do you take it seriously?"

"Me personally?"

"You and your fellow doctoral candidates."

"You mean compared to other parts of the Bible?"

"Do you take it seriously?"

"Well, if one assumes the Bible is not necessarily divinely inspired, then there's a case for some of the other books being more believable."

"Of course. What are you, some kind of campus politician? Just say no if you mean no. It saves time, and you may not have that much."

"What does that mean?" Bernie asked, his voice rising.

"You're lucky I have a fondness for the Jews, ridiculous as they are."

Bernie's voice rose further. "What does *that* mean?"

"So easily corrupted." Roselli sipped his water. "Revelation. The book is crazy. Still, the mealy-mouthed stuff about a second Judgment gets you off the hook, biblically, doesn't it?"

Bernie looked at the casino owner. "Who are you? Why are we talking about this stuff?"

Roselli waved the questions away impatiently. "This is more important than you think, and you don't seem to think very much anyway, so save your questions. I'm going back to the Old Testament now. Exodus and Deuteronomy refer to the Jews as the Chosen People. If Jews don't believe in Heaven, what were they chosen for? The Holocaust? What is the thinking there? Do you consider these things in your studies?"

"Wait a minute. I didn't say Jews don't believe in Heaven."

"You disappoint me, Mister Goldman. I thought we could have a meaningful discussion, an exchange of ideas. I don't often have the opportunity. Lots of yes men, know what I mean?"

He didn't stop to see if Bernie knew what he meant.

"Christians wrestle with the Bible because it's equivocal on too many issues they deem important. Attaining salvation, predestination, the very different personalities of their God between the two Testaments. It really doesn't hold water very well. You know, there is not a single shred of historical evidence, no trace whatever, of the supposed migration, the events of Exodus."

"That doesn't mean they didn't happen."

Roselli cocked his head, amused. "It's important to the Jews that it did happen, of course. Well, it did happen. Not like the romanticized book version, but it was a factual event. I can vouch for that."

"You can – vouch for that?"

"Of course. Back to Revelation 20. The Millennium." Roselli leaned forward, his gaze penetrating. "It says an angel with a key will lock Satan in the Abyss for a thousand years. The Dark Angel will emerge after that time and gather his armies for a great battle. Gog and Magog. A battle that will be lost and the Serpent cast into a lake of sulfur for everlasting torment. I'm paraphrasing now. Have you studied that?"

On the edge of his vision, it was as though something moved in the painting. Bernie Goldman looked across the table for a long time before answering. He was wrestling with an impossible possibility. He measured his words.

"Yes, in a historical context."

"What does that mean?"

"We did not seriously consider the possibility that much of Revelation could be accurate."

John Roselli leaned back. He seemed to be satisfied with this part of the discussion, Bernie thought.

"Yes. Not necessarily accurate. Even if some of the other parts are accurate," Roselli said. He looked at Bernie's head. "You know, even your own stupid *Shulchan Aruch* says you don't have to wear that yarmulke until you walk four cubits."

"That was superseded by the *Mishna Brurah*."

Roselli smiled. "Yes, but not now, not here. You're not eating, or at prayer, or engaged in a ritual act, or in a synagogue – that's for sure - , or studying something sacred. Well, maybe that, sort of. Are you going bald?"

"Bald? No, I'm not going bald."

"Jews go bald. I bet you're going bald."

Bernie yanked off his yarmulke. "See?!"

"So look what just happened. You violated your precious *Mishna Brurah*, even though you really didn't, just for vanity's sake."

Bernie put his yarmulke back on. He spoke slowly. "And what did that prove?"

John Roselli rolled his eyes. Bernie realized with a start that something seemed to be moving behind the pupils.

"It proves exactly what I just said. And they're going to let you graduate? Anyway, what nonsense it all is, don't you agree?"

"What do you mean?"

"Try to keep up. The nonsense with the head covering. Your God made you; you think the top of your head is an embarrassment to him?"

"It's a sign of respect."

"Does he need the adoration? Why do you do it?"

"Tradition has its value."

"And you took it off at the drop of a hat, as it were." He smiled at his own joke. "How easily the Jews are corrupted. I told you I had a fondness for them. I regret this was on a childlike level. I expected more. As I said, I was hoping for a meaningful discussion. Still, you answered the important question."

John Roselli stood. He walked to the door and opened it.
The two guards were standing outside.

"Take Mister Goldman here and see him out. We are
through."

"Wait a minute," Bernie said. "What important question?"

"How could your people be smart in some things and you so
dumb? The Millennium question, of course." He started to leave.

"Wait! Where's –" He was hesitant to name his friend.
"Where's my friend?"

"Goodbye, Mister Goldman." He turned away.

"Why do you have a fondness for the Jews?" Bernie called
out.

John Roselli turned around, the trace of a smile on his face.
"Because you killed Christ, why do you think? And because you
followed each other, one by one, into the changing rooms and the
showers. Even though you really knew. The insanity of faith over
reality. Remarkable.'

'Mister James is out front. He's feeling a bit run down."

5

Without a word, the guards escorted Bernie Goldman through a maze of corridors to a small, steel door. He was allowed to walk freely. One of the uniforms opened the door and gestured Bernie through as the other guard handed him his driver's license. He found himself on a side street, an alley really, alongside the Oasis. The door closed behind him. Bernie suddenly realized he didn't have his baseball cap. He reached out to grab the door handle, but thought the better of it. He had no desire to go back inside the Oasis, especially not for a seven dollar hat.

And there was no handle, anyway.

A chain link fence lined the other side of the narrow roadway, and beyond was the casino and parking lot next door. Las Vegas Boulevard was to his left, perhaps a hundred yards away. He could hear the traffic and the area at the end of the alley was bright. Twilight was approaching and the strip lights had come on.

He took a deep breath in the fresh air, inhaling freedom for the first time in hours. It was exhilarating. He had quite a story for Wesley, quite a tale. He wondered if his partner had been put to the test as rigorously as he had. As Bernie walked toward Las Vegas Boulevard and his rendezvous with his fellow grad student, he could already anticipate the pair of them telling their stories to the other doctoral candidates over rounds of drinks and dinner at Monti's, back in Tempe – high adventure, danger, derring-do – he'd stood up well under rigorous interrogation. He was out of the Oasis, wasn't he? Safe and sound, minus only his baseball cap, and without giving any money back. He was already likening the experience to Abu Ghraib, Guantanamo, Lubyanka. The more he thought about it, the more he figured he had probably talked his way out of being waterboarded.

Bernie was halfway to the street when he realized two things: first, he had twelve hundred dollars worth of Oasis checks in his pocket, and not cash. The knowledge that he had to go back inside to the cashier's cage chilled him. Secondly, the lights on Las Vegas Boulevard were flashing red. Something in Bernie Goldman's stomach urged him to walk faster; by the time he got to the street he was trotting. Directly in front of the Oasis driveway he saw an ambulance, a double decker bus, and two cop cars, wig wags flashing. He rushed forward. A yellow tarpaulin covered a still shape in the street.

For a reason he did not understand, he felt nauseous.

"What happened?" he asked a bystander, a middle-aged woman in a green pants suit.

"The Deuce hit a guy," she said. The woman saw Bernie's uncomprehending expression. "The Deuce. It's the double decker bus there. Runs up and down the strip. Young man ran out right in front of it. I saw the whole thing. He looked like he'd seen a ghost and was looking back toward the casino. Never saw the traffic. It was terrible."

Something caught Bernie's eye, something in the street perhaps ten feet from the body.

A red cap.

He's feeling a bit run down.

6

West Palm Beach, Florida

Reverend James Warren, pastor of Palm Beach Presbyterian Church at 316 Primrose Lane, sat in his small office in the back of the sanctuary listening to the steady drumming on the window. He swiveled in his chair and looked through a veil of grey rain at the new sanctuary, under construction behind the old church. A pair of workers carried a long stack of lumber inside, apparitions in the mist. It was an interesting picture, and maybe one he could work into Sunday's sermon if he could figure out a meaning for it. Stations of the Cross? That wouldn't do for Presbyterians. Maybe back at the Oasis – he cleared his thoughts.

The project was behind schedule, he thought, with all the rain they'd been having. His eyes strayed to the photo on the old credenza next to the window. An eight year old James Warren stood between his parents, one leg in the air. The shot was too far away to make out their features, except he could tell they were all smiling. He had on his Speedo bathing suit, orange with blue piping. The picture was faded now. Behind them was the giant slide at the water park in Phoenix. It had been his birthday, and about the last happy event he could recall. He wondered what had happened to the Speedo.

He had no memory of the accident. He'd been asleep in the back seat, still grasping the Transformers he'd traded classmate Scott Bergman for after P.E. class. He'd given up Flamefeather and Quake – not a particularly good deal – but James had tired of the same characters and really wanted Getaway, so they'd made the swap. The unsuspecting Needlenose had clambered over the seat divider and been ambushed by Getaway, lurking on the other side. After a fierce one-sided battle, Needlenose had been vanquished, and James nodded off. When he awoke, he was not inside the family Chevrolet anymore, which had been a creamy beige leatherette, beige and dark tan, a fine desert for the Transformer war, but in a white place, a hospital room back in Phoenix. Things were attached to him and the action figures were gone. So were his parents.

Although he was nine years old when the family Chevy careened off the Black Canyon Freeway and down the arroyo, he found as an adult the recollections of his mother and father were dim, jumbled, unclear. Childhood memories seemed pleasant enough, but rather than warm and comforting they were somehow not personal, like watching an old movie. When he tried to concentrate on his parents' features, the film was scratched, grainy, or too far away like the picture on his credenza. Warren had only an impression of his mother's smile and the sway of her auburn hair. His father was a pair of aviator glasses and the smell of Avon Legacy aftershave. He felt oddly a spectator to his own early years.

He remembered the morning of the accident, though, when his mother had startled his father by saying "Good morning, Reverend" as she served the two of them pancakes and bacon. The new seminary graduate had grinned and winked at James as she planted a kiss on his forehead. Afterward, they piled into the Chevy for the ride to Sedona, two and a half hours north of Phoenix, where Philip Warren was to be officially ordained a Presbyterian minister in the breathtaking Chapel of the Holy Cross. The ride ended in twenty five minutes.

The dreams had started months later, in the Oasis Home for Boys. As time passed, the nighttime images became clearer as the reality of his early years became less so. Somehow in the recurring dream he was not young James Warren in the back seat, orchestrating great Transformer military campaigns, but rather his father Philip. It was weird. It was beyond weird, because sometimes in the dream he thought of his mother and she wasn't his mother at all, but rather his wife. When that happened, he willed himself awake with desperate effort. He became terrified that one day he would not be able to do so. Warren was not a psychologist, and his knowledge of Freudian concepts vague, but he feared that possibility greatly. There was no way to tell if what he dreamed bore any relation to what had actually happened that morning, and there was no reason to think it did, really, but then why was it the same each time?

Something was on the highway ahead, black wings flapping, likely a raptor feasting on road stew but too big for a raven or crow. A turkey vulture, perhaps, with a six foot wingspan, although it was hard to tell as the Chevy closed at seventy miles per hour. Here, the Black Canyon Freeway sliced the desert straight to the horizon, north to the red rock country. In the featureless terrain distance was difficult to judge.

The car was on cruise control, heading for Sedona and the weekend ordination ceremonies. Philip/James Warren was a careful driver, especially with his family in the car, and so he eased the Chevrolet to the right lane and raised his foot above the brake pedal as a precaution. Any second now, the thing would beat itself into the air, its meal interrupted, but suddenly Philip/James gasped as he realized it was not a bird at all, but, he saw with disbelief, a *person* bent over the bird, a person all in black, and he caught a glimpse of white at the collar, and the flapping wings that were really the arms in a black surplice, loose, over the black cassock so that was why they seemed like beating wings, except that the vulture was struggling and flapping underneath, and what was this *thing* in the road that looked up with red running from its mouth, looking straight at him as the Warren family hurtled down upon it?

Philip/James Warren realized with another shock that he had waited too long, frozen in disbelief, and that the apparition had launched itself up and into the right lane, directly towards him with arms outstretched, and the only way to avoid hitting it was to turn the wheel hard, hard onto the shoulder. In his haste he turned too far too fast and he felt the car going, and it was going, and now it was turning over and tumbling and the last thing Philip/James Warren saw as he careened past the black figure and down the embankment was the old priest, his face a blur, slashed with red. Each time, it seemed, he saw the visage a bit more clearly, and James didn't know if he wanted to look or if he wanted to look away, afraid he would recognize it with a terrible knowledge, or worse, see that it was himself.

7

Twenty three year old Las Vegas Metropolitan Police Officer Wade Cahill had been assigned to Traffic Bureau, South Sector Area Command for five weeks. His partner, Ted Hostetler, was looking through the other end of the telescope. He'd been LAPD for most of his working life, moved to Nevada four years ago and would retire in two more. He'd seen just about all there was to see in Los Angeles, the rest in Glitter Gulch, and thought Las Vegas Metro was a good way to wind down into retirement.

Hostetler considered the rookie a gigantic pain in the ass.

This was a good example. They were covering Sector M2 and this guy had run out into the street in front of the Oasis and been hit by a bus. Period, end of story. What did Cahill want to do, measure skid marks? The Deuce had been plodding along like it always did and the passenger interviews all verified that it hadn't been speeding. The driver had not had a chance to stop.

"Yeah, but why did the guy run out like that?" Cahill asked his partner, who wanted to get on with things. They had interviewed three or four pedestrian witnesses and, Hostetler figured, if the newbie had his way he'd take statements from everyone within two blocks of the accident.

"Come on, Cahill, we've got all we need."

"They said the guy looked terrified."

"Wouldn't you look terrified if you were about to get flattened by a double decker bus?"

"I mean before that. He was looking back toward the Oasis, like somebody was chasing him. They were very definite on that."

"I heard 'em. Then how come nobody saw anybody coming after him?"

"I don't know, but how else could you miss a double decker bus? They all said he looked like he'd seen a ghost. He wanted away from there so fast he didn't think to look."

"So what?" Hostetler asked, shaking his head. "We don't have dick. Maybe he had an argument with a patron. Maybe he stole some chips. Who the hell knows?"

"Officers?"

Cahill turned and saw a middle-aged woman in a frog colored pants suit.

"Ma'am?"

She pointed to a young man, nicely dressed, sitting on the curb. "That guy? I think he might have known the dead person."

"What makes you say that?" Cahill asked.

"Well, I'm not sure but he came up to me about two minutes ago and asked what happened, and then he looked in the street and got real upset. He came out of the alley there. Then he just went over there and sat on the curb."

The young man on the curb did look upset. He held his lowered head in his hands.

"Wait a minute," Hostetler said. "He saw the victim before the body was covered?"

"Well, that's the thing. No, he didn't."

"All right, thanks, ma'am. We'll check it out."

One of the EMTs beckoned to Hostetler, who headed towards the ambulance. As Cahill walked over to the curb, the young man looked up.

"How long is he going to lay there?" It had grown dark. Somehow, the shape in the street looked smaller.

"Probably another half hour," Cahill told him. "There's a procedure to all this, when there's a traffic fatality. I know it looks terrible, but it's necessary."

The young man nodded, said nothing. He put his head back down. Cahill realized the woman might be right. Behind, officers from another unit rerouted pedestrian traffic, kept it moving. A small knot had gathered across the street.

"How did you know him?" Cahill ventured. The man didn't seem surprised at the question.

"I think it's my friend."

It, not he, Cahill noticed. Death created immediate distance.

"What makes you think that? Did you see what happened?"

"No, but I think that's his baseball hat."

He nodded towards the red hat, still in the street. "We were in the casino for awhile and I didn't see him and when I came out he was in the street."

Cahill had been on the scene for twenty minutes before the woman said the guy came out of the alley. Wade's fledgling cop mind began working. What had taken him so long? Why had they split up? Had there been an argument? And why had he been in the alley? That wasn't a regular casino exit, he was pretty sure. His friend, if that's who it was, had fled the front doors.

"Why did you two split up? Was there an argument?"

The man on the curb registered surprise. It seemed genuine. "No, no, nothing like that. We just played different stuff."

Cahill nodded. "Feel up to taking a look at the body for identification?"

The young man looked up quickly. "Didn't he have his wallet?"

"It's just procedure."

The young man swallowed hard as he stood up. "I guess. If I have to. Is he— was he—"

"It's not pretty."

Cahill's remark was an understatement. Wesley James would require a closed coffin. The front left tire had run over his head, flattening it quite a lot and leaving tire tracks across the left side of his face. The right eye had come partway out of its socket and the right ear torn almost completely off. Cahill lifted the sheet and snapped on his flashlight. Bernie Goldman nodded his head, then ran for the curb and retched noisily. After a time, he gave Cahill his full name, home address and room number at the Flamingo, head between his knees.

"Are you going to call Wesley's parents?" Bernie asked as he looked up. His forehead was slick with sweat, even in the low humidity, his face the color of dough.

"Someone will."

Bernie sighed as he wiped his brow with a handkerchief. "I think I should do it. I met them once. I need to do it."

"Someone will call anyway."

"Let me call first. It's the least I can do."

8

"When was this?" Davey Cahill asked his nephew. They were sitting in a coffee shop just off Russell and Las Vegas Boulevard South, a few hundred yards from South Central Command Headquarters.

"Couple hours ago," Wade Cahill replied. "I just thought something seemed hinky about it."

The young officer, still in uniform, had finished work fifteen minutes earlier. He probably wouldn't have gone out of his way to mention the strange accident except that his uncle had called and asked if they could meet for coffee after his shift.

Wade, born and raised in nearby Henderson, had wanted to be a cop since grade school, when Uncle Davey had let him ride in a black and white one Saturday morning. Davey Cahill was now a Las Vegas homicide detective and it had been only natural that his nephew had applied to Metro. Wade loved every minute of his work and would take the Sergeant's exam as soon as he qualified.

"Where's the guy staying – what's his name?"

"Bernard Goldman. He's at the Flamingo. I got the room number written down. He said he'd stay in town until the victim's parents came in to take the body back."

"And you asked him why he was in the alley?"

"He said he came out that way from the casino. I walked down the alley, though, because I didn't think there's an exit there." He didn't mention that Hostetler about blew a head gasket when he walked all the way down to the end of the building. "I didn't see any, just a side door. A utility door, not an exit. I know you guys are responsible for suspicious deaths so, maybe it's worth checking out."

"That's good police work, Wade."

The waitress arrived with a cupcake. There was a lit candle stuck in it.

"Happy birthday," she said, putting it down in front of the patrolman.

"It's not until Saturday," Wade said with a smile. "Thanks, Uncle Davey."

"Hey, kid, I don't know if I'll be able to see you this weekend, so I figured I'd catch you tonight."

Davey handed his nephew a package, obviously wrapped by the detective.

"Should I wait til Saturday?"

"Hell no, open it now."

Inside was a laser sight for Wade's AR-15 semi-automatic rifle. The perfect gift, they both thought.

*   *   *   *   *

*

Davey Cahill hadn't mentioned anything, but the traffic accident his nephew described set off an alarm bell. He'd investigated three deaths in the past seventeen months that had some ties to the Oasis Hotel and Casino.

It was a puzzling affair. Cahill had used his friend, Special Agent Tim Moss, as a sounding board during their weekly seven a.m. breakfast meetings. The two were the same age, at the same point in their law enforcement careers, and had met four years earlier when Moss was transferred to the Las Vegas FBI field office and Cahill was going through his divorce. Unlike some relationships between locals and the feds, they'd hit it off right away, often sharing information, theories, hunches. The detective had been grateful for a friend during that difficult time.

Lately, they'd been grazing at the Excalibur buffet. It was cheap enough and the food a notch above the usual cop franchise joints.

"How many deceased?" Moss had asked, shoveling in a mouthful of scrambled eggs, stained red from hot sauce. The guy had a stomach made from a steam boiler, Cahill thought.

"Three. All from out of town."

"Everybody's from out of town. How recent?"

"The last one was four weeks ago."

"But they weren't homicides, you're saying."

"I'm wondering. Look, all three had gambled in the Oasis within hours of their deaths."

"Were they hotel guests?"

Cahill shook his head. Moss was skeptical. "Well then, so what? That's not much."

"Yeah, maybe. I looked at the surveillance videos. Two of them were eighty sixed by hotel security for counting cards. The same day."

"Yeah? That is mildly interesting. What about the third one?"

"No record. I interviewed the guards and a casino executive, Jack Richards."

"Richards? I know that guy, he's the floor manager. Did they seem guarded? Cooperative?"

"Cooperative but unhelpful."

"That's a lot of work, Davey. You need to get a life. I can't believe you're still not screwing that dance instructor. What happened to her, anyway?"

The FBI agent always wanted to know who he was dating and all the details. The detective never gave any, but Moss was undeterred. Cahill ignored his friend.

"The first was a computer engineer named William Baldanian, twenty six, from San Francisco. Sixteen months ago, takes a header off the I-15 overpass at Flamingo. Ruled a suicide."

"Oh, yeah, I remember. Dumb bastard crashed through a taxi windshield. Lucky nobody else got killed." Moss mused about the Las Vegas cabbies. "I wonder how come they're all from Eritrea now? How the hell'd they get here?"

"Some are from Ethiopia. I don't know why."

"You don't know why the guy took the swan dive or you don't know why the cabbies are from Eritrea?"

Cahill ignored Moss again. "Anyway, eight months later, a medical saleswoman, a Janet Mills from Helena, Montana, age thirty two, she chokes on an artichoke heart in her room at Harrah's. A goddamn artichoke heart. Third guy, six weeks ago. Cal Tech student named Henry Wiggins changing a tire on I-15. Jack falls. Wheel lands on his chest, asphyxiates the guy."

"Jesus Christ. I didn't hear about that one."

"Coroner said he suffocated, stuck under the car. Must have taken a minute or so. It was dark, nobody saw the kid. Terrible, isn't it?"

"Yeah, that sucks. But I don't see the big red flag here, except they all died under bizarre circumstances. Coincidence, more likely."

Maybe, Cahill thought. But these had been three smart people, probably capable of counting cards and arousing the defensive systems of the hotel. Had the place escalated to a permanent solution? It sounded preposterous.

"Anyway, I don't know where to go from here. I tried looking back further, but there's no real way to correlate the data."

"Yeah, I guess," said Moss. "What was that broad's name again? The dancer?"

9

Cahill turned up East Flamingo and pulled up by the tall palms directly in front of the Flamingo entrance. The hotel, originally built by Bugsy Siegel and named after his girlfriend in 1946, was right on Las Vegas Boulevard with practically no setback. Parking was difficult. He turned down the visor, identifying the car as a police vehicle, and went inside.

Within the first five minutes Detective Cahill knew the young doctoral student was being evasive.

"How long had you known Mister James?" Bernie sat on the bed in his hotel room while Cahill sat in the chair by the writing table. The shiny plastic headboard looked like a mattress on its side, and went up to the ceiling. Davey Cahill couldn't imagine who'd designed it, unless it was Bugsy himself.

"About a year," Bernie had replied. "We're in − were in different doctoral programs at ASU."

"I understand. You drove into town this morning?"

"Right." The young man shook his head slowly. "God, seems like a week ago now. It's about three hundred miles, so we split the drive. Stayed overnight maybe halfway and got into Vegas a little before noon. Checked in here as soon as they could get us in, maybe one o'clock."

"Where'd you stay last night?"

"Kingman. Some place in Kingman. Best Western, off forty."

"Come up ninety three?"

"Yeah."

"Was the Oasis your first stop?"

"Yeah, we washed up, took a crap, that stuff, then headed out."

"Did Mister James have his own room here?" Davey Cahill had already checked.

Bernie gave him a look. The bed was a double.

"Hell, yeah. Course. What else? We're not—"

The detective nodded. "Okay. Why did you choose the Oasis?"

Bernie shrugged. "It was just our first stop. We were going to hit a bunch of places."

"I see. So it could have been any of a number of casinos."

"That's right."

"Why did you split up inside?"

Bernie Goldman had just the slightest reaction to the question. He shifted his weight slightly on the bed. The pause was for a fraction. Most would have missed it.

"Wesley wanted to play blackjack. I wanted to play roulette."

"And what happened?"

"That's what happened. After awhile, I got up and looked around for Wesley but didn't see him."

"And then?"

"After awhile I went outside and ..."

"There he was."

"Yeah."

"What were you doing in the alley?" Bernie Goldman's reaction this time was more pronounced. He scratched his neck.

"I don't know. I wasn't paying attention to what door I went out."

There was a pause. The detective let the silence gather weight. When he spoke next, it was with gravity.

"Mister Goldman, I'm going to have a look at the surveillance video in the Oasis for the whole morning, up until both of you left the Oasis.   Those recordings are very thorough and complete. Is there something you'd like to tell me?"

10

Cahill was prepared to allude to the possibility of holding Bernie Goldman as a material witness, but it proved unnecessary. The young Ph.D. candidate coughed up right away. He related that he and Wesley James had driven up from Tempe to count cards, and that they'd split up outside the Oasis. Shortly after beginning play, he'd been intercepted and held for interrogation. Bernie had no idea if Wesley had been similarly detained. He said he was questioned by casino personnel and let out the side door after the ordeal. He had no names to give the cops.

The story seemed simple and straightforward, and rang true, but something was missing. Bernie was vague about his time in the casino back office, saying they wanted to know about his card counting system and had asked questions about his partner. Cahill was pretty sure that was fancy. The hotel could give a damn what system Bernie and his partner had used; it obviously hadn't worked very long. The house weapon was intimidation and the young man hadn't mentioned much about that.

"How much did you win?" Cahill had asked.

"Uuh— there's the chips over there. Maybe twelve hundred bucks."

"You haven't cashed them?"

"No, I just didn't think about the money. My friend was dead." The kid shifted on the bed again. His body language spelled evasion big time. Besides, he would have cashed out before leaving, before learning he no longer had a partner.

"I'm going to pay the Oasis a visit," Cahill said. "Want to come along and you can cash those?" The cop wasn't going to the casino until the morning, but he was interested in the answer.

"Uuh— that's all right. I'll do it later."

That was also bull hockey, the detective knew. So Wesley James streaked out of the place in terror, right under a bus, and this guy Bernie Goldman was so scared he hadn't cashed his checks. Twelve hundred dollars was no small change for a grad student.

"Do you want me to cash them for you?" If Cahill had his checks, the likelihood was the kid wouldn't bolt.

There was only a momentary hesitation. "Sure," Bernie said.

Detective Cahill left a few minutes later with Bernie Goldman's winnings, after writing the young man a receipt on his note pad. He told the doctoral student he'd call his cell phone when he had the money and they'd link up early the next afternoon before Wesley James' parents got into town. He phoned Jack Richards at the Oasis, the casino executive he'd dealt with when he had reviewed the video of the earlier victims. Cahill told him he wanted to see the afternoon's surveillance video at eleven in the morning, if convenient. Richards said the hotel would cooperate and he'd have the material ready.

As he drove home, Davey Cahill mulled over the odd events. Something terrible had happened that morning in the Oasis Hotel and Casino, something frightening enough to cause one to flee to his death and the other to forego his money.

But what?

11

Cahill was a thorough investigator. As part of his inquiry into the three suspicious deaths he had researched the Oasis' history. The hotel/casino had opened in 1955, two months before the formation of Nevada Gaming Control Board, and thus no formal filings had been required. He'd reviewed the newspaper coverage through the years. The hotel had a history of hosting legendary gaming events, including major tournaments in poker, blackjack, and chemin de fer, the European version of baccarat that allowed for player skill. The Oasis was steeped in tradition and preferred by many older gamblers not enthralled with pirates, pyramids or pyrotechnics. As a consequence, the casino had always done well over the years, even when other operations experienced leaner times. On several occasions the hotel had played no-limit games against some of the wealthiest people in the world. The casino had taken several big hits, but had come out ahead most of the time and enhanced its reputation as host to the world's professional gamblers. The Oasis had the distinction of holding the floor game with the highest recorded minimum bet, when the baccarat table was set at two hundred fifty thousand dollars during a heavyweight championship weekend. The table was full and people waited to get a seat. Sometimes they hadn't had to wait long.

The original non-restricted gaming license was issued in 1959 by the newly formed Nevada Gaming Commission to a Philip Nero from Boston, Massachusetts. Cahill found little information on the man, who died in 1967. The detective raised an eyebrow when he learned Nero had owned a vending machine company. There were rumored ties to a second Las Vegas strip casino, the

Sacramento, as well as to the Savilla Capri in Havana, the only casino not nationalized or shut down by the Castro regime.

The license had been transferred to John Roselli in the spring of 1966. Curiously, there was no record of Roselli's original license application, which was theoretically not possible. Neither had he appeared before the gaming commission, despite the requirement to do so. What was that all about? Cahill decided to keep looking for the missing paperwork when he had the time.

While there was a fair amount of publicity regarding the hotel, there was not much on Roselli. The Oasis was not a public company. Roselli owned the operation outright and since its acquisition lived in the penthouse atop the hotel. In a similar move, Howard Hughes rented the top floors of the Desert Inn later that same year. Cahill knew Hughes had not appeared before the gaming commission either, probably because he agreed to fund a university medical school. Apparently John Roselli hadn't offered any enticement, at least one the detective could find. If Hughes tried to keep a low personal profile, Roselli's was nonexistent. He was occasionally confused with a well-known organized crime figure of similar name, Johnny Rosselli, who at that time fronted for the mob in Las Vegas. John Roselli was not a public figure and had never issued a public statement or held a news conference. The only exception had come in the late 1960's when he had been compelled to testify at U.S. Senate hearings on racketeering and organized crime. Questioned by Senator Darby Hicks, junior legislator from an eastern seaboard state trying to establish its own gaming industry, Roselli responded to questions about his possible affiliations with known members of organized crime by referring to a file.

Detective Cahill read from the transcript:

HICKS: Are you denying you ever met Mr. Sam Giancana?

WITNESS: Yes.

HICKS: Do you deny you ever met Mr. Anthony Spilotro or Mr. Michael Spilotro?

WITNESS: Yes.

HICKS: What are you doing there? I notice you keep looking in a file when I ask you these questions. For the record, what are you looking at?

WITNESS: I am looking at pictures of the various individuals as you name them, so I can be certain about my answers.

HICKS: Who provided you with that file?

WITNESS: I provided myself with this file.

HICKS: May we see it?

WITNESS: What for?

HICKS: We can subpoena the file. It is in your best interests to produce that file.

WITNESS: Very well. Here's a copy.

(Witness hands copy to clerk who hands file to Sen. Hicks).

HICKS: What? What the hell is this?

(Shouting, commotion)

Davey Cahill chuckled. Everyone knew the story. The senator had fallen directly into Roselli's trap. The casino owner had assembled pictures of each crime figure talking with or standing next to Darby Hicks. When Senator Hicks tried to have the photos withheld, Roselli had simply turned around and handed copies to members of the press corps. The shots caused an immediate sensation and the day's hearing had been adjourned in an uproar. Roselli had never been questioned again and the junior senator had not been re-elected. The attempt to legalize casino gaming in his state evaporated.

Other than the one instance, the Las Vegas Sun had made little mention of John Roselli. The casino owner stayed under the radar, Cahill found. Some years ago he was reported as being a scratch golfer on the hotel course, and an A ranked tennis player on the Oasis clay courts, and that was about it. Cahill wondered if the man had ever met Howard Hughes. Maybe not, since both kept their own company.

The net result of the detective's efforts was interesting but uninformative. Davey Cahill resolved to try and find out more about the reclusive owner of the Oasis Hotel and Casino.

12

By the time the detective arrived at the Oasis, Jack Richards had keyed the hard drives to the video recordings of Goldman and James' visit. The hotel was ahead of many other casinos, a few of which still used tape; the Oasis employed Pivot3 RAIGE™ state of the art High Definition storage with a Universal Video Management System (UVMS) capable of downloading streaming video for review. Finding the pertinent images was now just a couple of keystrokes.

They shook hands by the front desk before Richards led the detective to the ops center. En route, he explained that the pair had been spotted as a card counting team and had been taken off the floor, questioned and let go with a warning not to return to the casino.

"I handled the interviews myself, Detective. You know how these things go."

Cahill nodded. He knew how those things went. He also noted Richards had used the word interview rather than interrogation.

"Who did you talk to first?" The cop already knew the answer.

"Blue cap."

"Which one was that?" Cahill knew that too.

"The Jewish kid." He saw Cahill's eyebrow rise. "Well, he wore a skullcap. Of course we knew they were partners but they didn't admit to anything. We put the fear of God into them and let them go."

Richards opened the door to the operations center and gestured Cahill inside.

"What about their winnings?"

"We didn't confiscate their chips."

"How much did they win?"   The checks were in his pocket.

"Just over a grand."

"Let's take a look."

They sat in the console chairs. The surveillance footage began with the two men talking in front of the hotel, and then entering the Oasis a minute apart. They were recorded during play. The images showed them intercepted separately and escorted across the casino to a corridor that led to the backroom area. There was no camera surveillance, of course, beyond the gaming area except for the counting room.

As before, Jack Richards seemed straightforward and cooperative. Since the exact time of the accident was known, Cahill and Richards reviewed the video for the minutes just prior. Wesley James was not seen; nothing showed the victim fleeing the Oasis moments before being run down. Richards explained that Mr. James had been let out the same door as his partner, and therefore not recorded further. The witnesses who thought they saw the young man flee the casino were obviously mistaken. James must have been in front, waiting for Goldman, and for whatever reason run into the street. The Oasis had nothing to do with it.

There was little else to accomplish during the visit except cash Bernie Goldman's checks. Detective Cahill thanked Jack Richards and left. On the way to the Flamingo, he phoned Goldman. Fifteen minutes later, he gave the doctoral candidate his money in the lobby of the Flamingo.

"Thanks for cashing me out," Bernie said, putting the money away. "You looked at all the tapes?"

"It's not tape now; they store the videos on hard drive. I saw you guys come in, play, and get escorted off the floor. There is no record of your friend leaving the casino. There would be no record if he was escorted out the same door as you were. Evidently whatever spooked Wesley James was outside the Oasis, not inside."

Bernie Goldman looked at the detective. "I don't know what to say. I wonder what happened out there."

"So do I. Good luck this afternoon with your friend's parents. I'll be in touch if I find out anything, but right now it looks like just an accident."

Bernie looked like he had something on his mind.

"Is there something else you remember?" Cahill prompted.

"Detective Cahill? There is something. It's kind of crazy, but it's— well, I'll just tell you. There were two guys that interrogated me. The first one was no fun, but the second guy was really scary. He said something funny. Weird, nasty."

"What's that?"

"When they let me go, he said 'Your friend's out front. He had that run down feeling' or something like that."

The cop looked at Bernie Goldman for a time. "If he told you that just before letting you go, Wesley James had already been dead for maybe fifteen minutes, according to the timeline here. They already knew, didn't they?"

He paused to let his message sink in. "These are hardball people, Mister Goldman. That's the kind of thing they would say, and know you'd never forget. I guess you guys came up here thinking it was a game."

"Sure we did."

"It is not a game."

13

Davey Cahill mulled over the newest strange death and its possible connection to the other Oasis fatalities as he drove. He was in no hurry to return to the station. He liked to think while he cruised along, a habit he'd picked up since the divorce. He hated the radio.

Things just didn't add up. Something was still missing, but what?

Las Vegas Boulevard was crowded, as always, with lanes closed for construction, as always, so the detective took the back way. As he cut over on Audrie Street and out onto East Flamingo, he thought of his nephew. Wade was turning into a fine cop. Since his brother's death to prostate cancer two years ago, Davey had taken on the role of surrogate father as well as mentor. It had filled a void. He and Margaret hadn't been blessed with children, and now that he lived alone he keenly regretted that circumstance. He worked more overtime than he should. His married counterparts kidded him about being single in paradise, but Cahill knew better, especially after the first year dating showgirls and waitresses and the dance instructor. He was ready to settle down again. Trouble was, in Las Vegas his line of work didn't exactly intersect with the Junior League crowd.

Cahill was not one to reminisce, but in a way he envied his nephew. The young patrolman had begun a rewarding and challenging career. He remembered his own first exciting days when the city looked nothing like it did today. He turned right on Koval Lane and cruised along behind the Monte Carlo and Planet Hollywood. Eighteen years ago, when he was a rookie in South Sector traffic patrol, neither hotel existed. He turned onto West

Tropicana and under I-15, almost without thinking. It seemed like every corner brought back a memory: a traffic stop, a burglary, one crime or another. He cruised down memory lane. Felony lane, really, he thought with amusement. He made a right onto Polaris, past a warehouse they had raided maybe a dozen years ago and found a load of crooked dice and cases of marked cards. Cahill turned up to West Harmon. Another right and he came to the corner of Aldebaron. He slowed and pulled over. Something had happened here; the street sign triggered a dim memory. What? Then it came to him. The scenery was no longer the same, but Detective Davey Cahill remembered an early morning traffic patrol as a rookie. Who was his partner, his first mentor? Underwood? No, not Underwood. He could picture him now – a big guy, gruff, very competent. What was his name? Wisner, Richie Wisner. That was it. Good cop, taught Davey a lot. They'd stumbled upon a mugging, strictly by chance. Funny, he hadn't thought of the incident in years, maybe since it happened. He wondered what had become of that brave jogger who had probably saved the life of the tourist who had wandered off the strip into no-man's-land.

As he mused, he never dreamed their lives would intertwine again, within a matter of days, this time with horrific consequences.

14

Las Vegas, Nevada - 1988

George Reynolds began the worst day of his life reflecting on his good fortune. He sipped cold orange juice, gazing out the picture window of his 23rd floor suite. Below, the Las Vegas Strip lights stretched off towards McCarran Airport, already awake and doing business. An early flight emerged from the nest of blue taxiway lights and flew off. He watched the aircraft bank past Sunrise Mountain and climb toward the traces of pink and blue intruding on the pre-dawn darkness. The scene was quietly breathtaking.

He chewed a strip of bacon and let his thoughts drift back to what already seemed another life: remote, an old black and white reel. He'd hung up his cleats and faced the grim likelihood of having to get a real job after graduation. But then, fourteen months ago, someone – Someone? - had pushed the fast forward button. The offer had come from England, unexpected, stunning the young goalkeeper, and off he'd gone to Crystal Palace spending most of his first year on the bench and marveling at the quality of play in the world's best soccer league. The London girls were friendly and the night life exciting. His salary was more money than he could spend, and he was making a fortune on the blackjack tables during the off-season.

Yessir, he was really on a roll. Life was terrific. How could it get any better?

A few minutes later, he stepped off the elevator in his jogging suit and threaded his way past silent slot machines toward the Las Vegas Boulevard exit. There was little more depressing than an empty casino in the early morning, he mused.

Not quite empty. The voice floated from behind a row of quarter slots. "Want a date, honey?"

A moment later she appeared, looking as though she'd been up two days running. George noticed the tear in her stocking, the bruised thigh, the discolored tooth. She stared at him with dead eyes. Her customers were desperate men, he thought, people who stayed out of the light. For a moment, he imagined their fierce couplings, grunts and scrapes in the shadows. He shuddered, offered a small smile, looked away.

The few remaining hookers hanging around the lounge and slot machines tried to make eye contact, their last chance to sell themselves before vanishing with the morning dew. Even the best hotels couldn't keep them out, any more than they could the roaches in the kitchen. Really, he supposed, who cared anyway? They were as much a part of the scenery as the constellations of light bulbs, the flashing slots, the neon cowboys.

George pushed through the front doors by the curved driveway and taxi stand. At that hour, only a handful of cabs awaited fares. The drivers watched incuriously as he stretched against a planter and loosened up.

The Strip lights were winking off as he began his run. He felt an exhilaration, drinking the full wine of life; he ran with a boundless energy as the first wash of sunlight seeped onto the city streets.

He could run forever.

15

Sunlight in the stillness of early morning bathes most cities clean. The filtered light carries an aura of expectancy, of impending vibrancy, important commerce and vital transactions waiting to occur.

In Las Vegas, it's like a hangover.

The cool night air had not yet retreated to the shadows.

"Leave the guy alone."

The would-be muggers looked up from their victim, lying like a side of beef on the Aldebaran Avenue sidewalk just off West Harmon. Blood had spattered on his white golf shirt, soaking the collar and obscuring the country club crest. The khaki shorts were flecked with droplets.

George Reynolds recognized long term crystal meth addiction from the pair's hollow eyes and gaunt, pock-marked faces. The shorter one grinned as he showed the pigsticker.

"You want a piece of this, asshole?" he said through yellow, ruined teeth. His **I LOVE STARBUCKS** tee shirt was barely readable through the grime. It would have been almost comical except for the man on the sidewalk and the knife: a wicked looking affair, thin, sharp on both sides, a military-type weapon designed to cut arteries cleanly so the blood wouldn't clot. He drew a picture in the air, showing what he planned to do inside George if he didn't back off.

The other attacker straightened up to maybe 6'2". He looked all of 140 pounds in his jeans and filthy tee shirt. Scabs dotted his face and neck where he'd scratched the imaginary crank bugs under his skin.

Light flashed in George's eyes as the blade caught the morning desert sun. He did not feature tangling with the pair and the knife, but the man on the ground needed help. A tourist, no doubt, some damn fool who had ventured off the Strip for whatever reason and now was light years from Las Vegas Boulevard and paying the price, a fat, middle-aged conventioneer lying on the sidewalk and leaking blood from the ugly laceration on his forehead.

Everything was still for a moment: the victim, splayed on his back, unconscious, the assailants, sweating and twitchy from whatever substance had fueled their morning, and George, appraising his next course of action. There was a suggestion of red, then movement in a nearby doorway. Out of the corner of his eye George saw the whore who'd lured the john into trouble. There seemed to be someone or something behind her, sliding in the shadows, in black, indistinct, but his attention was on the danger in front of him. Physically, he knew he could take the two rail-thin, wasted attackers, but getting past the knife could be dodgy. The meth head had offered him an out. It would be easy to nod and continue jogging, telling himself they were just going to rob the man on the ground after softening him up, and that wasn't worth risking serious injury.

But he didn't know what the crazies were going to do any more than they probably did, so he stood his ground.

"Let the guy go. Get the hell out of here."

"It's your funeral, jerkoff."

The two muggers looked at each other and smirked. The smaller man hitched up grease-stained baggy pants riding a foot below his underwear. He crouched low and started forward slowly, knife at the ready. George moved sideways. Scab Face moved in the opposite direction to meet him. As he did so, George noticed the tire iron he'd been holding against his leg. Great, he thought. That evens things up. He took a breath, trying not to imagine how the blade would feel sliding between his ribs and puncturing some necessary organ. He moved up onto his toes, ready to—

A screech of tires and a whoop noise.

"FREEZE RIGHT THERE!"

Where had the cop car come from? The old expression wasn't always true, George thought with relief. The hooker started to run but didn't get ten yards, stumbling in her high heels and skinning her knee as she splatted on the pavement. Her wig flew off and landed two feet away, a yellow octopus on the Aldebaran sidewalk. She let out a stream of curses and scratched the cop's arm before he kicked her in the stomach and cuffed her up. Even so, she scrabbled on her knees to retrieve the wig but the cop booted it into the road.

Twenty five minutes later, the two perps and the whore, blood oozing down her leg, had been taken away. An ambulance had picked up the tourist, who would have to explain the broken ribs and forehead gash to his wife in Milwaukee or Peoria or wherever. George had given his statement and contact information to the two officers who had cruised upon the scene.

"London, hey?" The uniformed patrolman, whose name plate read CAHILL, looked at George's driver's license as he stood in the shadow of the nearby building. The crispness of early morning had vanished as the Nevada sun fired up.

"It says Palm Beach here." The young cop looked maybe twenty three, twenty four, the same age as George Reynolds.

"I know. I live in Florida about four months a year. Listen, there wasn't anyone else in the doorway over there, was there? I thought maybe I saw someone else."

Cahill looked puzzled for a moment. "No, nobody else. Just the whore."

"Sure?"

"Yeah. Where could he have gone? We'd have seen the guy. Anyway, what do you do?"

"I play footb— I play soccer. In England."

"You mean professionally?"

"That's right."

"No shit? Hey, Rich, look at this. The guy's a professional soccer player. Your kid played, didn't he?"

Rich closed the door of their cruiser and walked over.

"Christ, the bitch is probably HIV positive or some goddamn thing," he grumbled, looking at his bandaged forearm. The EMS tech had dressed the scratch after disinfecting it. He looked George over.

"What team you play for?" he asked. George glanced at his name plate. Patrolman WISNER was a veteran, much older than his partner.

"Queens Park Rangers. I just got traded."

A delivery truck rumbled by. The driver slowed, eyeballed the scene, moved on. There was no other traffic.

"Yeah? That's the Premier League, right?" He turned to Cahill. "This guy's big time, Cahill. What are you, midfielder or something?"

"Goalkeeper."

"No shit? Hey man, you risked getting cut up. Your hands and all, you know?"

Officer Cahill held up his hand, drew a line with his finger across the palm. "We see a lot of defensive wounds, he means." To the goalkeeper, the cop looked too young to have seen much of anything yet.

"Well," George said, "I'm just glad you guys came along when you did."

"You were lucky. We're just on routine patrol, you know? South Sector Traffic. We don't get by here that much."

"You got guts, buddy," Wisner said. "Listen, you'll get a call from the detectives, probably, in the next day or so. You say you're not leaving town until Thursday?"

"That's right."

"Okay, call the number on the card if your plans change." The cops moved toward their cruiser.

Officer Cahill turned. "And hey, thanks. Not a lot of people would've done what you did."

Later, back on the 23rd floor of the Oasis Hotel and Casino, George thought about the encounter. It hadn't seemed that scary at the time, especially with adrenaline rushing through his system as if he was facing a one-on-one breakaway in a packed stadium. It sure as hell seemed scary now, though, as he stood naked in the shower. He shuddered. The cop was right; he could have been maimed. It was crazy to have risked his career, maybe even his life.

You got guts, buddy.

Yeah, they could have been spilled all over the street. Still, what the hell else could he have done?

16

From his vantage point by the mezzanine railing, John Roselli eyed the crowd gathered behind table forty two in the blackjack pit below. Another whoop told him the kid had won again. The casino owner, impeccable in black tuxedo, shot his cuffs as he descended the staircase. An elderly worker in overalls polishing the brass handrail nodded respectfully as his boss approached. A finger pointed to a blemish on the stanchion by the floor and the old man scurried to the spot, rag in hand. Roselli headed towards the action. Despite his modest height and slender build, the crowd parted to let him pass.

Roselli entered the pit and moved to the blackjack table. He nodded to the dealer, an attractive, slender blonde whose name tag read CARRIE and underneath, Michigan. She spread the two decks on the table, stepped aside and clapped her hands, showing the palms. Carrie melted away, but not before smiling at the clean-cut, winsome young man who had been her only customer for the past half hour at table forty two, whose sign proclaimed a minimum bet of one thousand dollars. The table stakes had been raised all over the strip; it was a crowded fight weekend in Las Vegas.

George Reynolds looked into the casino owner's eyes from behind his stacks of orange, pink and gray checks.

He looked into charcoal. There was a current of warm air, suddenly. A dankness, a momentary whiff. Roselli broke open new decks as he stared at the player.

"Good evening, Mister Reynolds." The eyes belied any cordiality.

"You know me? Who're you?"

"My name is John Roselli."

The young man smiled slightly and nodded, as though their meeting might have been expected.

"You shutting me down?" George inclined his head towards the onlookers behind. "Everybody loves a winner." His smile broadened as he gazed at the array in front of him: castles of money on a field of green.

"Not at all."

Behind, the crowd strained to hear the exchange. A tension now vibrated the air. Roselli ribbon spread and inspected the decks for blemishes, imperfections, missing cards. Satisfied, he shuffled expertly; the cards fluttered into order. The casino owner extended the decks for George to mark the cut. The ornate ring with its large oval brown stone contrasted with his graceful fingers and impeccable manicure. Roselli cut the decks and burned the top card as Reynolds pushed an orange check into the betting square.

A ten and a six went to the player; the house up card was a jack. George beckoned and received the five of clubs for a perfect total of twenty-one. He sat back with an assured smile as the casino owner turned over a queen. Roselli moved to gather in the bet. Startled, George looked at his five, which seemed to shimmer, to lose focus as the light flickered for an instant. He blinked. When the moment passed, he was staring at the three of clubs.

"What the hell!?"

"Just so," said Roselli with a slight smile as he racked the thousand dollar check.

"Jesus!"

"He can't help you just now."

George looked around. No one seemed to have noticed what he had seen. He narrowed his eyes and stared at Roselli, then pushed forward a stack of pumpkins for a ten thousand dollar wager. Behind him, the crowd buzzed.

Roselli dealt himself a blackjack and took George's bet. Reynolds sat for a few seconds, then stood up.

"That's it. Cash me out."

Roselli beckoned for assistance. A floor man appeared with a rack and began loading George's checks.

"So nice to have you with us, Mr. Reynolds," said Roselli. The knot of people loosened, drifted away.

17

The heavyweight title fight down Las Vegas Boulevard at the Mirage had ended early, as Evander Holyfield kayoed Buster Douglas in the third round. George Reynolds had attended the weigh-in earlier, and seen the bloated Douglas sag the scales at an astonishing 246 pounds. He'd gotten a ten thousand dollar bet down on the trim Holyfield before Jimmy Vaccaro, the sports director who ran the Mirage sports book, could adjust the odds. It had been a very profitable evening.

George, who had enjoyed the bout from the sixth row in his seat provided by the Oasis Hotel and Casino, returned to the hotel for a late supper. The Oasis Grille was a cut above the usual casino restaurant, and with a major fight card in town the place was full. The hotel was noted for its fine food as well the accommodations. George hadn't been disappointed. He leaned back at his corner table as the maitre d' lifted the bottle from the silver bucket alongside and poured the last of the Clos du Mesnil '95 into his glass. In the ambience of the dining room, the early morning confrontation near the I-15 overpass had receded to an almost surreal incident in his mind.

"Was everything satisfactory, Mr. Reynolds?"

George nodded. "Yep. Wonderful. Thanks." In truth, George could have been drinking White Star and not known the difference, which was about $675.

A small bow. "Sir, it's all taken care of. The Oasis Grille thanks you for being our guest."

"Thank you." George wished he'd known beforehand it was all going to be comped. The meal would have tasted even better, he thought.

As he rode the elevator to the twenty third floor, George looked at his Breitling Bentley 6.75. Nine-thirty. After midnight in Florida, his off-season home. He was ready for bed. From hard-earned experience, he knew not to count cards with his batteries less than fully charged. He also realized his playing days at the Oasis were over, even though Roselli had not formally barred him from the blackjack tables. He wondered if the hotel owner would turn his picture over to Griffin Investigations for circulation among the other casinos in town, but he suspected not. Perhaps that's why he hadn't been barred outright, at least publicly. The man had a ruthless reputation.

He mulled over his plans as the elevator doors opened and he walked down the hallway to his suite. As he'd told the cops, he would be leaving in two weeks for London. He'd seen little action his first campaign, finishing with a tie and two losses. What the hell, that was better than some. At least he was still in the league. Most of his college teammates were sitting behind desks somewhere, cleats gathering dust in the closet, bodies thickening.

George was using the Oasis gym and eschewing desserts. He ran daily to stay in shape and had roughed out his course from the hotel, starting on West Harmon, across the I-15 overpass to the Union Pacific tracks and back. He had seen some interesting things while running that route, none quite as engaging as the morning's mugging.

He had wanted to get in as much blackjack as possible before the season. The London casinos were always crowded and the rules less favorable, which pretty much nullified his advantage. There was also the likelihood of being recognized, sometimes gratifying while enjoying the city nightlife but a deal killer at the tables. Nevada was the best blackjack forum, but Roselli was queering the pitch in Las Vegas, it seemed. No matter what, he figured he had at least another day of play in town.

Not that he needed the money.

18

George reached his suite, inserted the key card and walked in. Funny, he thought he'd left the light—

Breathing, very close, and a whiff of grilled onions. George whirled to see two large unfriendly looking men in black inches away. For big men, they must have moved awfully fast.

This probably wasn't good, he figured.

"Oh, shit. Sorry, wrong room." He turned to leave.

One of the thugs grabbed at his arm. He yanked away but the second man slammed him backwards into the wall and punched him hard in the stomach. George let out a whoosh and doubled over. He fought for breath.

"Christ, be careful. There's a hundred dollar lobster in there."

Suddenly he straightened and aimed a kick between the man's legs. It was the thug's turn to fold up. George threw a punch that connected on the man's neck. As he turned towards the second assailant, he was stunned by a blow to his temple, and then the house lights went dark.

The cool wind on the balcony woke him. His head hurt like hell, and he felt groggy. Lights danced across his vision. Did he have a concussion? But then George realized he was looking at the strip upside down. How could that—

Terror hit him with high voltage. He was being held over the railing, one thug on each ankle. He was suddenly fully awake.

"Jesus Christ, hey!"

"Better quit wiggling around, shithead." The voice was gravel from a dump truck.

George willed himself still. Blood dripped from his nose, down into space. He saw the wind catch the drops, hurl them away. His breathing was harsh, rapid.

"A little message from Mister Roselli. You listening?"

"Yes!"

The thug who had spoken nodded to his partner, who let go of George's other ankle. He hung by one leg, now.

"Are you sure? You paying attention?"

"Yes! Yes! I'm listening!" George resisted the urge to flail around; he remained as still as he could.

The man nodded to his partner, who grabbed George's other leg again.

"Mister Roselli doesn't like card counters in his casino. Understand?"

"I understand!"

It was blowing maybe fifteen knots on the twenty third floor balcony. Across the top of George's vision, a stream of cars crawled up and down Las Vegas Boulevard. The night was crystal clear. Stars twinkled below his feet.

"You're never coming back here. Got it?"

"Got it, yeah, I got it!"

"Cause if you do, next time we'll see if you can fly, asswipe."

"I get it!"

The men made no move to bring George back to safety. He felt his cell phone slip out of his pocket and fall away. He watched it tumble and disappear.

"Really, I get it! I get it! Christ!"

"Mister Roselli hears you're still playing kickball in Europe. That so?" The man's tone of voice was almost conversational.

What?

"Kickball? Soccer. Yeah, yeah, it's true. What's that got—?"

The second hood spoke for the first time. "You guys have a good season?"

"What? What the hell does that—?"

"I SAID – did you have a good season?"

"Yeah, yeah. Shit. Lemme—"

"Mister Roselli wants you to have a good season next year, too."

George felt himself being hauled up until his legs were over the rail. Suddenly one of the men jumped up and came down on George's right shin as it rested on the rail. There was a loud crack and incredible agony. George screamed and passed out.

Fifteen minutes later, siren wailing, the ambulance sped down W. Charleston Boulevard towards the University Medical Center Trauma Center, weaving in and out of the heavy weekend traffic. Inside, a paramedic ripped open a sterile pack.

"Hold on, fella. Morphine's on the way."

19

It was 8:40 a.m. and already 88 degrees in Las Vegas. Three West had been busy since Judy Feher had started her seven to three shift. University Medical Center, like the other Las Vegas hospitals, was seeing the aftereffects of fight weekend revelry, with its share of cracked heads, accidents, stabbings, gunshot wounds, drug overdoses and alcohol poisonings. The Registered Nurse was sitting at the DISPENStation, using the touch screen to obtain the nine a.m. meds for her patients. She longed for a smoke, which of course was out of the question anywhere on hospital grounds. Even the outdoor sitting areas were non-smoking now. Her new patient, George Reynolds, had been brought into the trauma center last evening and arrived in Three West around six in the morning.

When Judy had come on at seven, Kathy Rohleder was rotating off. She shared her shift notes with her friend.

"The new guy in three thirty four, Reynolds. They brought him down from recovery an hour ago. He's still out."

"What's the story?" Judy asked.

"It's a terrible injury. Right leg. He was in the O.R. three hours."

"Who did the surgery?"

"Doctor Hartman. They started around midnight. He said he was lucky to save the leg. He'll be in before noon."

In fact the fractures to the fibula and tibia were compound, complex and comminuted – multiple shards of bone with extensive tissue damage.

"What happened?"

"Some sort of accident on the strip."

"Has he been awake at all?"

"No." Kathy poked her friend. "He's a handsome one, you'll see. Word is he's a soccer star in England. Was a soccer star in England. Chart says he's twenty four years old."

"Okay."

"Just like you."

"Stop that."

"Only two years younger than me."

"Hey, you've got a date this afternoon, anyway. Don't you? Who is he?"

"Guy from the Riviera. Runs the baccarat operation."

"I thought we said we'd never date anybody from the casinos."

"Yeah, well, do you see a bunch of surgeons lined up to take me to dinner? How about just a proctologist to the cafeteria?"

Judy had looked in on George Reynolds just after Kathy left. He hadn't awakened, and her friend was right. He was boyishly handsome. She hoped he was tougher than he looked, because the news wasn't good at all.

She was almost through obtaining the morning meds. The DISPENStation was a sophisticated medication dispensing system designed to eliminate the possibility of controlled substance pilferage. The physician specified the medication on the patient's chart, which was scanned into the system and utilized by the pharmacy to dispense the appropriate drug and dosage in locked compartments below the touch screen. In theory, it was foolproof. If a nurse dropped a pill or anything untoward happened to a dose, the signatures of two other nurses were required for replacement.

These were the orders scrawled on George Reynolds' chart by Doctor Leonard Hartman:

Hydrocodone: 1 tablet every four hours for pain

Judy had thwarted this otherwise foolproof system by simply substituting a chart that read two tablets. She wasn't an accomplished forger but had found most physician signatures illegible scrawls, easy to replicate. The information was scanned; once in the system she restored the original chart.

She touched the screen for her patient in Room 334. The drawer unlocked and Judy withdrew the two hydrocodone pills. By the time she entered George Reynolds' room, she had freshened her makeup and the small paper cup contained a single tablet. The young man was awake and reading the Las Vegas Sun, propped up against two pillows, right leg heavily cast and in the air. He lowered the paper.

"Good morning, Mister Reynolds."

George looked up and saw a most attractive, slender blonde with green eyes. He smiled and put the paper aside.

"George, please. And you are . . ." He peered at her name tag. ". . . Judy Feher. Pleasure's all mine," he continued. "Cocktail hour?"

Judy smiled and nodded. She handed him the cup and another of water. He downed the pill.

"Mmm, tasty."

"How do you feel this morning?"

"Well," he said with a grimace, "I suppose if I were a horse they'd have shot me."

"Any pain?"

"No, thanks."

Judy liked his sense of humor.

"Can I make it to the bathroom when I need to?"

"Oh, goodness, no. Just ring."

He closed his eyes. "I'd sooner die, I think."

"That'll be the least of your worries."

"Yeah, a real icebreaker. I don't guess we're going dancing tonight, do you?"

"I think that's a good guess. Okay, I'm off now," she said, picking up the paper cups. "See you a little later this morning."

"I'll be here if you need me."

She'd had athletes before, mostly from UNLV football. Then there was that motorcycle daredevil the year prior who jumped fourteen school buses in a hotel parking lot, and cleared most of them. They were all the same. Good natured wiseasses. They were tough as nails until they realized they had to use a bedpan. They'd rather burst. The women couldn't care less.

From his banter, Judy figured this one hadn't realized the severity of his injury. Doctor Hartman would arrive later in the morning. She was glad he was in good spirits now – he would need, she thought, a great deal of comfort by noon.

And he did have that smile.

20

QPR flew Doctor Leon Childers, the team's orthopedic surgeon, in from the U.K. Childers examined George, looked at the x-rays and conferred with Doctor Hartman. Afterward, the goalkeeper was stunned to learn from the physicians that his professional soccer career was over. Judy wanted to console her patient, but it was a full day before he spoke a word. When he did, he seemed to have accepted the news.

"Both my careers ended the same night," he said, propped up against the pillows in Three West. Judy had brought lunch on his third day. Despite what George had heard about hospital food, this stuff seemed edible. There wasn't much to be optimistic about, but at least he could eat.

"What do you mean?" Judy asked.

"I got barred from playing blackjack at the Oasis. I've been counting cards since college. I don't know if they gave my picture to Griffin."

Judy, a lifelong resident of Las Vegas, knew what her patient was talking about. All the casinos subscribed to Griffin Investigations, the agency that supplied information and pictures of known card counters, cheats and unsavory characters.

"That's terrible," she said. "What a horrible coincidence."

"It wasn't a coincidence."

It took Judy several seconds to realize what George had said. She was shocked.

"No, that can't be true. They don't do that kind of stuff anymore."

"Tell it to the Oasis."

"My God. Can you go to the police?"

"The cops? You're not serious."

George put a piece of bacon atop his slice of liver and onions. It really wasn't half bad.

"It was a hell of a day. I was jogging early in the morning and I came across a mugging. Then I get barred and my leg broken. If it wasn't for bad luck, I wouldn't have any at all." Something under his cast was itching like mad. He tensed his muscles, but it did no good.

"Oh, my goodness."

George chewed as he reflected on his future. "These guys, these doctors have been wrong before. Goalkeepers can play until they're almost forty. It's mostly a reflex position. Chelsea signed a thirty eight year old keeper the other week. I'm twenty four. I've already proved I can play in the Premier League. Even if it takes me two years to come back, I'll be there."

Judy hoped the young man was right. He'd brightened remarkably quickly. George Reynolds seemed goal-oriented, she thought, no pun intended, and he'd given himself a whopper. He took the paper cover off a small dish and peered inside.

"Got any Red Hots for this apple sauce?"

21

Doctor Hartman discharged him in three days. Judy
arranged for George to begin therapy in Palm Beach six weeks
hence, after the cast would come off. He was preparing to check in
to another hotel for two nights, then fly back home. Judy had picked
up his luggage from the Oasis. When the R.N. volunteered to let
George stay at her apartment until his flight, he demurred. It would
be no trouble at all, she assured him.

"Of course it would be a lot of trouble," George said. "Are
you kidding? I can't get around anywhere at all."

"That's right, you can't. So it's settled."

She drove him to her apartment in North Las Vegas, a
pleasant two bedroom unit on Boulder Highway. Turtle Creek
featured a central pool and clubhouse, nicely landscaped. Getting in
and out of her Accord was an awkward affair, and George was glad
he wouldn't have to navigate his way through McCarran and onto an
airplane, even with first class seating. Fortuitously, she had a ground
floor apartment and a small yard with a well-tended garden.

That first night, Judy cooked linguini with white clam sauce.
They sipped wine as George kept her company from a stool behind
the kitchen counter, his cast propped up on the adjacent stool.

"I'm not sure chardonnay is supposed to go with linguini,"
she said.

George shrugged. It tasted fine to him, maybe just as good
the Oasis' Clos du Mesnil '95. "It's perfect."

He looked up and around. She'd placed baskets here and
there above the cabinets. Ferns and other plants poked out.

"Looks terrific. You're quite a decorator."

"Thanks. Why don't you tell me how you got to be a soccer star?" she asked, stirring the pasta as it simmered in the pot.

"I'm not a star, I'm just a player. Second string at that." George leaned on his crutch and shifted his position. "We didn't have a lot of money – my dad was a prep school science teacher in Palm Beach. Those jobs don't pay too well, but I got free tuition. I guess I was the poorest kid at the place. I played soccer and was lucky enough to get a couple of scholarship offers. The best school on the list was Lehigh University. I played four years for the Engineers. We played a tournament in England against the under-21's, and that's how I wound up getting signed."

Judy stirred the linguini and peered into the pot. "Okay, this is just about ready. I'll help you to the table as soon as I get this off the stove."

"I can do that by myself," George said, climbing down and hopping over to the breakfast nook, carrying his crutches. He looked at the small vase in the center of the table. It held two red velvet roses.

"These from your garden?" There were six or seven rose bushes outside the window, all of different varieties and colors. The weakening sun cast a warm glow on the flowers outside and through the window. It was indeed a cheery scene.

"Yes," she said, bringing over two small salads with gorgonzola cheese and balsamic vinegar dressing. Judy set the food on the table and sat down. "Would you like to say grace?"

George was taken aback. "Aah, maybe you could do that." He couldn't remember the last time anyone had prayed over a meal. He closed his eyes as Judy said a few words.

He tasted the linguini. "This is delicious."

"Thanks. How did you learn to count cards?" she asked, winding a mouthful around her fork. "I'm sorry if this seems like an interview."

George smiled as he shook red peppers on his plate. He held the shaker like a microphone and spoke into the little holes, evoking a smile from Judy.

"I took a statistics and probability course sophomore year. Boring as hell. In class one day, the professor talked about blackjack being the only casino game where you can predict what's going to happen. All of a sudden it wasn't boring anymore. I read a couple of books and began to practice and found I had an aptitude for it. I started to play in Atlantic City, which wasn't that far away. By the end of my junior year, I was self supporting. In fact, I bought a secondhand Toyota so I didn't have to take those god-awful bus rides to the casinos. I think I was the only person on the bus under eighty. The thing was filled with respirators and oxygen tanks."

George paused for another mouthful of pasta.

"My senior year, I did something I really wanted to do."

"What was that?"

"Like I said, I didn't grow up rich, like a lot of kids on Palm Beach. I took some of my winnings and sent my parents on a cruise through the Panama Canal."

Judy was taken aback. It was a most thoughtful act for a young man.

"What a wonderful gift. I'll bet they loved it," she said.

"It's probably the best thing I ever did. When dad died, it was a great comfort to me." He ate a forkful of salad. "Atlantic City's a dump, like a movie façade. Look behind the glitter, and it's all slums. At least you've got regular neighborhoods. I can't imagine you growing up here, though. So tell me. It's your turn to talk."

Judy's story was simpler, and there was one parallel.

"I really wanted to be a physician. My father was a Methodist preacher. You know what those guys make – less than your dad, I bet. Unfortunately, I didn't pull straight A's and I wasn't a soccer player." She smiled. "I'm glad I went to nursing school and I enjoy what I do."

"Do your folks live nearby?"

There was a pause. "They've passed on."

"Oh, I'm sorry."

"My mom died when I was in college. Breast cancer. My father died two years ago. He was on his way to say the eulogy at a funeral and was killed on I-15 driving to Woodlawn Cemetery. I'd have given anything for the chance to have sent them on a vacation."

There was a silence. They watched as a ladybug crawled out from inside one of the roses and stopped on a petal. Judy brightened.

"We have a dinner guest," George said.

"I love ladybugs. I hope you like chocolate cream pie with homemade graham cracker crust and real whipped cream."

In fact, it was George's favorite dessert.

22

He stayed longer than planned, spending a great deal of time reading by the pool while Judy worked her shift. Lew Reed, George's agent, called with the news that since the goalkeeper hadn't yet reported to QPR and taken the physical, he was still technically on the Crystal Palace roster. There would be a compensation package, but Reed asked his client to be patient while things were sorted out. The agent was optimistic the team would be generous in their settlement. George told Judy hadn't expected to get any funds at all and he'd be happy with whatever they came up with.

Meanwhile, he used the small community exercise room at least once a day, awkward as it was. He said he never remembered being physically idle and that the facility was a godsend. For the first time in awhile, Judy looked forward to coming home from work.

The first Sunday, she asked the goalkeeper if he wanted to accompany her to church.

"It's not too far. I go to Westminster Presbyterian, over on West Lake Mead."

The question caught George by surprise. Judy noticed.

"Maybe with the cast it might be too difficult," she said.

"Aah, yeah, that's probably right." Later: "Church and all. It's really important to you, isn't it?" She'd seen him looking at some of the books on her shelves.

"Yes, I've always gone to services. Especially after my parents died." It was obvious to Judy that religion wasn't a big part of his life. It presented a challenge she was sure she could overcome by example, pushing away the knowledge it was a mistake made by women since the dawn of time.

"I thought you said your dad was a Methodist preacher. How come you go to a Presbyterian church? Are they pretty much the same?"

"Everyone was kind and solicitous after he was killed. I just felt I needed a change after awhile."

George nodded and smiled. The sunlight, filtered by the garden, cast a soft glow around his head. He looked beatified for the moment; Judy almost gasped. She felt pulled off the shore by a wave of emotion, swept into an unknown sea, and for the briefest instant wondered what creatures lived in its depths.

Women had been readily accessible to George Reynolds since high school. They fluttered around his boyish smile and schoolboy charm, butterflies in his garden. This was especially true in the U.K., an American playing professionally on a London club. He was comfortable with the ladies, treating their presence as a natural phenomenon, almost as if they were his teammates, with an amiable affection. He drew them in: stars in his constellation, slowly circling in a galaxy of, they would invariably feel, a grand but not quite clear design. He had the gift of not taking women for granted, of sharing some unknowable understanding, some undefined but intimate knowledge. His easy smiles promised wonderful secrets. He was interested in what they had to say, and whether or not they became lovers seemed secondary.

It drove them crazy.

On the third night she came to his room. The sheers were drawn and there was enough light for her to see his face as he turned to her. She lay next to him, without words, and they kissed, and she eased on top, careful of the cast, and for a brief time she was sure the shattered leg had left his mind. He was tender, and his hands were magical. It was awkward, but not so awkward that she didn't climax again and again, and call his name.

Later, she wondered whether or not his injury had anything to do with his gentleness. She found herself crying for the injustice that had happened to him. He didn't ask why she wept, but smiled softly and wiped away the tears and they drifted into a peaceful sleep.

George never left. They became engaged two days before the cast came off. He was moronic, trying to get down on one knee and falling over on her carpet.

"Judy, I love you. Will you marry me?" he said from the floor.

She didn't know whether to laugh or cry. It was a moment she'd looked forward to since first laying eyes on George Reynolds, and dreaded as well. She took a breath and summoned all her courage.

"I'd love to marry you, George. But there's a problem."

23

Judy had rehearsed the speech in her mind several times, but it was no good. George had gotten up from the floor when he saw how serious she was and maneuvered himself into a chair. Hesitantly, she told him how she had gradually become hooked on painkillers. She'd planned to give the matter a light brush, if that were possible, to say this was not an uncommon problem among medical professionals, with the easy availability, the need to perform at a high level over long hours, and that she functioned perfectly, and would quit, but she couldn't say those things. She found that she couldn't be anything but frank and honest with George. Judy told him she'd been trying to stop for a year now, and admitted she wasn't winning the battle.

He said nothing until she had finished. She looked on anxiously as George sat, head down for a few moments. When he looked up, he spoke slowly, measuring his words carefully.

"Judy, I can't tell you I know very much about this kind of problem. I've seen guys using steroids in the locker room, lots of painkillers and other stuff, although they've been cracking down the past couple of years. I know it's gotta be tough.

'Right now I'm going to need a lot of help getting myself back on the playing field. It's not going to be easy. You've been terrific and I know you'll help me every step of the way. I guess what I'm saying is that maybe we're both injured in different ways. And I'll do no less for you than you would – than you already have – for me. This news doesn't change my mind. I love you and I'll help you however I can. There's professional help available, I know, and money's not a problem."

She flew off the chair and embraced George, leaking tears that ran around her smile. Judy gave her notice and made plans to fly back with him to Florida. They decided to get married in George's home town. She called various churches and decided on Palm Beach Presbyterian, sight unseen, after speaking with Reverend Taman, the pastor. There was an opening in five weeks. George booked the reception at the Colony Hotel.

Judy had a last night out in Nevada with Kathy Rohleder, eating their favorite Italian dinners at Carmine's, a small Italian place on Simmons Street.

"Remember when he first came on the floor?" Kathy asked, cutting a huge meatball with her fork. "We kidded about him. Who woulda thunk it?"

After espresso, Kathy cried and hugged her friend. Judy made her promise she'd be maid of honor at the wedding. They vowed to stay close.

The next day, as the plane rose from the runway and circled to the east, she looked down at the city. She wondered if she would ever see Las Vegas again, and found to her surprise that she didn't much care if she didn't.

Not then. Not for the next seventeen years.

24

North of Phoenix, Arizona – 1990

Two hundred and fifty seven miles southeast of Las Vegas, twelve year old altar boy James Warren was alone in the sanctuary of Holy Name Roman Catholic Church.   He gathered up the Communion goblet, water and wine cruets and other objects from the credence table adjacent the altar and placed them on his tray. The Holy Mass, attended only by the Sisters of the Immaculate Conception, had ended and the church was deserted. James sang softly, nervously to himself in a high pure tone. The notes vanished in the semi-darkness. The few dim lights illuminating the crucifix above the altar and the statues around the interior cast lengthy shadows across the footpace and pews. The long crack in the floor zigzagged down the center aisle like dark lightning before darting under the Confessional. Rows of columns rose up and disappeared into the gloom.

The tray was heavy and as the boy turned his foot caught on his cassock. He stumbled and the tray tipped; everything fell with a crash, tumbling down the steps and scattering in the darkness. Warren gasped; it sounded like a bomb going off. He prayed Father Corr hadn't heard. Hopefully not – the ancient priest was hard of hearing. James bent to pick up the sacred objects.

From the rear, a loud slam echoed throughout the church. The sound seemed to play on, repeating from behind pillar and pew. The altar boy froze as footsteps sounded on the marble floor.

"H- hello?" Warren peered into the blackness.

The sound was as a shovel trailing on cobblestones.

"Hello? Mass is over," Warren said.

"Mass *is* over." The voice was deep and frightening. A dark, hooded figure became visible in the cavity beyond. Warren froze as the apparition grew nearer, stepped on the black lightning.

"Come worship with me, James Warren."

Warren dropped the tray again and ran for the small, wooden door to the left of the sanctuary.

"Father Corr! Father Corr!"

Warren rushed through to the sacristy, slamming the door behind. He turned the key. He hated the place, normally; it was a frightening room almost as uncomfortable as the church. Filled with old, dark furniture, Gothic images, robes and other vestments, the walls seemed to lean in, stifling the visitor. Bookcases were everywhere, spilling over with books and religious trinkets. A Tiffany lamp cast its weak light on Father Corr, who sat motionless in his leather chair. His eyes were white, clouded with cataracts; his skin, like the old chair, was dry and cracked. The grey head turned towards the young altar boy, who stood panting, leaning against the closed door. A hand raised; a bony finger beckoned.

"Come here, boy! Don't make me wait! Disrespect is a sin!"

The voice was sandpaper across the wood.

Warren staggered to the priest as something pounded on the door. Tears coursed down his face as he drew near the ancient cleric. Father Corr extended his hand wearing the ornate ring with large, oval brown stone. When James Warren kissed the ring, the priest whined eerily. He reached for the boy's face and wiped away tears. His hand moved downward as suddenly the door splintered and the hooded figure burst through.

*   *   *   *

James Warren woke from his nightmare with a gasp, arm raised to ward off a blow. He shook his head in a moment of bewilderment before sitting up. There was silence except for the rhythmic breathing of the eleven other boys in the dormitory.   In a little while he lay down and tugged at the sheet, the worn thin blanket.

Outside, moonlight silvered the old stone building, the lawn and the sign that read:

THE OASIS
CATHOLIC HOME FOR BOYS
Father Patrick Corr, Headmaster
Thomas J. O'Brien, Bishop
Diocese of Phoenix

Inside, James Warren watched the shadows lengthen on the ceiling. He managed to stay awake for almost an hour, desperately trying to recall his parents' faces.

25

West Palm Beach, Florida – Present Day

Her name tag read Judy Reynolds. The former Judy Feher, George's wife of sixteen years, had aged little. Her unlined face was a blessing of heredity as well as good skin care; her mother at age sixty two still attracted glances in the grocery store. As Judy sat behind the teacher's desk in the West Palm Beach high school classroom, she looked at her attendance sheet. There were to be fourteen women. Twelve were seated and another came through the door. It was 8:28 p.m. on Friday night.

This was her fourth class since she began the program two years earlier. Her passion for the work had overcome an initial unease in front of people; she now looked forward to beginning each new class and the opportunity to help her fellow professionals.

Judy noticed that the women generally avoided eye contact with each other. They seemed to range in age from mid-twenties to perhaps fifty five. She found it interesting that each group so far had looked and acted pretty much the same. There was no conversation. She turned and looked at the white SMART board, covered with equations and other mathematical calculations. This class was apparently solving for two unknowns. She doubted if she could do that anymore.

It became 8:30. Judy stood and walked to the front of her desk. She began:

"Good evening. My name is Judy Reynolds. I am a Registered Nurse and have been for almost twenty years. How many of you are here under court order?"

The women looked at each other. Slowly, six hands went up as the fourteenth woman came in, signed the attendance sheet and hurried to an empty seat.

Judy leaned back against the desk. "How many of you are doctors?"

Another pause. This time three hands gradually rose. Judy nodded.

"Nurses?"

All the remaining hands went up. Judy's soft smile said we're all in this together.   "In the medical profession today, we have a secret problem of epidemic proportions. Our ease of access to prescription drugs, high stress environment and often a compulsive personality type all exacerbate the problem. You are not alone, but may feel as if you are, with no one to talk to, no place to go for help, until now."

Judy paused and looked around. "I know I did."

     *   *   *   *

Saturday morning brought a brilliant blue cloudless sky. George wandered into the kitchen, where Judy was seated at the counter. She looked up from the yellow soft cover book and papers scattered in front of her laptop.

"Hi," she said. Until a few months ago, the Reynolds had a single desktop computer in the family room wall unit, but Judy had been online so much recently she had purchased the laptop and gone wireless. George was beginning to worry she was becoming addicted to the thing.

"Hey. You were up early." He opened the refrigerator, grazing.

"There's frozen waffles in the freezer."

"How was class last night?"

"The first meeting's always the same," she said. "I did all the talking."

Most of her classes didn't open up until the second session, and by the third everyone had something to say. In fact, it sometimes became difficult to maintain order with fifteen or so women eager to share their experiences. The course had enjoyed a remarkable success rate.

"Want one of these?" He held a waffle over the toaster.

"No thanks."

"What's that?" he asked, indicating the materials on the counter with his head.

"Investing for Dummies," she said. "We've got a lunch meeting at the church."

"Really? Good for you. I can't wait until you take over the household finances."

George, who did all the bill paying and investing, was only half-kidding. The Reynolds' lakefront home on North Lake Way in Palm Beach was one of the more expensive properties in an expensive town. The goalkeeper's salary from his U.K. soccer days had been close to a half million pounds, and between those funds and his blackjack winnings he and Judy had purchased the home fifteen years ago. Now it was worth a not so small fortune, although the housing crisis had shrunk its value by perhaps thirty percent over the preceding three years. The real issue was liquidity. The collapse of the stock market had taken its toll on their investment portfolio; George's capital had been dwindling. Money was something he had put off discussing with Judy, who seemed more interested in the finances of her church.

When Palm Beach Presbyterian had appointed his wife treasurer some months ago, George had been surprised. She'd had no formal financial or accounting training. During their marriage, her financial expertise had been limited to spending her part-time hospital paycheck as mad money. She was taking her new responsibilities seriously, and had asked several questions about investments and the stock market recently. George had to admit he didn't even know what a financial derivative was, exactly.

26

At twelve thirty, while George was eating reheated pizza and watching Chelsea take the lead over Tottenham Hotspur at Stamford Bridge, half a dozen cars were parked in the lot of the old Palm Beach Presbyterian Church at 316 Primrose Lane.   The most extravagant feature of the place was the setting: a wide expanse of lawn, some eighty feet of well-tended greenery leading to the forty five year old sanctuary.   Behind, the partially completed new house of worship sat surrounded by orange construction fencing, wheelbarrows, materials and machinery.   The land continued on for another acre, where the new parking lot would have gone, except the ancient cemetery had been discovered in the weeds.

In front, near the roadway, the low sign set in the grass read:

Palm Beach Presbyterian Church
Rev. James Warren, Pastor
Visitors Welcome!

Inside the building, in a modest conference room, five people sat around a small, plain table crowded with a Bible, a pitcher of water, five glasses, and a manila file.   The room was simple painted wallboard, with a single cross on one wall.   There were no moldings and the door was light hollow core, the windows inexpensive aluminum frame, pitted with age.   The room was clean, but deterioration through time and decades of use could not be hidden.   The asphalt tile roof needed replacement; only constant patching kept the rain out.

The meeting had been hastily called. Aside from Reverend Warren, the other four attendees were deacons and elders of Palm Beach Presbyterian. Seated next to Judy Reynolds was Tom Swayne, an affable and handsome twenty four year old who ran his father's hardware store on Congress Avenue in West Palm. Across from Tom sat Dexter Wilcox, forty one years old, a slight man whose heavy glasses seemed to outweigh him. The remaining deacon was Joe Dykes, oldest member of the group at fifty three, a stocky city code enforcement official whose thinning hair was dyed unconvincingly black.

After the remains of a fast food lunch were cleared, a grim Joe Dykes spoke for several minutes. As he finished, he closed the file in front of him. Sunlight streamed cheerily in the single pane windows and slanted across the table, but no one took notice. Everyone around the table seemed in shock, trying to come to grips with the news they had just received. They looked at each other. No one had anything to say for a time.

James Warren became conscious of a morning dove as its soft coo floated in. It must be right outside, he thought.

"It's probably best we keep a lid on this," Joe said, finally.

Judy felt the food in her stomach rearrange itself.

"What'll we do?" asked Dexter.

"Nothing until after we get back from the convention. There's not enough time," Joe said. "We can't use anybody from inside the church."

"Pray for a miracle," Reverend Warren said.

"Pray it doesn't rain," Tom said.

*   *   *   *

That night, in fact, it did rain. While her husband was over at a neighbor's watching a middleweight title fight on HBO, Judy Reynolds sat curled in her bedroom chair with the lights off looking out at the rain veiling West Palm Beach across the water. The green channel marker lights winked slowly, turning the drops on the windows into emeralds. She watched them tremble and slide down the glass.

The overhead fan seemed to be sucking the air from the room, screwing the ceiling down towards her. She shuddered and took a breath. Time to rearrange her thoughts, push her anxiety and Palm Beach Presbyterian into a box and close the lid. She'd put on a new face as if it were makeup. George would be home soon.

27

Las Vegas, Nevada

Every few months after Sunday mass at Prince of Peace Roman Catholic Church Davey Cahill drove to Woodlawn Cemetery and visited Lonny's grave. Almost a century old, the forty acre site was on the National Register of Historic Places. Mature oaks and palms graced the grounds. The detective found it ironic that Las Vegas Boulevard ran from McCarran Airport to the strip, past the downtown grind joints and on to the graveyard, a kind of weird natural progression.

Cahill was thankful his brother rested in the shade, near Veterans Circle; standing in the sun just after noon was equivalent to being inside a pizza oven. He stood before the grave and said hello. After three Hail Marys and an Our Father, he walked over and sat on the nearby bench, shaded and right across the footpath from Lonnie's resting place. He reminisced about growing up with his family. He missed his brother. He missed his parents. He missed Margaret, too, and what the hell, he even missed the dance instructor. What a life. He sighed. After a time, he said goodbye to Lonnie but rather than leave the cemetery he remained and thought about Bernie Goldman and the Oasis Hotel and Casino.

As Bernie and his confederate had learned, Las Vegas casino gaming wasn't a game at all. Cahill also knew there was a possibility the James kid had indeed run out the front doors of the Oasis. Richards and his staff had ample time to excise the video; the event would probably have been momentary. It was easy enough to do. The casino executive had already lied, failing to mention he hadn't been Bernie Goldman's only interrogator. So who was the second man? And why cover that up? What was going on? What had happened behind closed doors in the Oasis back room? What had happened in the casino itself?

Cahill didn't believe in coincidence. There were now four young adults cut down, probably all after running afoul of the gaming personnel at the Oasis. He'd not been able to link any earlier accidental deaths or suicides to the casino, and, as he'd mulled over with Tim Moss, there really there was no practical way to do that anyway.

He hadn't yet had time to concentrate on John Roselli, the hotel owner. If indeed the Oasis was responsible for these events, the guy at the top must be aware. He'd have to make those kinds of decisions. There was no advisory board, no management committee, nothing but John Roselli and the few executives like Jack Richards. He'd find the time to investigate the guy. Not like the U.S. Senate, but quietly, from the bottom up, digging and scratching and seeing what came up out of the ground.

It was quiet in the cemetery, still and quiet, except—

Perhaps forty yards away, in the direct sun, a figure dressed in black cassock was standing before a grave. He appeared to be speaking, perhaps in prayer. The man, obviously a priest, appeared very old, although Davey couldn't see his face clearly.   He wondered how the old man could stand there, dressed in black, shimmering in the noontime heat. He seemed to sway back and forth, and Davey wondered if he was perhaps in need of assistance or just in prayer. He was about to walk over when the cleric knelt down and placed something on the grave. Davey guessed the guy was all right, and turned his thoughts back to John Roselli and the Oasis. He'd call Tim Moss and ask if the FBI had a file on the casino owner.

When he looked over a few minutes later, the priest was almost out of sight, moving slowly down the lane and around a bend. He was almost a mirage, a black stick figure undulating in the heat that was radiating upward, two feet in the air.

Davey got up and walked past the grave where the visitor had been. He glanced at the tombstone:

Rev. Peter Feher
1937-2007
He is with the Father

Something protruded from the grass in front of the stone. What was it the priest had left?   Davey bent over. It was a cross, jammed into the ground, but it was upside down. Cahill was taken aback. He hadn't seen anyone come by the grave after the old priest tottered off. He bent down and pulled out the cross, rubbing off the dirt before he planted it right side up.

Christ, he thought, you gotta be a cop even in this place.

He started towards his car. If he'd have turned around before leaving the footpath, he would have been startled to see the cross upside down again.

28

Palm Beach, Florida

After the fight, which had proven more hype than action, George came home to find his wife in the library, preparing for her weekly Bible Study class following Sunday services. George sat in a chair opposite and picked up the Palm Beach Post lying on the small table between them. "What time's your flight Thursday? I'll take you to the airport."

"Six fifteen a.m."

"Ouch."

"It's all right, you don't have to drive me. Reverend Warren said he'd pick me up."

George nodded. He crossed paths with Jim Warren three or four times a year, and thought the minister a likeable fellow, well-meaning but naïve. They had a careful relationship, making the effort to stay on common ground during their occasional interactions.

He skimmed the front page. "Seems kind of funny. A national Presbyterian convention in Las Vegas."

"I didn't pick the city."

"Well, can't say they're preaching to the choir. They probably got a cheap deal."

"I almost didn't sign up."

George lowered the paper. "Listen, honey, that stuff's way in the past. Could've happened anywhere."

"Yeah, well, but it didn't."

Judy's eyes lowered to her Bible, but they weren't moving.

"Did you tell any of your old nursing buddies you were coming?"

"I thought about calling Kathy Rohleder."

"I remember her. Pretty good looking. Married that casino guy."

"She was my best friend at the hospital but— I just didn't." She paused. "She probably doesn't even live there anymore."

"Easy enough to find out."

Silence. Judy lifted her gaze out the window. The sky had cleared. A white sail reflected moonlight above the shimmering water as the vessel slowly passed the channel marker. It was all so pretty.

Wasn't it?

From eighteen years experience, George knew when things were wrong.

"What."

"Nothing."

Something inside his wife was trying to come out. He looked over at her.

"What."

Suddenly Judy jumped up and ran from the room. As she hurried up the stairs, George heard a sob.

"What'd I say?"

Startled, he followed her up and into the bedroom where he found her sprawled on the bed crying. He had no idea what he'd done now.

Minutes later, a stunned George Reynolds sat in the upholstered chair looking at his wife. Judy was slumped against the headboard with a tissue. For a time, neither said anything.

"So you just decided to put the church's construction fund money into the stock market, and didn't tell anybody?" he asked, finally.

Judy looked over at George. "Yeah."

"And how much money is— gone?"

"Two hundred and eighty five thousand dollars."

A heavy silence. Outside, it had started to rain again, ticking against the windows.

"And you could just do that?   Write checks on your own authority?"

"Yeah. I guess."

She guessed?   "Out of the construction fund account?"

He waited for her to – he didn't know what. She pulled another tissue from the box.

"Well— I mean it's not exactly a separate construction fund. There's only one account. Well, two accounts, really."

Just a detail, George thought. One or two accounts.

"Anyway, I read all that stuff about growth stocks and wind power companies and oil and all, and it was all going to go up and then I read about day trading—"

"Day trading?!"   George was astounded.   He knew something like ninety percent of all day traders went broke. He thought for a minute as she looked at him like a wounded koala. No wonder she'd been spending so much time on the computer. He could have suspected, really, if he reflected on her personality and past struggles. He'd just missed the signs.

She began to cry softly. George waited while she composed herself. She grabbed a pillow and hugged it.

"And you didn't tell anyone at the time because . . . ?"

"I was going to surprise them," she sniffled. "I thought we'd make a lot of money."

You can bet this will surprise them, he thought. "So they had this emergency meeting yesterday and that's what it was about?"

The words tumbled out. "Yes. They said the whole construction project is in danger, and the roof isn't dried in so it's even worse if it rains. Which it stupid did. They said we needed an immediate audit from an outside firm.   They're going to hire somebody as soon as we get back from Las Vegas."

"And you kind of didn't say anything?"

"Yes."

"And you're in charge of the dough."

"Well, I am the treasurer. I don't know. It's not very—organized, I guess."

Two hundred and eighty-five grand down the tubes and they're just finding out. Judy was right, it certainly wasn't very organized. Did all churches operate this way? George hoped not, but maybe. He recalled reading stories in the Post about church money gone missing now and then. Usually it was a deliberate act committed in an atmosphere of trust. Two priests from nearby Boynton Beach had gone to prison for embezzling almost a million dollars; amazingly, many parishioners had defended them. No wonder all those fakers and showmen were on TV Sunday mornings. All week long, come to think of it. A few years earlier, the all-time con artist Bernie Madoff had decimated the Jewish population of Palm Beach, running through the town like swine flu. Madoff had committed the unpardonable sin of ripping off his own people for billions. George's eyes narrowed in thought.

The rain had begun again. Faraway lightning flickered against the window pane, turning the emeralds to diamonds. It occurred to George that Judy probably had not read those newspaper articles, nor seen the television stories, and that she had no idea she could go to prison.

29

Across the water and two or three economic strata away in West Palm Beach, James Warren also watched the rain from his small study. The occasional lightning flash lit up the Palm Beach Presbyterian steeple at 316 Primrose Lane. It looked solid and reassuring, but his church was in trouble, and he didn't understand it. How could such a staggering sum of money be missing? It wasn't like reconciling petty cash, for Go— for Pete's sake. It had been his idea to ask Judy Reynolds to be treasurer. True, she wasn't a trained accountant, but Judy was intelligent, diligent, capable. It had seemed like a good idea at the time. It *was* a good idea. He simply had no clue what could have happened to the funds; he was half convinced it was a bookkeeping error despite Joe Dykes' statements at the meeting. They'd just have to start the audit as soon as they got back from Las Vegas. The money would probably turn up somewhere, probably in some account they'd overlooked. Wouldn't it?

Las Vegas. Mixed feelings, there. Aside from the excitement of the place, it was but a few hours from Phoenix and –

He wished Betsy were home. Somehow whenever his wife went on another mission trip he seemed to need her for one reason or another. She was the only one he'd ever told about the Oasis Home for Boys, the only person who understood how Jim Warren's life had been shattered that one morning on the Black Canyon Freeway and the years of hell that had followed.

But he was here, and she was – somewhere else.

Thunder rumbled several seconds after the electric flash. The storm seemed to be moving away. Maybe he'd read in bed. He'd been wading through *Finding God at Harvard,* and usually managed two or three pages before drifting off. He got a lot farther whenever he picked up a Michael Crichton thriller.

He got up and wandered into the bedroom. He saw that he'd left his dresser drawer open and forgotten to hang up his pajamas. He felt guilty that he didn't always make the bed when Betsy was away. He knew he should.

30

"Who knows about this?"

Somewhere, water was dripping slowly. It happened sometimes, when the rain came from a certain angle; most likely it dripped down a flue. George hadn't found the leak.

"You," Judy Reynolds said through a tissue.

George shifted in the armchair. He never used it. It looked comfortable, but wasn't. Maybe it had springs in it, or something.

The goalkeeper's mind was spooling up, now. Just like the old days at the blackjack tables.

"Me. For now, anyway. You'd have to tell them before they do the audit. Can't just let them find out when you all get back from Vegas."

"I know. I should have spoken up at the meeting, but I— I was afraid. What am I going to do?" She sagged back against the headboard. Outside, the wind had shifted; the rain drummed on the north windows.

"It gives us about ten days, maybe," George said.

"Ten days?"

George got up and came over to the side of the bed. He sat down on the edge, smiled and ruffled her hair. She looked at him with wet eyes, sniffled, and smiled back gratefully.

"We can't just write a check," he said gently.

"I'm sorry."

George got up and went to the window. Puddles had formed on the lawn, reflecting the streetlight. He spoke softly. "The last time I was in that town, it ended my career." He paused. "Careers."

Her eyes widened and her hand flew to her mouth, now an
O.

"Oh, no, George. You can't do that!"

George took a breath, suddenly needing oxygen.
Unconsciously, he reached down and rubbed his leg. He walked to
his dresser and looked at an eight by ten picture. As he did so, he ran
his finger down the wooden frame.

"Please! Don't go back there!"

"Got any other ideas?"

"I— I don't—" She trailed off.

George turned and looked at his wife. She shook her head
helplessly.

"It's all right." Sure it was. "I'll see if I can get on your
flight," he said. "We'll just tell them I decided to go along. Do they
know what I used to do?"

Judy nodded. "Everybody knows. They ask me about it
sometimes."

George was mildly surprised. No one from the church had
ever asked him about his former Las Vegas vocation. He turned and
looked at the picture. The sky was brilliant blue, a rare occurrence
during the 3 p.m. matches in England, and the sunlight lit up a
younger George, frozen in time, as he dove for a shot in front of a
packed Selhurst Park.

The small print read:

Crystal Palace F.C.
Goalkeeper George Reynolds

He remembered that fine day against Liverpool, an F.A. Cup
quarterfinal match played at home. He had been full of adrenaline
and anticipation. He recalled the shot as well. He hadn't contained
the rebound, but he had stopped the ball that had a ticket for the
lower right corner. Liverpool had won, 1-nil, and George could not
have saved Ian Rush's volley that had found the net with ten minutes

to go. They had played the Reds level for eighty minutes in front of a delirious crowd, and it had been glorious.

The sun will always be lighting me up, and I'll always be in one piece at the top of my game, as long as I have this picture, he thought, and smiled.

31

George Reynolds entered a darkened room. It was hard to tell, but he appeared to be in some sort of small casino. John Roselli stood behind a blackjack table. He smiled and beckoned George over.

"Been waiting for you, Reynolds. Big game here."

Something seemed wrong to George, something out of kilter. He approached cautiously. He glanced to the sides, where dark shapes writhed in the shadows.

"What in hell is that?"

Roselli chuckled. "Precisely. Floor men? They're my floor men. Can't be too careful these days. Lots of cheaters and card counters, know what I mean? A good floor man blends right in."

Suddenly, flames burst from the walls with a whoosh, illuminating the blackjack table. The fire warmed George's face. Sweat began to trickle down his brow, into his eyes. He reached up and wiped away the moisture. His shirt was sticky, now. From somewhere, the sound of groaning metal. Was this normal?

"It's hot. Jesus."

"He can't hear you."

George ran his finger under his collar. "Like a toaster in here."

"Sorry, the a.c.'s on the fritz. Been out for awhile, but we're all used to it."

George looked around nervously. Something really wasn't quite right. For one thing, Roselli's shirt was black, the tuxedo and tie white. The table felt was a blood red color, awful to look at. There was only one player stool. The flames seemed to be growing *nearer, pushing him toward the table where Roselli stood, ready to deal the cards. There was another sound, now, as well, a low wailing. He looked at the casino owner. His features seemed to darken, the edges of his face grow deeper.*

George sat at the table. It was a hand held game.

"How many decks?" George asked out of habit. Sometimes two decks could look like one, depending on how the dealer held the cards.

"Just one." Roselli burned the top card with a smile. "Get it?" he asked.

He dealt a hand. As George picked up his cards, they burst into flame. He screamed but couldn't let go as his hands caught fire.

Roselli laughed. "Got a hot hand, goalkeeper?"

George awoke with a gasp. His face was slick with sweat. He sat up and drew a shuddering breath.

Judy stirred. "You okay?" She reached over and patted his arm.

"Yeah— yeah, I'm all right. Go back to sleep."

He pushed aside the covers and moved to the window. The rain was heavier now, cascading down the glass in sheets. A dim ache sifted through his leg.

"Jesus," he said.

He can't hear you just now.

32

Judy felt a growing foreboding, waves on a spring tide of
guilt. She wanted to embrace the hope that George would save the
day, her hero, but when he decided to go she'd felt a rush of anxiety
instead of relief. She tried without success to talk her husband out of
accompanying the church group to Las Vegas. They agreed to keep
their cover story simple: she told Reverend Warren her husband was
going just to keep her company and to see if he would be permitted
to play a little blackjack. The minister was delighted. Once George
made his decision, he seemed to come alive and went about
preparing for the trip with a zeal that disturbed Judy. He had kept up
with the game, which had undergone changes over the past eighteen
years. George had read the Ben Mezrich books *Bringing Down the
House*, the story of the six MIT students who had taken card
counting to perhaps the ultimate level, and *Busting Vegas*. The latter
described the system that relied on as little information as the
identification and location of a single card in a shuffled shoe. The
results had been devastating, the take in the millions before the
players were identified. But George was a lone wolf, and played
without a partner, and was of the old school, so he took his dusty
Blackjack to Win paperback off the shelf. The pages were dog-eared
and the binding was falling apart, but it was the real stuff. The
anonymous author, known only as The Grey Knight, had decimated
the casinos years earlier during his raids on the Nevada landscape.

Judy had her Holy Bible, and he had his.

There were new rule variations, all unfavorable to the player.
Single deck blackjack had been as difficult to stamp out as malaria,
no matter how hard the casinos tried. The ideal game for a card

counter, many casinos had poisoned the rules by paying 6:5 instead of 3:2 on a player blackjack.   It didn't sound like much, but meant that for a ten dollar bettor playing a hand a minute, using error-free basic strategy but not counting cards, his hourly losses would soar from $3.50 to $8.35.

George went online and updated himself on the exact nature of the game currently being played in each Las Vegas casino, once a painstaking and difficult task but now made easy with the internet. With the information obtained and graded, he assembled the list of viable targets. Ironically, the Oasis had as good a game as any on the strip, but of course he would never go near the place.   The smaller downtown casinos had traditionally offered some advantage to the serious blackjack player, with many single deck and two deck games and the most favorable rules.

Many of the hotels on George's list had not existed when he left Las Vegas eighteen years ago, but a new operation didn't guarantee anonymity. He knew that floor men, dealers, croupiers and pit bosses were localized nomads, often drifting from place to place. Casinos had been known to lay off gaming staff simply in an effort to change their luck; there was a chance he might run into someone from the old days in a new hotel. George was fairly sure his picture was not in the Griffin book, but if so the shot would be almost two decades old. The odds of getting barred outright seemed negligible. He wondered briefly what had become of John Roselli, who, he figured, would be around seventy now, if he was still alive. It was not a thought he dwelled on.

George sat at the library desk, cleared of the usual papers and bills. He dealt blackjack over and over, playing a two deck game for both dealer and player. Initially, the house's check pile was much larger than the player's. The speed wasn't there yet, and he knew he had to be a lot sharper, but he was gratified how quickly the rudiments of the game were coming back after almost two decades. Time passed unnoticed as the sun tracked across a clouded sky, gilding the edges of the low cumulus puffs. After a time, they crowded together into a gray slate.

Judy came in with a pimiento cheese sandwich, a couple of Oreos and a glass of milk on a tray.

"How's it going?"

"Like riding a bike." He picked up the sandwich and took a bite. "Mmm, delicious. Hey, thanks."

Judy looked at the cards and checks in front of George.

"George . . . I'm sorry," she said softly. Outside, the sky sputtered.

"Don't say that. I'm beginning to look forward to this, anyway."

"I don't know if that's good or bad." She paused. "Please tell me the truth. Can you do this after so long?"

George just shrugged.

"How much money will you – will we bring?"

"I figure I can pull together maybe thirty five, forty thousand on short notice." He sipped his milk. "You know it's money we can't afford to lose."

Judy's hand went to her open mouth. She closed her eyes and spoke softly. "Oh, my God. What have I done?"

"Aah, we'll be okay. Probably." Both knew it was just words. She turned and stared out the window.

"I don't remember rain like this."

George wore a thoughtful expression. He didn't remember rain like that, either. It seemed relentless. He put the food down and picked up the cards. Judy patted his shoulder and left the library. He dealt hand after hand. His fingers moved swiftly now. Checks moved back and forth; George's pile grew larger. If he had been listening he would have heard the water drumming on the roof and the windows.

33

The night before leaving for Las Vegas, Reverend James Warren was keyed up. He'd hardly traveled out of state since taking the reins at Palm Beach Presbyterian, and his anticipation had grown as the day neared. The last Presbyterian convention had been in Orlando, just three hours north. He enjoyed that city, the amusement parks, the fine restaurants; he had an annual Florida resident pass to the Disney attractions. He'd been there often, but Vegas would be new and exciting. Warren had looked online for a couple of hours, planning his time in Nevada. Not that it was a vacation, really, but then again why had they chosen Las Vegas if not to enjoy the place a little bit?

An old auto buff, Warren relished seeing the great antique car display at the Imperial Palace. He couldn't wait to be awed by the pirates and pyrotechnics at Treasure Island, the indoor canals at the Venetian, the Pharaoh's tomb, the giant Luxor pyramid that shot its 30.2 billion lumens (he'd looked it up in the Wikipedia) high into the troposphere. He read up on the shows and decided he'd love to see just about any of them except the female impersonators. Female impersonators made him uneasy. He looked forward to an excursion to a real ghost town and another to the Hoover Dam. He was fascinated to learn that of the 112 men who died constructing the massive work, the last man killed was the son of the first to die – thirteen years later to the day.

Warren felt a kinship with the desert, the stillness of the stark landscape, the sense of great distance: the high, deep blue sky with its crystalline high clouds and jet contrails crisscrossing like celestial tic tac toe played against the heavens. It was where he had spent the first half of his life, just north of Phoenix, gazing up at those alabaster tracings, wondering, trying to read the celestial poetry written by the jet engines, wondering if they were writing to him, much as T.S. Eliot had wondered about his mermaids. He had looked up and wished he were onboard, winging away from the Black Canyon Freeway that had taken his parents, from the Oasis Home for Boys, from the Sisters of the Immaculate Conception.

And Father Damien Corr.

Still, the desert had been his home.

Home is where the . . .

He left the thought unfinished.

Warren climbed in bed early (he'd made it up that morning), having heard how difficult it was to sleep in Las Vegas. But it was no good. He was too hyped. He turned this way and that, glanced at the clock which seemed to stop whenever he wasn't looking. At 1:20, he sighed. Maybe I should get up, he thought. It didn't help that Betsy, his wife of eight years, was still away and he was alone. He didn't know how long it was before he fell into a fitful sleep.

*   *   *   *   *

He was back at the Oasis, and he was twelve years old. Father Corr had summoned him to his quarters. As he entered, the old feelings of horror and revulsion returned, and his stomach roiled.

"Wait, you don't understand," he told the ancient priest, fighting the bile that was heaving upward. "I'm grown up now. I don't belong here. I don't sleep in the dormitory anymore. I sleep with my wife Betsy." He retched, and his throat burned.

But that wasn't really true, for Betsy wasn't there, she was off again on one of her mission trips, sleeping in tents and talking strange Indian talk and Spanish in some godforsaken place along with the youth minister and a dozen teenagers building yet another—

And anyway, Jim Warren's entreaties fell on deaf ears, literally, as the old priest's hearing aids dangled from his collar. And then Father Corr pulled out the largest, sharpest knife Warren had ever seen, it glistened it was so sharp, and he rose up from his chair and began chasing the boy, hearing aids jangling on their cords, screaming epithets all the while, and Warren realized with dismay he really was twelve and Father Corr was way bigger than he was and he couldn't run because his legs were stuck in molasses or something and he tripped and fell on the Santa Fe tracks and he could hear the whistle of the—

What? The Santa Fe was miles from the Oasis, running on the edge of town through the desert, and that didn't make much sense—

He woke, sweating and breathing hard. He hadn't dreamed of the old priest in – how long? – maybe a year. Yet the emotions were as vivid as ever. He shook his head slowly and turned over his pillow.

We are all prisoners of our past. There was a hackneyed line. Boy, wasn't it the truth, though. But then he had another thought, a phrase from the Eagles song:

So often times it happens
that we live our lives in chains
And we never even know we have the key.

That was better. He had the key, he was sure. Somewhere.

He didn't remember much in the morning, but his breath quickened when something in his raisin toast reminded him of the old priest's ring.

34

George was cart wheeling past floor after floor, broken leg flapping, down and down. Occasionally he would see Judy on a balcony below, and she would reach out and try to grab him unsuccessfully. He—

- woke with a start and looked over at the seat next to him. Reverend Warren, seated by the window, was reading *The Gospel According to Pontius Pilate* by James Mills. On the aisle, Judy dozed. Across the row, Joe Dykes, a nightmare all by himself in polyester and checks, slept, mouth open and drooling. The ambient jet noise didn't quite cover his snoring. Next to Joe, Dexter Wilcox read a magazine while Tom Swayne looked out the perspex.

George considered his traveling companions. He knew Judy was fond of Tom Swayne, the congenial hardware store manager, telling George the young man had struggled since the Home Depot store had opened on Palm Beach Lakes Boulevard. She'd fixed Tom up with Jane Pont, a Sunday School teacher along with Judy at 'PB Pres'. When the pair had announced their engagement six months later, Judy had been overjoyed.

On their last night at home, before they turned the light out, Judy had filled him in on the other members of the PB Pres delegation.

"Dexter's okay, but he lost his job about a year and a half ago. You met him once at the Sisters in Christ luncheon." George remembered the little man struggling with the heavy trays; they'd both been volunteered as waiters by their wives.

"What did he do?" he asked, hands behind his head on the pillow.

"He's a mechanical engineer."

"He looks the part. Those glasses look like they could start a fire in the sunlight."

Judy giggled. "He got laid off from Pratt & Whitney and it took him almost a year to get another job. Now he manages some tile and lumber company."

"Who's the other guy?" George asked.

"Wait, I'm not done with Dexter. His wife Marcy tells everybody they don't sleep in the same bedroom, and that it was her idea."

"You gotta be kidding me."

"No, she does. She even told me. I guess that year off work stained their marriage. She's about two inches taller than he is and five years younger. He's forty one."

"Figures, I guess. Did I ever meet her?" George was curious.

"No. Joe Dykes is the other guy. He works for the city. He's some kind of building inspector or something. His wife Debbie says he's always telling her he works for a bunch of assholes who lack vision and guts."

"Everybody thinks they work for a bunch of assholes who lack vision and guts. Is he that beefy guy with the phony hair dye job?"

"That's him. Debbie said he wants to move to Montana when he retires in two years."

"Yeah? What's Montana got?"

"Who knows? Debbie said she wishes he would, 'cause she's not going anywhere."

"Christ, you women are worse than men. Everybody tells everybody everything."

"Of course, how else would it work?" she'd said.

"Telephone, telegraph, tell a woman."

"Nobody's used a telegraph for fifty years."

"It's an old joke." He turned out the light.

35

George sat up in his coach seat on the Boeing 767, reached into the pocket of his sports jacket and pulled out a new package of cards. He unwrapped the cellophane as Warren peered out the window.

"Is that Lake Mead down there?"

George leaned over the minister and looked below.

"Yep. Won't be long now. See the Hoover Dam?"

"Wow. Looks huge even from up here. I read up on it. Did you know the last guy to die—"

"—was the son of the first guy. Thirteen years later to the day."

Warren smiled and nodded. Well to the north, high, wispy mare's tails brushed the sky. The minister pointed to the horizon.

"That's God's palette, you know."

George followed Warren's finger. "I guess maybe so."

"Airline pilots are lucky. They get to see His paintings every day."

"You're a poet, Jim."

"Sometimes I think that's a greater affirmation of faith than all they taught me, all the books and all."

"You got that right."

Across the aisle, Joe Dykes drooled onto his shirt as he slept. George nodded towards the city works inspector.

"Think that's an affirmation?" George laughed.

Warren smiled. "You know, George, I'm really glad you decided to come. I know this is new territory for you."

"Las Vegas?"

"No, no, I mean the Presbyterian Convention."

"Yeah . . . new territory."

You don't know the half of it, George thought.

"I hope you'll have time to attend a few of the seminars," Warren said.

George smiled. "How about if you do the praying and I'll do the playing," he replied. The minister chuckled. The goalkeeper genuinely liked Jim Warren, but knew he would have neither the time nor the inclination to participate in the convention activities. The near-impossible task of seeking financial restoration for P B Pres would take all his energies, his skills, and a measure of luck. Nobody gives away money without a fight, and the casinos knew how to fight.

George pulled down his tray table, extracted the jokers and shuffled the new deck. The minister watched George's rapid and practiced hands make a few one handed cuts and shuffles, limbering up and showing off. He did a few simple card tricks, then allowed Warren to cut the cards and dealt him three blackjacks in a row.

"How in Heaven's name did you do that?" Warren asked.

George laughed. "Well, it wasn't in the name of Heaven."

"You can do amazing things with those cards."

George had never forgotten what had happened to his five of clubs eighteen years ago. "Not like some people I've known," he said.

The plane had begun to descend.

George leaned over and pointed out the window.

"There's the strip. See it?"

Warren peered below.

"The Promised Land, eh, Jim?" George asked.

"I doubt that."

The aircraft banked and turned on final approach. As both men looked out the window, the cabin lights flickered. There was a reddish glow. A gaunt figure dressed in black passed by in the aisle. Neither George nor Reverend Warren, gazing at the city below, took notice. Joe Dykes woke with a start, coughing on spittle. On the aisle, Judy felt a chill and shuddered. Tom Swayne thought he smelled something foul.

Twelve hundred feet below, something black fluttered across the threshold of McCarran International runway 25R.

36

Detective Davey Cahill watched as Special Agent Tim Moss pushed in a last mouthful of scrambled eggs soaked with hot sauce and sprinkled with crumbled bacon.

"Christ, Davey, you're turning into a monk," Moss said. "I still remember that dance instructor broad. She was hot."

"How do you know? You never met her."

Moss prodded. "Those dancers, they move like cats." Cahill ignored him.

"Those dancers, they screw like lemmings."

Cahill, unaware of the mating habits of rodents in general, shook his head slightly and looked at his friend's plate. "Do you ever order anything else?"

"Stop changing the subject. What do you mean?"

"Same thing, every week. Scrambled eggs, bacon, sausage, hash browns. Hot sauce on the whole mess. Then a little sugar doughnut and a slice of melon."

"Hey, melon's good for you. Cleans your palate."

"I know you don't eat like that at home or you'd need a bookmark to find your belt."

Moss shrugged. "Are you kidding? All I get is dry toast and cereal. Mary wonders why I'm not losing any weight." They laughed. Cahill was fond of Moss' on-again, off-again girlfriend. Their relationship reminded the detective of sunspot cycles: warm, quiet times marked by bursts and flare-ups, spectacular coronas and dark spots. Moss seemed to thrive on it.

Cahill took a bite from his Danish and sipped coffee. "Listen, Tim. I'm doing a little background and I wonder if you guys have a file on someone."

"Who?"

"John Roselli."

"Johnny Rosselli? Sure, we had one. The file's as thick as my arm."

"Not the dead wiseguy Rosselli. I mean John Roselli, the owner of the Oasis. It's not the same spelling, you know?"

"This connected to that Oasis stuff you asked me about a couple weeks ago?"

Cahill nodded. Moss pushed his plate aside, picked up his coffee cup. "I don't think so. No, there's nothing on him, I'm pretty sure."

"I wonder if I could take a look at your Johnny Rosselli stuff anyway. Maybe it's possible something from my guy got put in your guy's file."

Moss looked dubious.

"I mean, it's possible, right?"

That afternoon, Detective Davey Cahill sat in a cubicle in the John Bailey Memorial Building on West Lake Mead Boulevard and stared at the crumpled, smeared copy of John Roselli's 1966 gaming license application. The document was almost completely illegible; the carbon hadn't stood the test of time very well. The application copy had indeed been misfiled by the FBI in the jacket on Johnny Rosselli, the Chicago mobster who had been involved in a CIA assassination attempt on Fidel Castro, and who'd had close ties to Santos Trafficante in Tampa before trying to swim across Miami's Biscayne Bay. Without legs and inside a weighted steel drum, the odds had been against him.

Aside from the name, and that of the Oasis, the only readable entry left on the application was an address for Roselli within the preceding five years. The typed answer was:

316 Primrose Lane
West Palm Beach, FL

"Son of a bitch," was all Moss could say. "I wouldn't have believed there'd be anything in there. I wouldn't even have thought of it."

Cahill shrugged. "Me neither, really. It just popped into my head that maybe with the same name there was a chance something would get in the wrong file."

"We've got an office in West Palm, you know. I know an agent there. I'll give her a call."

"Thanks. I owe you a beer."

"You meet Haley, you'll make it a whole bottle, not just a draft," Moss said with a grin.

37

Las Vegas, Nevada – Day One

The motley delegation from Palm Beach Presbyterian exited the jet way at McCarran International and was immediately assaulted by a slot machine symphony of rapid-fire bells and electronic beeps. George slowed and a distant smile crept across his face.

"Aah, the sweet music of my youth."

Judy looked quickly over at her husband, concern on her face. George took her hand and squeezed it reassuringly.

"Hey, not to worry. It'll be all right. You'll see."

Joe Dykes was the last to exit the corridor. He stopped still, mesmerized by the action. Like Reverend Warren, Dexter and Tom, he had never been to Nevada. He'd had driven to the Indian casino once, some years prior, with his bowling team. He had lost two hundred dollars, and still blamed the Seminoles for it, telling his teammates the games were crooked and all Indians were drunks anyway.

But this was Las Vegas.

George headed in the direction of baggage claim. As the group passed the rows of slots, the light dimmed momentarily and the ceaseless cacophony became muffled. At the faint sound of groaning metal, Joe seemed to notice something. He slowed and glanced back with a questioning look. In the back row, a flickering darkness enveloped a gaunt figure in black cassock as he pulled a handle. A reddish liquid cascaded out and splashed across the floor, accompanied by strangely dissonant bells.

"Hey, what—" Joe blinked hard. When he opened his eyes, the young black man in the back row raised his arms as a machine lit up and rang continuously.

Tom Swayne pulled Joe forward and they stepped onto the moving walkway towards baggage claim. The group spent the next twenty minutes picking up their suitcases. When they walked out to the taxi line, the temperature hit them like a firewall.

"My God, it's hot," Joe said.

"Yes, but it's a dry heat," said Warren, parroting a Chamber of Commerce slogan.

"So's a furnace," Tom observed.

The long line snaked back and forth but moved quickly. They split in two for the cab rides to their hotel. Warren, George and Judy piled into the first taxi, taking in the sights as the cab rolled down Paradise Road. The sky was cobalt, the air crystal clear on a typical Las Vegas sunny morning. With the three hour time change it was not yet noon.

"Reverend, when does Betsy get in?" Judy asked.

"In two days. Her mission trip gets back tomorrow, and then she flies out here."

The minister's wife had been in Guatemala for a week with a missionary group building yet another school for the rural Indians, who by this time, George figured, were all college grads. The whole region should be covered with schools and churches and orphanages, except for the hurricanes and mud slides and earthquakes that seemed to knock them down as fast as the volunteers put them up. George wondered idly if the Lord didn't like the Presbyterians meddling in other cultures, or merely wanted to keep them busy. They just couldn't let well enough alone.

Religion, he thought. Christ.

As they drove, he marveled at the size and magnitude of the new casinos and their oversized, lavish outdoor displays, all paid for by the two dollar bettor, two and a half million of them a month, thirty million a year. A ceaseless migration on eight hundred fifty flights per day, groups just like the stewards of Palm Beach Presbyterian, arriving at the number one destination in the United States.

George had to admire what he saw. Eighteen years, and the town had transformed itself again. Out with the family vacation spiel, in with the new slogan.

Whatever happens in Vegas stays in Vegas.

There was New York! Grab a bagel! A few steps, and the Eiffel Tower right around the corner! Have a baguette! Your wallet is your passport! Egypt, with a beacon that could be seen from space! What next? Perhaps on the next block, that statue of Saddam, hoisted again, given new life in a new desert, maybe with a miniature Baghdad, exploding merrily and crackling with small-arms fire! No? What went there? The old Dunes? Gone! The Stardust? Vanished! The Aladdin? A memory! The Sands, Landmark, Hacienda, Pioneer . . . the old carpet joints, casualties of war imploded into oblivion, like the dreams of their patrons. All reborn with new life, bigger, better, ready to play! You pays your money and you takes your choice!

Hey, I'm back!

It was almost as though he'd never left, except that it wasn't.

George tried to place the ghosts of junkets past, corpses in the vale of tears that was Las Vegas, his adventures in Bugsy Siegel's 1945 dream come true. Bugsy and Walt Disney, the men who had shaped America's playgrounds with a deck of cards, a pair of dice and a rodent.

The Imperial Palace, with its wonderful car exhibit? Yes, there was the old Palace, but it sure looked tired and in need of a makeover. The MGM Grand? Moved down the street, leaving the old building and tragic memories of the fire behind. And there . . . where Evel Knievel didn't quite clear the fountains. Las Vegas Boulevard and Flamingo Road – ground zero. The crossroads of the world, the Pearly Gates to Perdition.

They passed a couple of Metro cops on bicycles, in their yellow shirts and black shorts, as though they were leading the French Grand Prix. They were talking to two young women on a street corner. The place hasn't changed all that much, George thought, underneath the glitter and sizzle. Maybe the girls are a little younger, but maybe I'm a lot older.

Memories.

For James Warren, of course, there were no memories. Las Vegas left him gaping— the monstrous outdoor displays, the sheer size of the place, everything larger than life. Casino after casino, hotel after hotel, the old rub joints and new state of the art palaces side-by-side in the Las Vegas Valley.

"Jim, do you know the difference between praying in church and praying in the casino?" George asked.

"No."

"When you pray in the casino, you mean it."

George smiled at his own joke. He leaned back, hands behind his head and watched the scenery roll by. There was contentment on his face. He looked happy, almost childlike. Judy bit her lip, wondering if she should be concerned. The cab driver had one of those bead things on the seat back and some incomprehensible mobile-type deal hanging from the mirror. As he turned the wheel, she noticed the strange ring on his finger. It had a large, brown oval stone. She thought it the ugliest ring she had ever seen.

38

"A *church*? You sure?" Cahill looked again at the typed address on John Roselli's gaming license application. There was no mistake: it read 316 Primrose Lane.

"Yeah, Palm Beach Presbyterian Church." The voice on the other end of the telephone belonged to Special Agent Haley Carradine of the FBI's West Palm Beach field office. "It's only a couple of blocks from here." She looked out the window down Flagler Drive. "I can see the steeple, actually."

"Has it been a church long?"

"Almost a hundred years. I asked. It's got an interesting history. It burned down in the 1940's, and before that it was some other church. Need me to dig any further?"

"No, I guess not. Listen, thanks for the help."

"Don't mention it, Detective. Glad to help a friend of Tim's."

Cahill hung up the phone, thoughtful. For whatever reason, John Roselli had listed the address of a church on his gaming license application. It made little sense, unless he just got the address wrong. The commission would have checked his background information, so why write a bogus address? Although in 1966 they didn't always check very rigorously. Maybe Roselli just made it up, maybe he'd been in the city and remembered the street, or knew someone from there, or whatever. It didn't seem worth the effort to actually dig into the church's past, perhaps looking at Palm Beach County property records, calling the local historical society or otherwise wasting his time on the whole deal. It was probably just a typing error, anyway.

On the other hand, he wasn't seeing the dance instructor anymore. What did he have better to do?

He could not know the answer would be almost anything, or that he would wish he'd never asked.

39

After checking in at the Sacramento, the Palm Beach Presbyterian group ate lunch at the hotel's pizza parlor. Reverend Warren, Dexter, Joe and Tom then went on to the convention to register. Warren said he'd sign Judy in so she could accompany her husband for the afternoon.

At 1:45 pm, George and Judy climbed out of a taxi in front of the Mandalay Bay. In the old days, George disdained cabs unless he was going from one end of the strip to the other, or traveling between Las Vegas Boulevard and Fremont Street. Card counting required the player to be in and out quickly, and no matter how clever, somebody would be watching if he or she was not losing money after a reasonable period of time. George's limits were thirty minutes when he was ahead, and an hour regardless. He used the walks between casinos, which were usually considerable, for exercise and to clear his head.

Now, at age forty two with an aching leg (despite the two ibuprofen he'd taken at lunch), Judy in tow, and limited time to reach their financial goal, he traveled by taxi. He was starting to pay for the airplane ride and hoped the painkiller kicked in soon.

As they headed for the front doors, Judy stopped. It was obvious to George she was anxious.

"What's the matter?" he asked. "Sure you want to do this? You can take another cab to the convention."

"No— yes. I— I'm— I don't know. Let's go."

George took her arm. "All right," he said. "Everything'll be okay. Promise."

They entered the arena. George meandered through the rows of blackjack tables. His mind clicked into another gear, despite the intervening years.

It was show time.

Old habits flooded back. Besides the number of players at each table and its betting minimum – easily determined at a glance, as the sign's color always matched the corresponding check denomination - he noted the locations of the camera domes, table lighting, positions of the floor people and what they were doing, number and denomination of checks in the dealers' trays, how far down the dealer was in the shoe or decks, location of the cut card in the decks, dealer speed, crowd conditions, spotters, security and a million other things down to the number of waitresses on duty and where the good-looking women were playing. The last item had occasionally proved important for reasons less obvious than the aesthetic. An attractive woman at the tables often occupied the attention of the floor staff and allowed him to slip under the radar a while longer.

Most card counters sat at third base, the last and leftmost seat, which gave a mathematical advantage in that everyone's cards but the dealer's would have been played, and therefore counted, before playing decisions were required. The trouble was, the house knew it too. George had preferred the center, primarily to preserve a one-on-one game. Third base in a solo session was just too inviting with all the empty seats to his right.

But that was in the old days. In recent years, most casinos had barred mid-shoe entry, in response to MIT and other card counting teams. New players had to wait for a shuffle to enter the game. The house had inadvertently given the lone counter a significant advantage, preventing new players from entering the game during favorable conditions.

Toward the rear of the gaming area, George found a table with a $25 minimum and three players who appeared in their sixties. George laid five one hundred dollar bills on the felt. The dealer, a pleasant looking young man, spread the bills, picked up and counted them.

"Change five hundred," he called out. The floor man, a heavyset, dark-haired man in his fifties, nodded and eyeballed George. The dealer counted out four bumblebees and four quarters and pushed them over.

George bet fifty dollars, his first wager in almost two decades, and play began.

For the goalkeeper, it was as though time had bent around and met itself. Sitting down at the blackjack table was as familiar as a cowhand climbing back in the saddle after a short stop at the saloon. The intervening years vanished like a snowflake in the Nevada sun. The tactile sensations – the sound of the shuffle, like leathery wings promising an exciting flight, the click of the checks, the smooth feel of felt, the snap of the cards, dormant for so long, even the processed air with its metallic, stale cigar smell – they burst forth in his brain like spores exploding seeds into the air. He was surprised. George had not expected these memories, these impressions, to be so strong. He knew these powerfully sensual, almost sexual images seduced thousands of people every day.

The floor man eased over, crossed his arms and casually observed the action as he slowly chewed his gum. Judy wandered over to the slots and began feeding quarters, seeking favor from one of the hundred and ninety seven thousand one armed bandits in Las Vegas.

George played for twenty minutes. The cards ran fairly true, with no surprises and no long streaks. After cashing out, he collected Judy.

"How did you do?" she asked, as they walked towards the rear of the Mandalay Bay casino, which seemed about two miles.

"Okay. That woman yakked my head off, but I kept the count, never lost the picture. It was good practice."

"What do you mean, okay? Did you win?"

George gave a chuckle. "Yes, we did. Come on, I want to show you something. It's the only sightseeing I'll get a chance to do here."

Fifteen minutes later, George and Judy were wandering through the hotel's Shark Reef, where twelve hundred species of shark, ray, reptile and marine invertebrates roamed through over ninety thousand square feet of marine aquarium. They stopped at the jellyfish tank, where the ethereal creatures pulsed and eddied in the weak current. It was surreal and beautiful.

"Wow," Judy said. "That's God's handiwork, isn't it?" They were as translucent purple hearts, silently beating with life.

For some reason, the majesty of creation brought Judy a jarring realization. George had won six hundred twenty five dollars in his practice session. Six hundred twenty five dollars down, two hundred eighty four thousand and change to go, she thought. George had pocketed just over a half of one percent of what they needed to win, not counting her own two dollar and seventy five cents profit. Despite his success, Judy felt a wave of nausea. They needed a hell of a lot of money.

40

West Palm Beach, Florida

As George and Judy wandered through Shark Reef, a hod carrier named Erubiel Sanchez from Oaxaca, Mexico took off his hard hat and wiped his brow at the Palm Beach Presbyterian construction site. It was almost quitting time and hot and muggy despite the rain. It was hot in Oaxaca too, but the air didn't turn to steam and drown a person with every breath. Erubiel felt like he was wrapped in wet visqueen. He was looking forward to a couple of bottles of Estrella, maybe even a six pack. Estrella was real Mexican beer, not for export, and nothing like the watered down brake fluid his country sent up to the States. It was not so easy to get. His cousin Cesar, who was staying with him through the weekend in Lake Worth, had somehow brought a couple of cases across. Erubiel had joked that when the beer ran out, so did his hospitality. Because he was an illegal immigrant, Sanchez could not go back and forth across the border like his cousin and so he had to rely on his relatives for the beer runs. And whatever else his cousins managed to sneak across.

This church job hadn't gone well. The new, larger sanctuary was being constructed behind the old facility on the property. What did they expect? They weren't supposed to use salt water aggregate. All the rebar would rust away in a few years, but they'd be long gone anyway. There had been a couple of minor injuries and supply delays. The project was behind schedule. The wet weather hadn't helped, nor had those lazy Caribbean workers from Montserrat or Haiti or some goddamn place. They drank that shitty Prestige which was not really beer at all, Erubiel knew, but something made with the sewer water that ran in the streets and gutters of Cap Haïtien. Not that he knew much about Haiti, but he had tasted the swill, and his uncle Esteban had been to Cap Haïtien and so he could picture the place in his mind, and that's how he knew they must make Prestige there.

Erubiel was not an engineer but he had been in construction for a long time and he knew there was something definitely wrong with the new sanctuary. He had seen the foreman talking with Mister Fekete, the big boss, off to the side. Erubiel made like he wasn't looking, but he followed the foreman's finger as he pointed to a large crack that ran from the ceiling almost halfway down the wall, parallel to the stained glass window behind the altar. The discussion became heated.

The next day, the crack had been plastered over. Erubiel wanted to ask the foreman about it but he knew better. Anyway, what did he care? It wasn't a Catholic church.

He carried a load of bricks in his hod. They were making steps out of brick for a short sidewalk running from the rear entrance of the new building to the paved driveway. What a pain in the ass. Somebody had screwed up again because the piles of bricks could have been dumped a lot closer. As he stepped across the board that spanned the five foot deep trench beyond the back wall, he noted the water was halfway up the embankment. It had begun to rain again, dimpling the surface below his boot. He hoped his truck, a 1983 Dodge Rampage he'd bought in Lake Worth for three hundred bucks and a set of socket wrenches, would start in the wet weather. The damn thing was temperamental and—

Just as he was halfway across the short distance, altogether perhaps eight feet, Erubiel stepped on a patch of mud on the board left by the foreman, who had gone around front to lock the doors.

Before he knew it, his legs had flipped up in the air. He smacked down hard on the board, right on his back, and bounced up and into the water. Goddamn it! He was soaking wet. He stood up. He'd been carrying the hod on his shoulder and it was nowhere to be found. He cursed under his breath and hoped no one had seen his humiliation. The bottom of the trench was soft and his boots sank as he waded for the embankment. He almost didn't reach it. As he began to clamber up, the wet soil gave way. He couldn't get a purchase. His other boot, in the mud at the bottom of the ditch, was sinking at an alarming rate. He heaved himself up and got one leg on the hill. He was thinking he was going to give the foreman what-for, all right, when the soil gave way again. Jesus Christ, his right leg was almost knee-deep now. Maybe he should take off his boot. It was full of water. It cost eighty bucks but—

He couldn't reach it. It was too far below. Erubiel felt the first tendrils of panic, but then he realized he was right by the board. He grabbed onto it and yanked, pulling himself up. There was a sharp, fierce pain that made him gasp. Somehow there was a nail in the wood and it had gone right through his palm. Because he was still sinking, he could no longer raise his hand up to free it. He was nailed to the board! He sank further, and now he was hanging from the wood. He feared his palm would tear through. His blood was spurting and running and mixing with the rain and it hurt like hell. And now the board began to slide towards him. He was pulling the board sideways, right off the embankment! It was slipping, faster now, and suddenly it came crashing down, but somehow his hand didn't come free, and his wrist bent back and there was a sickening crack and another shocking wave of pain as the bone splintered. Suddenly he wished someone had seen his pratfall.

There was red at the edges of his vision. Erubiel began to scream for help, but the rain was coming down heavily now, a real downpour, and it was drumming on the equipment and everything else and muffling his voice. He felt the water at his neck. Jesus Mary and Joseph! There was someone at the top of the embankment! An old man, dressed in black, looking down at him. He couldn't see clearly because of the rain and the shock but he appeared to be – a priest? What the hell? But the old man made no move to help, he just stood, staring. Erubiel opened his mouth to scream as loud as he could and saw that the old man did too, as if mocking him, but then the old man wasn't an old man at all but something else entirely that launched itself off the embankment and into the water with a great splash, much faster than Erubiel dreamed it could move, and he saw with horror the ripples come straight at him as the old priest waved goodbye on the embankment and then there was a tremendous pain in his side and some incredible force wrenched him under and the water poured in and he choked, and he tried to draw another breath as the old priest waved goodbye but now there was only the water and he wished for a split second he was back in the state of Oaxaca drinking his own goddamn beer and then he thought only of the agony and felt the shock of cold muddy water in his lungs and then he felt nothing at all.

42

Las Vegas, Nevada

That first night, George and the Palm Beach Presbyterian delegation managed to link up for dinner. After the Mandalay Bay, George had played low stakes blackjack at the nearby Luxor and Excalibur casinos, regaining proficiency. He picked the fastest dealers and crowded tables. Under the difficult conditions, he won three of the four sessions while Judy watched from afar or pulled a few handles on quarter slots. All in all, he had done well and was satisfied he was playing error-free blackjack.

On their modest budget, the group went through the Roundtable buffet at the Excalibur. They'd hit a low point; the three hour difference and long plane ride had enervated them. Over dinner, Warren, Joe and Dexter debated an upcoming "Grace versus Works" lecture – George had asked if they were female wrestlers, and even the preacher had to grin - while Tom chatted about hardware and other more earthly topics. Dexter had to tell Joe to tone it down so the surrounding tables weren't in on the discussion. Throughout, George swallowed his pride: he used to spend more on dinner for himself in Las Vegas than their entire tab.

They split up after supper. Joe, Tom and Dexter wandered down Las Vegas Boulevard as the sunlight faded over purpling hills. The trio felt the pulse of excitement as the strip lights came alive. As they walked up the driveway to the MGM Grand entrance, gleaming limousines, white and black and reflecting a million lights, pulled up to the portico, disgorging or picking up handsome men and sleek, tan, beautiful women dressed to kill. At least the women looked sleek and tan and beautiful and dressed to kill to the church trio, quite unlike the Sunday morning dress ups at home.

Adrenaline kicked in, exhaustion vanished.

Moments later, Joe, Tom and Dexter stood at the head of the steps to the MGM Grand casino pit. Dexter had picked up a gaming guide and was leafing through the pages as Joe and Tom watched the action before them. Dexter looked up and around.

"Hey, this is exciting. I'm not even tired anymore."

"Long way from Palm Beach County," Joe said.

People came and went: down the stairs, carrying their dreams in their wallets and purses, or up, having left them in the dealer racks. The temporarily lucky ones were generally still down on the floor, feeding slots, shooting craps, playing blackjack, roulette, baccarat or one of several poker variations. Few would actually leave the place with wider wallets.

"Time to have some fun, boys!" Joe said with exuberance, as he clapped his hands and rubbed them together. He looked at Dexter, who was reading the pamphlet.

"I don't need that booklet. I know how to shoot craps."

"How do you know that?" Tom asked.

"The Army. That's what we did. I was a supply sergeant."

"I thought you said you were a helicopter pilot," Tom said.

"Well, I need the booklet," Dexter said. "I don't understand craps. I don't even understand the name."

Joe led the men down the steps. They threaded their way through the crowd, eyeing the action. There were people at every open craps table. Whoops and hollers here, groans and curses there. Joe made a big deal out of sensing the "auras" of the various games. He suddenly stopped at a table where a tall, stunning redhead, perhaps thirty years old and wearing a tight, low-cut sequined black dress, stood and observed the action. She had an air of distance, of promises made to men who were nothing like the deacons of Palm Beach Presbyterian. Joe pushed aside an elderly Korean so the trio had room on the rail. Tom stared at the woman, open-mouthed. He found her spectacular.

Joe turned to Dexter. "Gimme your money," he said in a low voice as he eyed the titian goddess.

"What?" Dexter was already confused.

"Come on. You said you didn't know how to shoot craps. We'll pool our dough and I'll show you how."

Dexter looked dubious.

"Come on, you're right here next to me. What do you think's gonna happen? Or do you wanna bet yourself?"

Dexter reluctantly reached into his wallet. "I'll lend— you can have a twenty."

"Jesus, what the hell? It's not like you come here every week."

"Well, I only got two hundred. Why? What'd you bring?"

"I got three fifty. Here, gimme the two bills and I'll put in the same, so we're an even split."

"What? No way! Let's start with . . . forty."

"Jesus Christ. At least give me fifty."

Dexter reluctantly handed Joe a fifty dollar bill. Joe matched it. He made a big show out of laying the money on the table as he glanced at the redhead. She made eye contact, and Joe felt a jolt of electricity. He swallowed hard.

"Is this all the chips we get?" Dexter said, looking at the two quarters and ten nickels. Compared to the other gamblers, they had a ridiculously small stake. It seemed to the engineer they had enough to last all of five minutes.

Joe ignored his new financial partner. He put a green check on the pass line as the croupier pushed him the dice.

"New shooter comin' out, folks, new shooter!" came the cry.

"Hey!! Twenty five bucks?!" Dexter yelled. "You're crazy! I told you I only brought two hundred!"

"Pipe down, for Chrissake, willya!? You're making me look bad!" Dexter hissed out of the side of his mouth, one eye on the statuesque queen.

Joe picked out two dice from the lot. He handed them to Dexter.

"Here, you do it."

Dexter looked surprised. "Me?"

"Now, Dexter, not next week."

Dexter brightened, suddenly warming to the idea. He threw the dice halfway down the felt. The stickman scooped them up and pushed them back to him.

"Sir, the dice must hit the rail," he said.

"Jesus Christ." Joe rolled his eyes. He looked at the redhead as if to say he's the asshole, not me, but she wasn't looking.

"Oh! I'm sorry," Dexter said. He picked up the dice and rolled again. Tom paid no attention; he was staring dumbly at the auburn goddess.

"Seven! Seven a winner, lucky seven! Pay the Pass line, pay the shooter! Come on, folks, hot table here . . ."

The lilting litany of the croupier.

A matching green check was laid alongside Dexter and Joe's bet; the dice were returned. Dexter stood there until Joe nudged him. He had a dazed expression.

"Hey! Wake up! Roll again, Dexter!"

Dexter nodded toward the bet. "What about—"

"Don't worry about it! Just roll the goddamn dice, willya?"

Dexter looked stricken with $50 of their money on the pass line. Joe rammed him in the ribs with his elbow and Dexter tossed the dice down the table. They bounced along merrily, caromed off the rail.

Eleven. They'd won again. Two more green checks.

Dexter's mouth was open, and then formed a grin. It was his turn to belt Joe. He punched him in the arm.

"Hey, this sure beats working!"

42

While Dexter rolled his naturals at the MGM Grand craps table 4, George split a pair of aces across the street at the Monte Carlo. He sat at third base, table BJ-17. The only other player in the hundred dollar minimum game was a well dressed Asian man, who occupied the third spot. Both had several thousand dollars in checks in front of them. Judy and Reverend Warren stood by a five dollar table several feet away. The casino was noisy and moderately crowded.

"Boy, this place is— overwhelming," Warren said as he looked around.

"It can be."

"Look at George and that other fellow. They haven't spoken a word to each other as far as I can tell. Isn't that odd?"

"Not really. They're in their own games. First time in Las Vegas, Reverend?"

"Yes. When you lived here, Judy, how could you— I mean, with all these distractions?"

"If you live here, you don't gamble. Not if you want to survive. Just take advantage of the shows and great meals. We'd go to the strip just on weekends."

"I guess that's smart."

A player got up from his first base seat at the five dollar table. He had a disgusted look as he brushed by Warren.

"Hey, pal, here's a seat if you want it," he said.

The minister was surprised. "Oh, me? Well, all right, I guess."

"The way this bitch is dealing, I'm not doing you any favors." The man walked away.

Warren sat down, confused. Judy stood behind. When he made no move to buy in, the dealer dealt a hand to the other players. Warren realized with a start he needed to get out his wallet. He extracted a ten as the dealer finished housekeeping. He held it out.

"Sir, you have to lay your money on the table."

"Oh," Warren said, and laid the ten down. He received two red nickel checks and the dealer began. When she came to Warren's spot, she stopped.

"Sir, your bet goes there." She indicated the betting circle.

"Oh! Sorry." The preacher moved a check into the circle.

And as he did so, James Warren became yet another of the thirty seven million annual Las Vegas visitors to lay his average stake of six hundred and twenty dollars down on the turn of a card, the spin of a wheel, the roll of the dice or the pull of a handle, four hours a day for 3.7 hotel nights in any of the seventeen hundred licensed gaming establishments in the city. And while most sowed their seeds to the wind, the state of Nevada reaped an annual harvest of nine billion dollars from their fallow hopes and failed dreams.

Whatever happens in Vegas stays in Vegas – usually all six hundred and twenty dollars. Nevada did not have nor did it need a personal state income tax.

The state called it gaming.

Warren received a jack and a ten. He picked them up. "Judy, what should I do? I've got enough points here, don't I?"

"Sir, please. Just one hand on the cards, all right?"

Warren jerked a hand away. The hand played out. The dealer busted and lay another red check alongside Warren's bet.

"Way to go, preacher!"

Warren, startled again, turned to see George standing behind him.

"George! Look! I won!"

George clapped Warren on the back. "Hey, lucky is better than good any day."

"Should I keep going?"

"Why not?"

Warren laughed and Judy smiled.

"Cocktails?" asked the attractive waitress. Warren was suddenly enjoying himself.

"Sure, why not? What've you got?"

Judy and the waitress rolled their eyes, George closed his.

Fifteen minutes later, Warren sat with Judy at a covered blackjack table in a closed section of the blackjack area. She drank a White Russian while Warren sipped his seven and seven through a straw. The preacher nodded towards George as he played across the row several tables away.

"Well, that was fun while it lasted. How long did I play, five minutes?"

"More like fifteen. It can be a real rush."

"Yes, I see. At least I did when I won a couple of hands." He nodded towards George. "He's doing very well. I had no idea how— I mean, I'm not used to seeing so much money in one place."

"Believe me, Reverend, neither am I."

Warren drained his drink. "Can we get another round?"

"Sure, but it's only free if you're at the tables. Playing."

"Oh. Oh, well." Warren shrugged and put his empty glass down. "You know, Judy, your husband's such an interesting guy. Wish I didn't just see him at Christmas and Easter."

"I wish the same thing."

"Do you still have friends in town here? I've been meaning to ask."

"I'm not really sure. I think I'll just let sleeping dogs lie."

Warren nodded. "We're all very proud of you, Judy. You're such a brave person."

She turned away.

43

The rail in front of Joe and Dexter was crowded with quarters, bumblebees and a few red nickel checks. They seemed to be everywhere. The table had gotten boisterous and crowded. People were two deep at the rail. Dexter couldn't believe their run of luck, couldn't take his eyes off the checks. There had to be over a thousand dollars there. A thousand dollars! He ran his fingers along them, felt the delicious sensation. They were lined up like Necco wafers. He almost wanted to suck on one. He tried to put them in order and count their winnings, but it seemed as though he was continually interrupted as they won another roll and Joe piled another stack indiscriminately on the rail. Then it was his turn again and this time he held the dice a full five minutes before crapping out. Maybe they should quit?!

Joe had been so busy with the checks and caught up in the game that he had forgotten about the redhead. He glanced up but she was not at the rail. He looked around the casino just in time to see her walking away with Tom, arm around his waist. He poked Dexter.

"Well, would you look at that, Dex. Who needs us?"

Dexter, still caressing their mother lode, followed Joe's gaze. "Jeez. Hope Jane doesn't find out."

"Who?"

"His fiancé, you asshole. Christ, you flirted with her at the Sunday Supper last month."

"How the hell's she going to find out?"

"Yeah, I guess. Unless he brings something home, you know what I mean?"

"Hey, whatever happens in Vegas . . ."

A waitress floated by. "Cocktails?"

"Sure," Dexter said immediately. "They're free, aren't they? Give us a couple of seven and sevens."

Joe, busy piling checks on the pass line, looked up with a startled expression. "Hey, what the hell you doing? You're not supposed to— what about all that AA stuff? You've been on the wagon since I've known you. What's that, eleven years?"

Dexter raised a reassuring hand. "Don't worry about it, Joe. I can handle it. That's what those meetings are for. I learned my lesson a long time ago. Hey, it's like we're on vacation. Besides, the price is right, hey?"

Joe looked dubious, but the dice had passed and it was their turn to roll.

      *   *   *   *   *

As Dexter blew on the dice and rolled yet another seven, George Reynolds was seated behind towers of purple and orange and a small stack of gray five thousand dollar checks. He had just won a thousand dollar bet at a five hundred dollar minimum table in the New York New York blackjack pit. Before going into the casino a half hour earlier, he had asked Reverend Warren and Judy to maintain a discreet distance if they were going to tag along. He was playing for real now. They had wandered off and he had begun with a five thousand dollar buy-in.

A floor woman, dressed in a dark Tahari pinstripe business suit, observed the action from her station. Slender, with a serious face that looked like it had seen it all, she had been watching table BJ39 for ten minutes now, since the handsome fellow in the middle seat had won several thousand dollars in his first fifteen minutes. She picked up the phone and dialed. Presently, a heavy-set man in his fifties, evidently the pit boss, came by and drifted over to observe as well. George had split a pair of threes against the dealer five and won both hands.

The goalkeeper, of course, was aware of the activity behind the table although he had never looked directly towards the station. He remembered the Oasis balcony eighteen years ago. It was time to go.

The battle was on. First blood had been drawn.

44

West Palm Beach, Florida

Martin Millhouse and Ricky Harris, fourteen year old ninth graders at The Benjamin School and best friends since pre-K, tolerated the P B Pres Teen Life program because the hot good-looking eighth and ninth grade girls from Palm Beach Day attended the Thursday evening meetings.   Debbie Poindexter was the exception. Debbie was not good-looking, nor was she hot, but she was very cool and very popular. Debbie had a source for oxycodone, a Schedule II controlled substance.

Being Presbyterian wasn't a requisite for attending Teen Life. Youth Minister Ted Moffitt embraced all faiths and creeds, figuring he could turn young, impressionable minds to the Way of the Cross. His Christian message was a soft sell at the end of the night's activity, usually around nine o'clock, and revolved around the theme that Jesus had been a really neat guy and probably had been a really cool kid. He kept the youngsters occupied with wholesome, fun activities for two hours and, he hoped, imbued some sense of Christian relevance.

In actuality, of course, nobody listened to the soft sell Christian message. The activities, like bowling or viewing an instructional video on STDs, were strictly dork ball. The middle schoolers spent the time sending graphic text messages about what they wanted to do to each other's organs after Teen Life while Ted was giving his sincere, mildly passionate talks. On this particular Tuesday evening, while the Youth Minister delivered Christianity Lite, Martin and Ricky were chatting up eighth graders Betty Ryder and Pamela Nickerson. Martin had heard that Pamela, who attended

St. Anne's, would let anyone feel her up as long as he didn't put his hand under her panties.

It was almost eight o'clock and not quite dark when Martin Millhouse gazed outside the conference room window and his eye happened to fall on Erubiel Sanchez' truck. The vehicle was parked back on the property. At first, he paid no attention but then he began to think about it. He nudged Ricky Harris. The rest of the attendees were gathered around the conference table. Ted Moffitt had come up with the idea of building a diorama of the new sanctuary on miniature church grounds so everyone could admire the building before it was completed. A few kids were working on it. Kathleen Delacourte had brought in coffee grounds for dirt, and even Martin and Ricky had to admit it was a pretty realistic touch. Martin and Ricky planned to torch the model after it was completed, the Saturday night after it was set up in the narthex. It would be a nice surprise for display Sunday morning.

"Hey Ricky."

"What?" Ricky didn't look over.

"Look out the window."

"What."

"Look."

Ricky reluctantly looked away from the overripe Cheryl Hornsby, who was leaning over the model, top buttons undone. Cheryl was an eighth grader going on twelfth. Ricky looked out the window. He saw nothing special.

"What, dude? I don't see a damn thing."

Martin pointed. "Look at that truck. Back there by the construction stuff."

Ricky looked at the old Dodge. "So?"

"So this. It's been in the same place since Sunday. Maybe before."

"How do you know that?"

"I remember. I saw it Sunday at church. It's in the same place, I'm telling you."

Ricky didn't find the concept particularly interesting. "So what?"

"So it's probably abandoned. Let's check it out after. Maybe there's a stiff in it."

In West Palm Beach, abandoned cars with stiffs in them were not that rare. Ricky realized it was possible. Better yet, an untraceable handgun in the glove box.

At nine fifteen, the Teen Life meeting dispersed. The boys got on their bicycles and rode around the block. When they returned, the church was deserted. They biked across the grass to Erubiel's truck. The cab was locked. A tarp was lashed across the bed.

"Let's see if there's anything under there," Martin said.

"You do it."

Martin looked around. No one was near. It wasn't completely dark; the security lights at the corners of the church were on. He took out a pocket knife and cut the cord, unthreading the line through the grommets until he could lift a corner.

"There's something here but it's too dark to see what it is."

"Take the whole thing off," Ricky said.

A minute later, Martin flung the top off and the boys looked inside the truck bed. They saw a wooden crate and a toolbox.

"Let's take these over to the light," Martin said. The toolbox was easy, but the wooden crate was another matter. They struggled to get it over the truck sides, then toted it to a pool of light on the grass next to the tool box. They were at the left rear corner of the church, out of view from the street.

The boys opened the old, rusty tool box and rummaged through a collection of well-worn tools, nothing of real interest. They turned their attention to the crate. It appeared quite old and bore stenciled markings on two sides:

DYNO NOBEL.
HECHO EN MEXICO
GUADALAJARA, JALISCA

There was other, smaller writing, faded and unreadable. Neither boy spoke anything beyond maid Spanish, anyway. The box was nailed securely. Ricky picked up a hammer from the toolbox and pried open the lid. He laid it aside.

"Whoa," said Ricky.

"Holy shit," said Martin.

There were five dynamite sticks in the box, which looked like it originally held four or five layers.

"You know much about this stuff?" Ricky asked. He reached in gingerly and picked up a stick. It had been bright red at one time, they could tell, but was now faded and old. He turned it over and examined it.

"What's that?" Martin said, pointing to the stick.

"Looks like crystals. The thing's wet, too."

"Can't see good, but yeah. The bottom of the box looks wet." Martin felt it with his fingertip, then sniffed his finger. He licked it gingerly.

For some reason, his heart began to race.

"It's wet, all right. The rain must've leaked in."

It was a wrong guess.

"Think's it's still any good?"

"I dunno. Looks kinda crappy. Maybe, though."

"What'll we do with this stuff?"

"Well, we sure could top torching the diorama," Martin said. "We could blow the real thing."

The boys guffawed.

"Should we put it back?" Ricky asked.

"Hell, no. It's ours, now. We gotta find a place to stash it." It was obvious they couldn't take the heavy box on their bikes, even if they had a place to hide the explosives. They thought for a few moments, looked around.

"Okay, look," Ricky said. "There's a lot of crap back there on the construction site. You stay here. I'll bike home and get a flashlight. Be back in ten minutes."

"Hey, bring a shovel, too."

Twenty minutes later, Ricky had returned with a flashlight and shovel. The boys toted the dynamite back to the construction site and poked around for a place to hide their arsenal. They wandered around behind the new sanctuary. Martin walked into a ladder and bashed his shin.

"Ow ow ow goddamn it!" he said as he hopped around in the dark, almost falling over a two by six. "Will you keep that goddamn light where I can see where the hell I'm stupid going?! There's crap all over the place!" He stumbled again on a piece of plywood.

"Goddamn it! Give me the goddamn flashlight!"

"Yeah, yeah," Ricky said, handing it to him. He jabbed the ground with the shovel as they went. The earth was particularly soft near the southwest corner of the new building.

"Grab some visqueen," Ricky said. "It's all around here."

"What for?"

"We gotta wrap the box, keep the water out," he said, poking the earth.

"Oh yeah," Martin said, shining the light around. He spotted a piece of the heavy plastic protecting a stack of Redi-Mix concrete bags. It was held down by bricks at the corners. He yanked it free.

"Here," Ricky said. "It's nice and soft here."

Martin looked around. "How're we gonna mark it? This construction crap will all be gone. They'll have flowers and hedges and stuff."

"No, we'll have it out of here in a day or two."

"What if we don't?"

"Okay, we'll put it right up next to the wall, right on the corner. How's that?"

"Perfect."

Ricky dug a hole four feet deep around the corner of the foundation. Martin offered to take a turn, but it was an easy job. The earth at the corner was loose and porous and it only took about ten minutes. They wrapped the case with visqueen, carefully placed it at the bottom and refilled the hole. They tamped and stomped on the ground and scattered the dirt around.

They stepped back and looked at their handiwork. No one would be able to tell.

"Perfect," Martin said again.

"Rock on," said Ricky.

As soon as they thought of a more secure place, they decided, they'd come back and move the box. They started back, walking along the drainage ditch, which was still half full of water.

Out of the corner of his eye, Martin saw twin specks of light not ten yards away. They were so faint he couldn't see them straight on.

"Hey," he said. "Shine your flashlight over there."

Ricky snapped the switch. No light came on.

"Shit."

"What?"

Ricky smacked the flashlight. "Cheap shit flashlight."

The specks moved. They heard a deep, low grunt. Something large and heavy moved.

45

Las Vegas, Nevada

Standing in the Oasis elevator lobby, Tom Swayne fidgeted and glanced at the security guard behind the small podium, who seemed to be giving him the fish eye. Was he doing something wrong? The young hardware store owner smoothed his shirt front. Just looking at his new companion made him weak in the knees. He pressed the elevator button every few seconds as he talked.

"There's five of us out here, ma'am," he said, forgetting about George. "It's pretty warm where we come from. It never snows. Just like here, I guess. You?"

The redhead dazzled Tom with her smile. "I'm Charlotte, Tom. From over the mountain. It never freezes over."

"Charlotte," Tom repeated dumbly. He nodded and pushed the button again. Presently the elevator arrived, followed by another on the opposite side. Father Corr, dressed in black cassock and priestly collar, stepped out of the second elevator towards Tom and Charlotte, who were entering the first car. Tom, gazing at his stunning companion, failed to notice. The priest followed them in and the doors closed. A reddish glow became visible under the doors, fading as the car rose.

In a few seconds, they had reached the nineteenth floor. Tom and Charlotte, arm in arm, emerged and walked down the corridor. As they approached Tom's room, he failed to notice a bright, flickering orange light from under the door. He fumbled with the key card as Charlotte smiled at him. As he opened the door, he turned to allow her to enter. She sauntered by and a whiff of Obsession quickened his breath. Tom eyed her as she passed, and as a result never noticed Father Corr as he slipped into the room behind them just before the door closed.

Tom took a stab at urbanity. "Would you like a drink?" he asked, without having checked if the room had a mini-bar.

She smiled her brilliant, toothpaste smile. "Where would you get it?"

Tom's suave demeanor dissolved. He looked around the room.

"Uuh—" It came to him in a flash. "I can order from room service." He was pretty sure he could. Did he need to order food with it?

"Why, do you think I need it?"

Did he what—? What was she saying? He sure could use a stiff one, he realized. He already had a stiff one, he realized.

"Why don't you just come over here?" She walked slowly over to the bed, sat down and crossed her legs. There was the sound of rustling nylon, and Tom thought it might have been the most erotic sound he had ever heard. She patted the bedspread next to her. Lust was degrading his motor control. He lurched toward the bed. Suddenly his face was on fire. He was gripped by passion and they hadn't even kissed yet. He knew he could handle things once they got going, but the first move was always his trouble spot. The first time he had kissed Jane, the wire on her braces—

He cut off the thought of his fiancé.

"Why don't you turn off all those lights?" she asked.

Yes, the lights! Two lamps were on. He walked over to the one in the corner and fumbled for the switch without finding it. Then he remembered the damn hotel lamps usually turned on and off at the base. He looked and felt around but there was no switch, no button, no nothing. There must be a switch on the wall! Suddenly he was furious with the lamp. If he didn't find the switch right away, he was going to break off the bulb and—

He found the switch. The only light now came from the bathroom, a reddish, flickering glow that for a moment struck Tom

as odd. But his loins were on fire and he didn't dwell on it.   He
walked over and sat on the bed.

"You look—" he started to say, but then her mouth was on
his, and her tongue a white-hot flame inside his mouth, and they both
hurtled down on the bed. As their clothes flew and they embraced,
Tom realized this woman was nothing like Jane, nothing like her at
all, and at that moment Jane had faded to a flaccid pale limp thing,
her body a toy, a vacant promise, a brush with womanhood bereft of
paint, devoid of true passion, and that when they had made love it
was a hesitant, bumbling act, comical, really, and she actually
reminded him of a fish flopping, pale and gasping, and this was
nothing if not incredible and passion he had never known, or
dreamed of, and he squeezed her breasts and felt the nipples— what?

Something was wrong. Where were her breasts? Why was
the skin so rough and what—

He opened his eyes and in the dim red flickering light from
the bathroom, which was now bright and raging, he stared into the
milk-white eyes of Father Corr, inches from his, and its tongue was
in his mouth, a foul wriggling serpent that belonged to this horrifying
thing and he recoiled and screamed, he screamed so loud he could no
longer hear the sound of groaning metal.

Father Corr sighed. "Does this mean you're not in the
mood?"

46

West Palm Beach, Florida

Ricky Harris banged his flashlight again. The light came on weakly just as the boys heard a heavy splash. He shone the beam into the water as something swam across the drainage ditch. It climbed out and stopped. Ricky banged the flashlight again and it beamed brightly. Now the gator was lit up, glistening and prehistoric. The eyes were even brighter. The creature was on the near bank, twenty feet from the boys.

"Christ, that's a big one," Ricky said.

"Twelve feet if it's six," Martin said.

"They're fast enough to catch dogs, you know." Ricky's neighbor, old Mr. Fletcher who lived with his married son and daughter-in-law, had fled in his motorized wheelchair when his noisy Shi Tzu had been mangled and devoured by an eight foot gator. Ricky's dad had found the incident hilarious, especially since part of the little creature was still on the chain attached to the chair. The neighborhood was considerably quieter now.

Martin picked up a rock and threw it. The rock bounced off the gator's head with no effect, except that Ricky thought it looked pissed off.

"Hit it again." He hefted the shovel. Martin picked up a heavier rock and really wound up. It hit the gator just below the eye.

Everything after that was a blur. The gator bellowed and charged into Ricky before he could bring the shovel down. Martin stumbled back, horrified, as the beast snapped Ricky's leg and dragged him towards the ditch.

"God! Martin, help!"

A split second of indecision.

Martin ran forward and picked up the fallen shovel. He began to beat the gator on the head with the edge of the blade. It felt like hitting a front end loader; there was no give at all. Ricky screamed as they neared the water. Martin continued to bash the alligator. Suddenly it let go of Ricky's leg and snapped at the shovel, breaking it in two. Martin grabbed Ricky's arm and dragged him backward. The gator watched. It almost seemed to be making up its mind. Then it slowly turned and slipped down the embankment and into the drainage ditch.

Ricky sank into shock as Martin tore off his shirt and fastened a tourniquet. He had never seen so much blood. He would have been terrified, but there was no time. He reached into his pocket for his cell phone and held his friend until the ambulance and two cop cars arrived.

The story made the front page of the Palm Beach Post, and was featured on the evening news, right after the nightly dog story. The boys told everyone they had just hung around after Teen Life, shooting the breeze, and were attacked as they walked to their bicycles. Martin Millhouse had saved his friend's life at great risk to his own and was hailed as a hero. He received commendations and a two thousand dollar college scholarship from the Junior League of the Palm Beaches. Ricky underwent emergency surgery. He'd eventually need a second operation but would regain full use of his leg. Neither boy mentioned the dynamite nor went near the box, which lay buried four feet under the southwest corner of Palm Beach Presbyterian's new sanctuary.

47

Las Vegas, Nevada

Nineteen floors below the grotesque ménage à trois in Tom Swayne's hotel room, George, Reverend Warren and Judy sat at a small table in the Sacramento's Redwood Lounge overlooking the casino action. It was close to eleven o'clock. Onstage, a three piece combo sawed on an old Elvis tune. Warren and Judy were drinking seven and sevens, while George pulled on a Hard Hat beer. Despite the hour, neither the lounge nor the casino was crowded.

"They were watching you tonight, weren't they?" Warren asked.

"Two on the floor, and the video, of course."

"Do they really do that? Are there that many card counters?"

George smiled. "Not just for counters. They've got to have video in case of any dispute, or cheating, a lot of reasons."

"Cheating?"

"Happens all the time. And not just the patrons. Dealers, casino employees. Slugs, coolers, false shuffles, pull-throughs, all that stuff. Lots of tricks. Two card drop, you name it. Somebody switched an entire shoe, once. That's why they're chained. People have tried everything, and they keep coming."

Warren shook his head slowly. "Amazing. A whole world I never knew about." He looked around the nearly empty casino and gestured with his drink. "You really like this place, this atmosphere?" To the cleric, the deserted casino, drained of people and energy, had acquired a sordid tinge.

"It's a house of worship in its own right. Every table's an altar. The prayers said in this place are probably more fervent than in your church."

"Speak for yourself," Judy said.

Warren sipped his seven and seven. "He's probably right, Judy. You know, George, you made more money today than I do in six months."

George chuckled. "You didn't do so badly yourself. Can they get decent help in Heaven these days? What's the pay? That one guy got thirty silver dollars, didn't he?"

Warren shook his head. He had a wry expression. "You can't fool me, George. You're not the cynic you pretend to be. I know you believe."

"That's more than I know, Reverend," Judy said.

"I believe in a jack and an ace when a pink chip is on the line," George said. "I believe in Hell, Jim. Maybe I believe in God, but I think his sense of humor is maybe not the way you think."

"I just try to be guided by the Holy Word and common sense."

George knew he was going to regret this, but it was too much. The guy led with his chin.

"Well, tell me this, Jim. You ever thank God?"

"Thank him? Sure. All the time. He's bestowed many blessings upon all of us."

"Do you blame him for the stuff that goes wrong?"

"Of course not," he chuckled. The band had launched into Three Dog Night while its audience debated religion.

"Whose fault is the stuff that goes wrong? The bad things?"

"Well, we are tested."

"So he is responsible."

"Responsible, no. This is an old argument. He doesn't intervene."

"I'll say. Do you take the Bible literally?"

Judy shifted in her chair. She was close enough now to belt him.

"The Bible is the Word of God."

Just an old fashioned love song, the band said.

George decided to let it all go. It wasn't worth it. He liked the minister, misguided as he was, and Judy would be unlivable if he persisted. Still –

"One last question, Jim." As far as George could tell, most religions considered Heaven their private club. We're in, you're out.

"Sure."

"Do Jews go to Heaven?"

There was a sudden sharp pain in his shin. Now both legs hurt.

"Reverend Warren, don't answer that," she said.

Warren grinned. "You don't think I can hold my own?"

"*You* may, but he's going to have a couple of sore shins."

Conversation drifted for a few minutes. Soccer, the persistent rain back home, the unending Middle East unrest. Talk petered out while they drank another round.

Warren leaned back and looked thoughtfully at George. "Were you brought up in a religious home, George?"

George shrugged. "Aaah, you know." He made a vague gesture.

Warren didn't know. He supposed George didn't want to talk about it. At least, that would be his guess considering the prior discussion.

"Judy tells me you were raised in an orphanage, Jim. How'd that work out?"

There was a subtle change in the minister's demeanor. He seemed to shrink within himself. He fiddled with his drink, almost spilling it.

"Aaah, you know." Sauce for the goose.

But George didn't let him off the hook. "What do you mean? How'd it work out?"

"It— it didn't work out too well. Not too well. There was this priest that ran things, Father Corr. He ran things." He spoke hesitantly, nervously. "I was his favorite altar boy. He tried to touch m— teach me things. I got out of the Oasis when I was sixteen."

"Oasis?" George repeated, thoughtfully.

"Yeah, that's it. The Oasis Catholic Home for Boys."

"Oasis, huh? That's funny."

Warren looked quizzically at George, misinterpreting his statement. "My father was a Presbyterian minister. I never really was Catholic."

"Oh."

"My parents were killed when I was nine years old. Accident."

"Sorry, Jim."

Warren nodded.

Judy yawned. "I can't keep my eyes open."

George looked at his watch. "Two fifteen a.m. back home. Stick a fork in me, I'm done."

"Too much adrenaline, I guess," Warren said. "I'll just finish this." He held up his seven and seven.

George and Judy got up from the table. George stretched and rubbed his bad leg. As he did so, he looked around the room. The only other patron was a stringy, washed out bleached blonde a couple of tables away. She looked to be in her early twenties, but could have passed for forty. She sipped on colored water, waiting in a deserted lounge in a deserted casino.

Well, that part of the town hasn't changed, he thought.

"Good night, Jim." He slapped Warren on the shoulder and took Judy's arm as they headed for the elevator.

48

James Warren watched the couple wend their way around the tables and out of the lounge area. He preferred to think George's needling was his way of questioning, that down deep the man was not a cynic but rather searching for the same answers as everyone. He was glad George didn't treat him with kid gloves. Everyone else did. It was the old locker room syndrome. All the dirty jokes stopped as soon as the minister came in the place.

They were an interesting pair, and he was fond of them both. They seemed so different, yet they blended well together, real companions. As pastor, he had counseled many marital partners who seemed to be at odds all the time. He could think of no reason why most of them should continue together, really, especially those couples who truly appeared to hate each other. They seemed to feed off each other's animosity. What sense did that make? What sense did any of it make?

Sometimes when he performed the marriage ceremony he felt ridiculous saying the words. *What God has joined together* etc etc. Sometimes he knew the young people personally and wouldn't give them six months, a year at best. But he was fooled all the time. The most idyllic couples flew apart like a nuclear warhead after three months under the same roof. Others, who seemed to have nothing in common, to hold completely polarized views, or come from different economic strata, they were happy together. Who could figure it out, really? Certainly not Jim Warren. The only thing he had gleaned from his observations was that if one of the partners knew he or she wanted to marry the other on the first date, the marriage usually lasted. From that, he had deduced that chemistry was more important than anything. Everyone had problems, everyone had rough spots. The couples that survived did so because they wanted to. And they wanted to because of – well, chemistry.

But that's all he knew, except that the human capacity for misery seemed boundless. Couples stayed together when they made each other miserable, when there was no hope. Common sense said enough was enough but they wouldn't bust up, wouldn't end the agony. It made no sense at all.

So whose dumb idea was it that he could counsel anybody, really, just because he donned the robes on Sunday? Half the time the people were older than he was, anyway; as a result he had taken to wearing the collar during those sessions. They'd come in, with hatred in their eyes sometimes, or a sullen resignation, but mostly with hope, and they'd look at him as if he were Jesus Christ personified. That's when he felt most like a fraud. He wanted to say, *Hey, I know I look the part, and I'm wearing the uniform, but what the hell do I know? I read a few books and went to a couple of seminars but the truth of the matter is I was lucky to wind up with Betsy. Otherwise I might be coming into an office like mine just like you.*

But of course he couldn't say that. He parroted advice from the stuff he'd read, spouted the platitudes served up like pabulum, and usually had a hollow feeling that went along with the words. In fact, he would be attending two seminars on the subject at the convention. It made him think of Betsy, who would join him in a couple of days. She was his bedrock, more than she knew, certainly more than he ever told her. He didn't know what he'd do without her. He resolved to tell her so: the kind of promises a man makes when his wife is away.

He'd met Betsy White while in seminary. She had been a sophomore at a nearby Bible college and they'd been introduced at a lemonade and sugar cookie mixer. Warren had shrunk from the horrors of the Roman Catholic Church and, after leaving the Oasis, vowed never to go near it again. But religion was like cigarettes, like many of the marriages he counseled – repugnant, yet so hard to quit. The Presbyterian seminary had filled the large hole in his heart (as they had put it) and assuaged his yearning. Like father, like son, it seemed. And yet, he'd been a water color marred with coffee stains. It had taken Betsy to – to what? – heal him, he supposed. If he was healed, that is. She was balm for his scar tissue.

When she had dropped out of college to marry him, it did not occur to James Warren that Betsy had accomplished her educational goals. The minister's wife always sat in the first row when he delivered his Sunday sermon, unless she was involved with Bible Study, Youth for Christ Missions or some other church activity. Warren often felt a pang of guilt when mounting the steps to the podium before delivering his address. Here he was, presuming to tell a church full of intel- a church full of people right from wrong, dogma from heresy, sin from sanctity, shit from shinola. Well, how many were listening anyway, besides Betsy? Mostly those who didn't need any advice. God bless the women of the church. He probably knew what they did at night, alone in the dark, but forced himself not to think about it.

The music had stopped. The band had taken a break, he realized. He felt a distraction to his right and looked over. A young blonde woman at a nearby table was looking at him, saying something and gesturing, something he did not hear. Was she talking to him? He had not noticed her before. She seemed young and quite pretty, if a bit thin.

"I beg your pardon. Did you say something to me?" he called out.

"I said hello, sport," and smiled. When she smiled, she beamed, Warren noticed. Her teeth were very white and even. Well, within reason. What did she want with him?

Fifteen minutes and two demis of ersatz champagne later, Warren's tongue was made of Velcro. He thought her name was very – nice. He almost told her there was no one in his congregation named Candy. As the two of them floated out of the lounge and toward the elevator, the minister pushed away the thought that he had neglected to tell her he was married. Or what he did for a living, for that matter.

49

Upstairs in room 1933, Judy had climbed into bed after another hot shower.   George emerged from the bedroom in nightclothes, rummaged in his suitcase and took out a magic marker and a couple of peel-off name tags that said HELLO MY NAME IS. Sitting at the small table next to the television, he wrote on the first tag.

"What are you doing?" she asked.

He held up the tag. "Camouflage. For tomorrow." The name read Dr. Chris Kirkland. He had penned in the name of the former Liverpool goalkeeper.

Judy looked at the tag. "What if there's an emergency? You might have to treat somebody."

"Actually, some guy passed out at the tables one time. I had to say I was a psychologist."

"That's a laugh. Can you do the arts and crafts in the morning?"

He closed the marker and got into bed. He fluffed the pillow and lay on his back with his hands behind his back.

"Good start today, Judy. I'm optimistic."

"Are you just saying that?"

"Yeah.   Listen, there's a big fight this weekend. When the high rollers come in tomorrow, it'll be easier."

"What do you mean?"

"The casinos will raise the table limits. They won't notice larger bets as much. Your church convention crowd sure aren't big bettors."

Judy looked off. "Just me. I'm the only big bettor. I bet everything the church had. That's why we're here."

"Stop that. What's done is done. What the hell."

She looked at him softly and caressed his arm. "What would I do without you?"

George shrugged. "Your friend the minister," he said. "He's a funny guy. I guess his upbringing wasn't exactly Leave it to Beaver."

"Doesn't seem it. Stop needling him."

George thought about a reply, picked his best option. "Okay."

"I know how you are, but he doesn't. He thinks you're serious."

George thought he *was* serious.

"You should get to know Betsy," Judy said.

"Who?"

"His wife, Betsy. You met her a couple of times, once at our house. She's really neat. It was the two of you who really— believed in me."

"Yeah? What'd she do?"

"Well, she's the one who encouraged me to teach the substance abuse class."

"She good looking?"

"She's perfectly attractive. Turn out the light."

George knew what perfectly attractive meant. He nodded and reached for the switch. He recognized the false sense of alertness, fueled by adrenaline on top of exhaustion. The feeling had done in many a would-be card counter. He made a conscious effort to relax. He drifted off just as James Warren and Candy Land wafted by his door on their way to room 1911.

      *   *   *   *

He tumbled through the air, broken leg corkscrewing. On the sidewalk below, Judy held open a toy net while standing on a small Oriental rug, wobbling back and forth to stay under her falling husband. She was unsuccessful. He hit with a splat. Judy looked disgustedly at her dress, sprayed with gore.

"Did you have to do that in here?"

George groaned, then woke with a start. He looked at the glowing digits and shook his head. Since deciding to return to Las Vegas, his nights had been troubled, filled with violent dreams. What did it mean? He looked over at Judy, who hadn't stirred. She'd slept like a baby, ever since they were married. He wished he had an on-off switch like she did.

He lay back down and consciousness dissolved. If his dreams continued, he didn't remember it in the morning.

50

The door to room 1911 opened. Warren, holding a paper bag, stepped aside and made an exaggerated gesture; Candy breezed in. He followed and closed the door.

The minister was tanked. He was also sixty dollars lighter in the wallet after she had worked him for the bubbly. How could he have spent that much? Warren hadn't been blotto since – when? – the Waggoner wedding. And that was two years ago. And he wasn't really tanked then, either, but had what Joe Dykes had called a pretty good buzz. He had danced with Betsy, and the bride, and had even hauled Mrs. Waggoner out of her chair to some Rolling Stones tune. He'd thoroughly enjoyed himself. It was the next day before he remembered Mrs. Waggoner was coming off hip surgery.

Candy gave a little wave and skipped into the bathroom. After she relieved herself, she douched with Krest Bitter Lemon Drink and applied Viva gel, smuggled in from Australia by a friend. Warren put the bag on the small table and took out a fifth of White Heather Blended Scotch along with two cans of diet Pepsi. He remembered having seen a couple of glasses with paper tops somewhere, but couldn't find them. As he waited, he rummaged idly through the promotional crap the hotel had piled on the table: a restaurant guide, show schedules, nearby attractions. There was a glossy tri-fold, a Las Vegas casino map. He opened it and tried to trace their route from the airport to the Sacramento. It was proving a difficult task.

The minister frowned. Something was wrong with the map, it seemed. Was it the streets? They didn't seem to connect, to go anywhere. And the casinos. The casinos were – what? He stared at the paper:

Mandalay Bay Unmatched dining, unmatc*ondemned to death*
Luxor Live entertainment, gourmet re*ceives the cross*
Excalibur You belong in a castle! Water*falls the first time*
Tropicana The Way Las Vegas Was Me*ets His Mother*
New York New York Rooms starting from $*imon of Cyrene carries the cross*
MGM Grand Enter Maximum Las Ve*ronica wipes Jesus' face with her veil*
Monte Carlo The best of Las Vegas Entertainme*ets the women of Jerusalem*
Planet Hollywood The House that Fa*lls the second time*
Paris Las Vegas Ooh La La Je*sus falls the third time*
Bally's Elegant Style. Timeles*tripped of his garments*
Bellagio   Contentment and Opulenc*rucifixion: Jesus is nailed to the cross*
Flamingo   Modern. Chic. Gourmet di*es on the cross*
Caesar's Palace   Experience the Luxur*emoved from the cross (Pieta)*
Imperial Palace   A first class resort centrally l*aid in the tomb*
Sacramento   Mirrors on the Ceiling, Pink Champag*olgotha*

The thing didn't make sense. He tried to think, always an iffy proposition, especially filtered through 86 proof. What was that Bible-texty stuff? He'd seen it before. Bible words? Then it dawned on him. But what were the Stations of the Cross doing—

The bathroom door opened and Candy, now locked and loaded with her makeshift but effective lemon spermicide and HIV-proofed with Viva gel, floated out with a big smile. She sat in one of the two upholstered chairs and crossed her legs. Warren forgot about the glossy tri-fold Las Vegas casino map and let it fall to the floor. In the room light, she looked much younger than she had downstairs. She was pretty, and without her make-up Warren judged she would look vulnerable. Her complexion was coarse, but so what?

"Glasses! Now I remember," he said. He'd seen the tumblers with paper lids in the bathroom. He wobbled in and suddenly realized much of the liquid he had ingested needed to come out.

"Just a sec," he said, and closed the door. He really had to go now. He fumbled with his fly as the need to go became urgent.

The fly seemed to be stuck.

Outside, Candy took her hairbrush from her purse, which contained little else except the toiletries essential to her trade. She began to brush her golden locks. She liked this guy, and for some reason she did not really understand had not approached this transaction in the usual way. Clearly he wanted her, but he was so fumbling and inept that she felt a real liking for the geezer. Actually, he wasn't a geezer at all, in fact he wasn't that much older than she was, but he did remind Candy of her own father, a Baptist preacher back in Cut and Shoot, Texas until he was run out of town for molesting two women in the congregation. Well, two women, he had argued, only if you count a harmless feel as a big deal. This was not going to be a volume night, she knew, but maybe she could take this guy for a kited price. Unquestionably, he would have no idea of going rates.

Inside the bathroom, Warren was on the edge of panic. The recalcitrant fly was not budging. His eyes were watering. He tried to work on the zipper but it was hard because he was hopping around. He *really* had to go; the urge was multiplying geometrically. He whipped off his belt and jerked his pants downward. They didn't fall, but Warren did. He jumped up and down and lost his balance, tipping over into the tub and clonking his elbow. Even through the alcohol fog, it hurt like hell. It took several tries before he righted himself and finally got the pants down over his hips.

"Aaah," he said out loud as relief washed over and out of him, accompanied by something that might have been the clarion of an angel, but wasn't.

It was the telephone. In the other room, Candy looked at the instrument. Candy Land was one of those who couldn't let a ringing phone go unanswered. She got up, moved over to the bed and reached for the receiver, even though she realized the call was probably not for her. She hesitated with a great effort of will, and after three or four more rings it stopped.

In a few moments, Warren emerged from the bathroom with two glasses, removed the paper tops and sailed them towards the wastebasket.

"Candy, there's no ice anywhere. We'll just have to make do."

The minister had left the bathroom door ajar. He didn't notice as, behind him, a flickering, reddish glow emanated. Candy continued to brush her hair and hum softly to herself as the minister poured two strong drinks, mixing them with his finger. He handed one to her and gulped his with a grimace. It felt like molten pitch working its way down. He poured another and collapsed back into the chair. His fingers belonged to someone else's hand, he noticed. He could make them work, sort of, but hardly felt the tumbler he was clutching. Although his mind was largely molasses, he became aware that she had moved to the bed and was brushing her hair. Her hair was very attractive, like a golden halo, kind of, spilling around her neck and shoulders. Not like— he didn't finish the thought.

The bed. He focused on getting from the chair to the bed. He knew he could do it, he knew it would be easy, just a step or two from here to there, as easy as biting an apple, or sticking a sword into an already gaping wound, and he also knew this step would be irrevocable, final in its execution. *One small step for a man* . . . and then he was there. She sipped, set her glass down and gently caressed his shoulders. Warren reacted with a jerk, spilling his drink. He turned and Candy kissed him; his lips were made of rubber. They fell backward onto the bed in a passionate embrace. A shadow moved on the wall behind James Warren. Father Corr's ringed hand seemed to melt into hers as she caressed his neck.

The glow from the bathroom intensified. Suddenly, Warren bolted to a sitting position and rubbed his face vigorously.

"No, no. I've got to stop this," he said. "I— I can't do this. I'm sorry."

He held his head in his hands and rocked on the bed. When he looked up, Candy was standing in front of him, pulling her dress over her head. Warren jumped up and backed against the wall. The room darkened to crimson; shapes writhed in the corners. He closed his eyes.

"Get thee behind me, Satan," he whispered. Father Corr's shadow appeared on the wall behind him. Candy, clad only in panties, climbed on the bed. On her hands and knees, she turned away and slapped her rear.

"How's *this* behind, Jim?"

It was all too much. What's a body to do? He lurched back onto the bed. The next five minutes were a white-hot blur of ecstasy filtered through White Heather Blended Scotch, and then it was suddenly over.

It was really over. Warren staggered into the bathroom and threw up. He retched from a great depth, and worried he might break a rib or heave up a piece of some organ. A torrent, a fire hose of vomit leaped into the toilet bowl. Oh, God, he started to say, but thought the better of it. It probably was a good idea not to call His attention to Jim Warren right now.

In the other room, Candy's thoughts were perhaps clearer. *Oh shit, I did it for nothing. I can't even do this right*, she rued. And then the phone rang again. It was too much. She picked up.

"Hello?"

"Hello?" came a feminine voice. "I— what? I'm trying to reach James Warren."

Candy bought time, tried to think. "Sorry?"

"I'm trying to reach Reverend James Warren."

Reverend? Well, whaddya know, she thought. "Who's calling please?"

The voice on the other end raised up a notch. "This is Mrs. Warren. Who is this?"

"Oh, well, I'm sorry, ma'am. This is the maid," she said, in a burst of not divine inspiration. Candy realized what time it was. "The night maid. I'm here to turn down the bed."

The connection wasn't clear. Candy heard "Who is that?" or "What was that?"

"The maid," said Candy. She reinforced the lie. "I'm leaving the chocolate now."

Hisses and clicks in the far off night, and then the sound of disconnect. Candy stared at the phone until Warren came out of the bathroom a moment later, toothpaste dribbled down his chin. He lay on the bed as Candy sat next to him. Warren was surprised to find that he was halfway sober, and that he wasn't really feeling any regrets at the moment, although it might be too soon to tell. In fact he wasn't feeling too much of anything except maybe air in his stomach, or else he still could be half in the bag. He realized he had joined a long line of illustrious preachers, priests, televangelists and the like in their common failing. Somehow, it was a comforting thought. At least she was over eighteen. Probably. And female.

"I knew you were married," Candy said. "I mean, besides the ring and all."

The minister was jolted; his mouth was full of metal shavings.

"What?" he croaked.

"I said I knew you were married. What I do for a living, just about all my clients are married." She paused. "But I didn't think any of them were Reverends."

What? "How did you know?"

"You had a phone call."

Accompanied by a great sense of foreboding, Warren's heart slammed into his chest wall. He dared not speak.

"Your wife sounds like a very nice lady."

James Warren knew what it was like to be electrocuted. "Oh, my God," he managed to gargle, in spite of his earlier resolution not to bring the Lord into this night. Voltage spurted around inside of him; he lost some motor control.

"It's all right. Don't worry, Father. I told her I was the maid."

It was almost a full minute before Warren could speak. "I'm not a priest," he managed.

"Not right now, anyway," she giggled. Candy's firm young breasts jiggled as she jumped up and hopped into the bathroom. Warren felt himself stirring again, despite everything. It made him wonder at the miracle of his own body. He had not known a miracle could be disgusting. Could this get any worse, even his apparent lack of remorse, which was so alarming in itself? He might have been more alarmed, actually, but he was suddenly so tired. He could sort it all out later. His last thought before sleep, just as Candy Land was giving herself a Krest Bitter Lemon chaser, was the nagging question he kept pushing back down to wherever it came from.

Should I go to Heaven?

51

The young altar boy James Warren filled small glass vials with Holy Water from the font, which was just a few inches deep. Absorbed in his task, he sang an old English hymn in a high pure tone.

"In England's green and gentle . . ."

The surface of the water rippled slightly, as if in a breeze. Warren peered closely as the water began to roil and bubble. Suddenly, the head of Father Corr erupted from the font, streaming seaweed and water. It opened milk-white eyes.

"Receive the Holy Water, boyo!"

Warren jerked awake with a gasp. He sat up quickly. As he did so, his head began to pound, as though thick motor oil filled the vessels in his temples. From somewhere, he thought he heard a shovel trailing on cobblestones.

"My God, will it ever stop?" he murmured. He turned and was startled to see Candy asleep next to him, facing away. He was horrified as the events of the past few hours came back in a rush. He tried not to think, to push it all away, but there she was in his bed. He looked at her in disbelief. Had this really happened?

Whatever happens in Vegas stays in Vegas.

He didn't remember where he'd heard that but it must have been on television. Boy, was that right. He sincerely hoped. Should he wake her, and usher her out the door? She evidently had some sort of sinus problem, because he could hear her faint snore. He gently pulled the covers down and stared at her form. She was just a kid, for God's sake. Good Lord, maybe he could be arrested?!? He remembered when they had waited for the elevator. There was a man, a security guard, standing behind a kind of raised up podium in the elevator lobby. He'd looked them over closely, but hadn't said anything. Warren remembered the officer's scrutiny had been disquieting, but he'd pushed it away. Truth be told, he hadn't wanted to think about it too much. What if there were security cameras in the elevator lobby? Or in the halls? Of course there were! Were they coming down the hall, right now, ready to yell "Search warrant!" and splinter the door down with that battering ram he'd seen on *Cops*? Maybe they had cameras!

Jailbait! Was she? She could be anywhere from sixteen to – what, thirty? Thirty two? No, she wasn't that old at all.

Cops is filmed on location with the men and women of law enforcement. All suspects are innocent until proven guilty in a court of law.

My God!

Warren took a deep breath. He leaned over and stroked her hair. Almost without thinking, his hand went down her back, smooth and sensual, and down. She stirred in her sleep. He jerked his hand away and pulled the covers back over her.

As he watched in horror, a withered hand, wearing the ring with the large brown stone, came out from under the covers and pulled them down. Warren screamed and jumped back off the bed at the sight of Father Corr, naked, lying there in an adult diaper. He was wearing a colostomy bag. He grinned at Warren with his milk-white eyes. The old priest reached down and yanked the bag free, spraying fluid and fecal matter around the room.

"Wanna play catch?" he said, still wearing a demonic grin. He heaved the bag at a fleeing Warren.

It's the only script we follow.

52

Las Vegas, Nevada – Day Two

Another brilliant, cloudless desert morning. As the sun broke the horizon, the city dozed. The lights had winked off and the only movement was the occasional cruising taxi, a pedestrian here and there, the airport. Las Vegas, in the early morning, always looked like it had partied too long the previous night.

In room 1937, Dexter awoke, disoriented. He looked over and saw Joe in the other bed and for several seconds could not place where he was. Then he remembered. They had decided to let Tom, the single traveler, have a room to himself. It was all right with Dexter, what the hell. Wilcox did not travel much, although Marcy had once persuaded him to take her on a Caribbean cruise out of Ft. Lauderdale. He had been startled at the change in his wife aboard ship. Suddenly bubbly and vivacious, the new Marcy barely resembled the day to day version he had been used to for fourteen years. She had enrolled in the shipboard aerobics class, and had pursued the exercises with a pneumatic vigor. When they ran into the instructor the third afternoon at sea, on the Lido deck, Marcy had introduced him. His name was Derek, and to Dexter looked like one of those 'California guys'. Derek had said several complimentary things to Dexter about Marcy, commenting on her great enthusiasm and sunny disposition. Dexter had felt an annoyance; the kid had taken liberties. He wanted to tell Derek that Marcy was none of his business and that she wasn't really like that anyway; she was actually pretty quiet and not overly enthusiastic at all. It annoyed him that Marcy would believe that crap, but when he looked at her she was sucking up everything the asshole was saying.

When, the following year, his wife had suggested another cruise, Dexter had declined, remembering the irksome Derek. What kind of a name was that, anyway? Some L.A. type deal, probably phony. Shortly thereafter, Marcy had enrolled in her classes at the Aerobitoreum. Dexter had tried to think of a reason to discourage her, but, since she had started working again, he could not complain about the money. It was hers anyway, sort of. The experience had made her grow taller, or stand up straighter, maybe, and she had lost that bulge just below her belly button that had appeared in the last few years. He could not completely place the change in her and he did not know why he disliked it. She seemed to be growing out of her pod, or something, and had started forming opinions about things. He had meant to sit down and have a talk with her about it all but just then he had gotten laid off by Pratt & Whitney and the whole deal became moot. There no longer was money for the classes and she wasn't listening to him anyway. But he'd shown her. He'd gotten another job, a good job. It had taken awhile but so what? Once he was working again he was in charge, and he'd let her know it, pretty much.

Dexter fumbled for his Casio in the dark. Joe had pulled the blackout curtains when they had gone to bed. The watch had cost only $39.95 and was waterproof down to sixty six feet, a place Dexter surely would never visit. It glowed 6:10 a.m. He lay there for five minutes, but it was no good. He slid out of bed. When he emerged from the bathroom twenty minutes later, Joe had not stirred. He opened the door and picked up the newspaper, but he was too hungry to read. He reached for the phone and dialed Tom Swayne's room. They were supposed to meet for breakfast at 8:30 Nevada time, which no longer sounded so good to Dexter. It would be almost lunchtime at home. He'd be starving by then.

Joe had awakened at the sound of the phone. He rolled over and squinted at Dexter.

"What the hell? Who are you calling in the middle of the night, for Chrissake?"

"Tom. No answer in his room." Dexter hung up. "Anyway, it's not the middle of the night."

"Maybe he's in the shower or taking a dump. Christ, it's too early to be up anyway. He probably stuck a pillow over his head."

Dexter put his hand to his forehead. "My head's pounding."

"No wonder, you moron. You must have had half a dozen seven and sevens. Better take it easy on the sauce, Mister A A."

The little man's face lit up. "Hey, I rolled a bunch of seven and sevens, didn't I?"

Joe propped himself up on an elbow. "Yeah, you sure did that, all right."

"Maybe a Bloody Mary'd fix my head." He got up from the bed and opened the dark curtain. Brilliant sunlight flooded the room.

"Gaah!" Joe yelled. "Now what the hell you doing?" He flopped back down and put a pillow over his head.

"I gotta eat. My stomach's rumbly. I'll call Reverend Warren for breakfast," Dexter said. He dialed 7-1911. Warren picked up right away.

"Hello?"

"Hey, Reverend. It's Dexter. Joe and I are going down for breakfast in a little while. How 'bout I call you when we're about to leave?"

"Breakfast?" The minister seemed befuddled.

"Yeah. I know it's a little early out here but it's way past breakfast time at home."

"Oh. What time is it?"

"It's about nine-forty our time. Six-forty here."

"Six-forty here," Warren repeated dumbly. He really sounded out of it to Dexter. He must have been asleep.

"Sorry if I woke you," Dexter said.

"Oh. No, you didn't wake me."

"Have you heard from Tom?"

"Tom?"

What was with Reverend Warren? Dexter thought. "He's not in his room. I left a message."

"Uh, no. I haven't heard from him. Maybe he's downstairs already."

"Well, all right. We'll call you when we're about to leave and then we'll pick you up on the way to the elevator."

"NO! No, I mean, don't do that. I'll go down and get a paper and meet you in the coffee shop."

Somehow Dexter thought he shouldn't tell his minister that USA Today was right outside his door. After hanging up with Warren, he tried Tom's room again.

"What are you, the goddamn switchboard?" Joe grumbled from under the pillow.

"Yeah, I'm the goddamn switchboard." Dexter hung up the phone.

"Listen, Dexter," Joe said quietly. He'd propped himself up on one elbow again.

"What?"

"We've done pretty well here so far, you know?"

"What are we ahead, maybe a grand?" Dexter asked.

"We're up, yeah, about nine hundred and sixty five dollars. Remember, I had to tip those guys five bucks." Joe was looking at Dexter with what passed for a sly look.

"What?" Dexter prompted.

"I was just thinking. What about the money we've made?"

"What do you mean?" Dexter was thinking that everything he was saying was a question.

"Maybe we shouldn't broadcast it."

"What do you mean?" Dexter repeated. He looked over at Joe, who had cocked his head and raised an eyebrow, silently asking another question. A question Dexter couldn't grasp.

"What are you talking about?"

"Well, the church is in the financial crapper, isn't it?"

"Seems so."

"If Reverend Warren finds out we've made a killing on a church trip, maybe he'd think we ought to— you know?"

Dexter caught the drift. He thought for a moment. "Gee, I didn't think of that." He tried to work it through. "Maybe that's right, though. We wouldn't be here if it wasn't on the church's dime. How about if, say, we give half?"

Joe wasn't buying. Or giving, for that matter. "What we're talking about is a drop in the bucket to the mess the church is in. But a thousand or two is a lot different to guys like us – guys who work for a living, honest guys who could use a few extra dollars and appreciate it more."

There was a pause. "I don't think that's right, Joe," Dexter said.

"Well, let's just think about it, all right?"

Dexter ran his hand across his forehead. "I don't know," he said, finally. "I'm going to try Tom again one more time."

Dexter listened to the phone ring and ring. Where *was* Tom Swayne?

53

James Warren woke to a sound he couldn't place. He rolled over and was jolted by what he saw, which wasn't Betsy Warren. The evening came back in a rush. My God! Had he done that stuff? The proof was six inches away.

He recognized the sound that had puzzled him a few moments ago. Candy was snoring again. Barely, but he could hear it. Fascinating in a degenerate sort of way, he thought. The whole thing seemed surreal, even though she was right there. He could reach out and touch—

NO! he thought. What was the matter with him? He remembered she had put her mouth—

The phone rang; he jumped. Who could that be? Oh, God, not Betsy again! What would he say? He hadn't thought that one out yet. He was afraid to answer no matter who it was, because maybe she'd awaken and the person on the other end would be able to hear her. Maybe it was hotel security, though, asking about last night. And if he didn't answer maybe they'd come knocking—

He picked up quickly. "Hello?"

When he hung up with Dexter a minute later, relief had given way to anxiety. Warren was on the edge of panic. He had to get Candy out of there, and right away. Maybe Joe and Dexter would come by anyway, even though he had told Dexter he'd meet them downstairs for breakfast. Or maybe Candy would be leaving, halfway out the door and trailing a stocking or something, when they came down the hall. That would be a real horror show! He reached over and shook her, perhaps a little less gently than he wanted to. She didn't stir. What?! He poked her now, a bit harder. He had a fleeting vision of a scene from *Barton Fink*, where Audrey lay dead next to Barton after spending the night, sheets stained with blood. This time he really gave her a shove. To his relief, she gasped a big breath and rolled on her side.

"Candy! You've got to get out of here! You've got to get out of here right now!"

Candy didn't seem too perturbed. She opened her eyes, stretched and smiled at the minister before lowering the sheet seductively.

"Hi, Jim," she said. She ran a hand across her nipple, which became instantly erect. He had a vision of Betsy's nipples, little pathetic pimples atop a fleshy, dimpled blob filled with cottage cheese. The closest they came to becoming erect was flopping over from one side to the—

Stop! What was— it felt like little roaches scurrying around in his brain, synapse to synapse, miswiring the whole thing. He grabbed the sheet and pulled it back up. "No! I've got to go! You've got to get out of here! You've got to leave right now!"

He jumped off the bed and grabbed her clothes, which were scattered here and there. Actually, mostly here; some small part of his mind realized Candy wore way less things than his wife. He shoved them at her.

"How about breakfast?" she purred.

My God, he thought. She doesn't get it. "I can't! I'm late! Please!"

Candy smiled and gave a little pout as she dressed. Doesn't she even wash? Warren wondered. He thought about the prior night. She still had his stuff inside her, he guessed. Ugh. What about disease? God! He hadn't even considered that! And he lectured his pre-marital couples about the dangers of— What *had* happened to his brain? Was it drowning in sperm? He pictured little creatures crawling up his penis, viruses and germs and little malignant things and God-knows-what right this very minute! Was it too late to cleanse himself in the shower? Was HIV waterproof? He couldn't remember!   He'd put the water on scalding and scrub like a maniac as soon as he got her the hell out of his room!

It seemed forever before she headed for the door, but really it was less than three minutes. He hastened to open it and peer up and down the hallway before letting her out, but as he went to move past she wrapped her arms around him and kissed him, a big, open wet one right on the mouth! He held his breath since he knew she hadn't brushed, picturing all sorts of STD things pouring down his throat. He felt slightly nauseated, and then, unbelievably, he became aroused as her tongue just about tickled his tonsils.

God! He thought. GET OUT! GO! RIGHT NOW!

Of course, she lingered in the doorway as she rearranged something. He resisted the overwhelming temptation to give her a shove. She turned a few steps down the hall, smiled and gave a little wave.

"Ta ta, Jim," she said.

Ta ta.

54

Joe and Dexter wandered into the coffee shop at a quarter past seven. The little man had finally gotten Joe out of bed by turning on the television. It had been too much. They spied Judy waving to them from a table where she, Warren and George were having coffee. As they approached, Joe stopped dead, slack-jawed. Warren was in a golf shirt but George was wearing a ministerial collar. Joe and Dexter sat down at the table, which held the remains of a hearty breakfast.

Everyone was in a light mood, it seemed, even Reverend Warren, whose polarity had reversed with the departure of Candy Land. The minister was so relieved to have her out of his room he felt like the time he had gotten away with stealing the chocolate cream pie from the orphanage refrigerator. The night had reinforced a valuable lesson he had learned at age ten: sin was only sin when you got caught. He had often tried to push it away, but there it was. You could always ask God to forgive you, and He always did. Not like people.

Dexter pointed at the collar and clerical shirt. "What is that, a disguise?"

"Holy shit! Is that yours?" Joe asked Reverend Warren.

"I'm afraid so."

"I've never seen you wearing one of those," Dexter said.

"I know, it's usually for counseling sessions and stuff like that. I brought it here just in case."

Joe pointed to the offending article. "You let him wear that?"

"I must admit I had some misgivings about this," Warren said. "He convinced me the outfit would throw them off the scent."

"They made a deal," Judy said. "George promised to attend one of the seminars if Reverend Warren lent him a collar."

"My missionary work for the trip," Warren said.

"There, there, my child," George said. "Absolution." He made the sign of the cross. "See? It's working already."

"Wrong religion, dear."

Dexter laughed. "Hey, Reverend. Your face is all red. What's up? Are you okay?"

The minister became even redder. "It's nothing, Dexter. Just had a real hot shower. The steam made my nose feel better."

"Oh, yeah. I know what you mean."

"How the hell do you know, Dexter? You don't take showers," Joe said.

"Any Bible quotes for us this morning, Reverend George?" asked Dexter. "Going to say grace?"

"The sad thing is, he looks the part," Judy said.

Laughter around the table.

Joe chimed in. "Hey, Reverend, maybe his Sunday sermons would be an improvement."

Warren shrugged.

"Going over to the convention center with us this morning, Judy?" Dexter asked.

"I could do the convocation," George said.

"*In*vocation. Yes. I'm attending two seminars today," she said. "Reverend Reynolds here will have to be on his own."

"That has a nice ring to it," George said. He ran his finger around the collar. Judy chuckled in spite of herself.

"Listen, has anyone heard from Tom?" Warren asked. "I checked with the front desk and he hasn't picked up my message."

"No answer in his room," Dexter said.

Joe laughed. "Maybe we oughta see if his bed's been slept in."

Warren furrowed his brow. "What do you mean, Joe?"

"Tom was doing all right, last we saw him. Had a real looker with him."

Dexter chimed in. "Looker? Or hooker!"

Joe and Dexter laughed.

"I'm really shocked," Judy said. "Clean cut Tom Swayne?"

"Your flock is wandering, pastor," George said. "Guess this trip won't qualify as a church retreat."

Dexter's head swiveled around. "Where's the waitress? I'm starved."

"How can a little man like you always be starving?" Joe asked.

"How are you doing, George?" asked Dexter.

"Okay," George shrugged. "I'm ahead a bit." In truth, the goalkeeper was up over ten thousand dollars.

"Did you see anyone from the old days? Any problems?" Judy asked.

"The one floor man at New York New York, I think I remember him from the old Stardust. Maybe the Dunes. He didn't recognize me, although he watched the action for awhile. No problem there."

"Are you going to play at the Hard Rock?" Dexter asked. "I heard the entertainment is terrific."

"I don't care about the entertainment. The Hard Rock is poison. So is the Wynn."

"What do you mean, George?" asked Warren.

"RFID." George saw their quizzical looks. "Radio frequency identification. Each chip is a miniature transponder."

Dexter, the engineer, was stunned. "You're not serious."

George nodded. "They can track every chip in the casino in real time. They're all embedded. If I'm betting five bucks and they see I have fifty grand worth of chips in my pocket, they can flag me as a potential card counter. They know what I've won and where and when I won it. If you and I have chips that get mingled, we can be tagged as a possible team. It's all transparent as glass. It goes without saying that bogus chips are no longer a problem in those places, and believe me counterfeiting chips is one of the biggest problems you never read about. They keep a real tight lid on that one."

Silence around the table. They were all dumbstruck at the twenty first century technology.

"I wouldn't have dreamed," Warren said, finally. "It really is another world."

"That's right," said George, aware of the twinge in his leg. "And it's not Oz."

55

By 9:30, everyone but George had gone on to the convention and the goalkeeper was playing a double deck game at The Sahara. He'd found a vacant table and had been enjoying one-on-one play for the past twenty minutes. At three hundred a hand, he was covering two spots rather than exceeding a single five hundred dollar base unit. It was another small strategy to allow him to play longer with less scrutiny. If he'd played a single hand for six hundred the dealer, a comely young brunette from San Francisco named Giselle, would have called out "Purple play!" and that would have invited the field hands.

Giselle dealt slowly and was in no hurry gathering the cards after each hand, allowing George plenty of time for a proper count. She also dealt down into the second deck, and as a result he was ahead several thousand dollars. He gradually upped his base unit bet. He occasionally put up a side bet for Giselle. While dealers and floor people generally split their tokes, it didn't hurt to bring them into the game. After all, they had some discretion in placing the cut card.

On the last hand before the red cut card came out, George put up a quarter check for the dealer and they won. Giselle tapped the checks on the metal tray and dropped the fifty dollars into her shirt pocket. It was no easy trick. The woman was heavily endowed and the shirt appeared a size small, George had noticed.

"Thank you, Father." She smiled as she shuffled the decks.

"You're welcome. Do you get back to San Francisco often?"

"Oh, sure. I love it there."

"He never really said it, you know."

"What? Who?"

"Mark Twain."

"What did he say? I mean, what did he not say?"

"The coldest winter I ever spent was a summer in San Francisco."

She laughed. "I never heard that one."

They were real buddies, now. George knew he had been under casual observation, but the actions of the floor men seemed routine. He had never exceeded a thousand dollars on any individual bet. A heavy-set man in his forties drifted over from the podium as Giselle finished the shuffle. He watched as George inserted the cut card.

"Morning," he said.

George nodded as he placed his bet and the cards were dealt.

"Staying with us, Father . . . ah . . . ?"

"Reverend. Reverend Robinson. Paul Robinson." George had given the name of the former Tottenham Hotspur goalkeeper. "No, I'm down the strip."

"In town for the convention?"

"Yes, my son," George replied. "Perhaps you'd like a pass for one of the seminars."

"Aah, thanks anyway, Reverend. I have to work."

"Too bad. I'm teaching later. Christianity and craps." A small part of George's brain wondered why he was always pushing the envelope.

The floor man looked confused. He handed George a business card.

"If you need anything . . . ah . . . Reverend, please let me know. I'm Tony Constanza."

George took the card and looked at it. They shook hands.

"Oh, sure. Thanks. Nice to meet you," George said.

Tony stepped back and continued to watch as the counterfeit Reverend Robinson doubled down with an Ace-seven against the four and won a thousand dollars. George glanced up briefly at the camera bubble, and out of the corner of his eye saw a second suit take up a position from another angle. It was time to go. He stood and gathered his checks.

"Change those up for you, Father?" Giselle asked.

"What? Oh, sure," George said, pushing all his checks forward. He knew the real purpose of changing up his checks was not to make it easier for him to transport them to the cashier's cage, which was but a few steps away, but so the house could get an accurate count of his winnings. In the past, he had often slipped a few high value checks into his pocket during play as a countermeasure.

But it wouldn't do to refuse allowing her to change him up. A real red flag, that would be. Giselle finished tallying and stacking, and exchanged little ones for big ones. She pushed them back to George.

"Nine thousand, three hundred, Father." She smiled sweetly. Maybe there's something to this outfit, George thought.

"Thank you, my child."

Tony Constanza leaned in. "Leaving us so soon, Reverend Robinson? Want some breakfast?"

George looked at his watch. "Thank you, no. Goodness, I've got a Bible Study meeting at ten. I've got to hurry." He started to step away.

"What hotel did you say you were staying at, Reverend?"

George turned. "Ten o'clock," he said, and walked briskly to the cashier's cage. "I'll try to stop by after."

"Nine thousand, one hundred, two, three hundred, Father," the cashier said, pushing a stack of bills through the cage.

"God bless you, my son."

Outside, he caught a taxi and told the driver to take him to Caesar's Palace. George realized he was tending to favor those older casinos on his list, whether from familiarity or nostalgia or what he wasn't sure. He supposed it was the comfort level he felt walking through the doors. He could recall their marquees fairly shouting out the old names in six foot letters, names from George's salad days like Wayne Newton, Elton John, Neil Diamond, Don Rickles— they were, in a way, an anchor. Anyway, he remembered which way to turn and where to go in those familiar places. It was amazing how little they'd changed, and how much he recalled. New carpet, new slots, most without handles or coins – that was about it. Sometimes, he wasn't even sure about the carpet. He saw the player was often connected to the slot machine by an electronic umbilical cord. George had shuddered, finding the grotesque mating ritual obscene.

As the taxi entered Caesar's drive and moved past the fountains, George removed the clerical collar and pasted the HELLO MY NAME IS tag on his lapel. They pulled up to the door and the driver reached up and turned off the meter. As he did so, George absently noticed the man's ring with the large oval stone, but didn't really place it.

56

The main hall of the convention center wing was a hubbub of activity. A number of meetings had just ended, and attendees streamed out towards a large, central area where tables were set out with juice, milk, coffee and pastries. Judy was eating a croissant and drinking a quick cup of regular when she spied Reverend Warren a distance away. She waved and he smiled and waved back. She held up her croissant with a questioning look, but he pointed down the hall and then his watch. Judy finished her coffee, put down the cup and headed down a side hall where the traffic thinned. She came to meeting room H303, where the easel outside read:

10 AM – 11 AM
SUBSTANCE ABUSE: NEW METHODS OF
TREATMENT

She glanced at her watch. The seminar would begin in three minutes. She tugged the heavy door open and went inside. She thought it odd the room was empty, and that the door had been closed. Judy walked past rows of chairs set behind long tables and towards the podium. This lecture would be the highlight of her trip and she wanted to be near the front. Meeting materials and cups of water were set on the tables in front of each chair. She suddenly noticed the background noise had become muffled, although she'd left the door open. The room seemed strangely dark, almost like a theatre, except for a screen near the podium that glowed with light. She began to feel uneasy, without knowing why. As she neared the front, the door clicked closed behind her. The noise seemed especially loud in the dead quiet room. She turned for a moment, feeling a chill, perhaps the presence of another, but the room was empty.

She sat hesitantly on the aisle in the third row. Did she have the meeting time screwed up? She was sure the sign outside and the program said 10:00 a.m. but that was evidently wrong. It seemed to have gotten very cold, all of a sudden. She guessed it was because they had set the air conditioning to compensate for a roomful of people.

She realized there were two paper cups on the table in front of her, two paper cups in front of each seat in the room. The larger cup was filled with water and the medicine cup contained a single pill. Before she could quite grasp what she was looking at, a picture snapped onto the screen. It was a hospital chart that read:

Patient's Name: George Reynolds
Hydrocodone ↕ 2 tablet(s) every 4 hours for pain

Judy's mouth fell open and her eyes widened in shock. She looked on the table and saw the meeting materials in front of her, in front of all the seats, were the identical chart.

Suddenly, from somewhere, scratchy, low fidelity music:

> *I hear music and there's no one there*
> *All day long the people stop and stare*

She bolted up, tipping the seat over, and began to pant rapidly. She backed away with a low moan, whirled and ran down the aisle.

> *I keep tossing in my sleep at night*
> *A pill or two and I feel all right*
> *It makes me high*
> *I wonder why?*

She banged into the heavy door and grabbed the handle. She yanked but it would not open. She saw a flicker reflected on the door, a red flicker, and whirled to see the screen had changed. The words now read, in bright red letters:

Need An Investment Advisor?
We Can Help!

She heaved again with a loud sob. The door flew open and banged against the wall as she rushed out and down the hall, now crowded with people who stared as they parted to let the wide-eyed, panting woman run past.

The music receded:

All day long the people stop and stare
There's no one home to listen to my prayer
I wonder why?
I could just die

I could just die...

57

James Warren munched on a sweet roll, seated at a table in the overpriced convention center food court. He hadn't known whether to order a snack or lunch. He realized he was starting to eat on Nevada time as well as Florida time. When they got back, he'd need to go on Weight Watchers or something. He looked at the sweet roll. It seemed to be made of chemicals held together with congealed wallpaper paste. Along with tepid coffee, the thing had cost him seven fifty, and it wasn't even warm. He could have used a good strong blend, maybe a nice piping hot cappuccino. He'd thought his next seminar started at ten, but found he had a half hour to kill before it began.

Considering the exertions and excesses of the prior night, the minister felt fortunate, if a bit sluggish. His head seemed all right now, until he imagined all sorts of pathogens crawling up inside his groin and spreading to important vital organs, courtesy of Candy Land. He knew there were no nerve endings in the brain, but it did feel as though something might be trying to crawl in through the stem, perhaps after navigating the spinal column. It was a thought he kept trying to push from his mind, along with whatever it was. He shuddered.

Warren looked around, but didn't recognize anyone else at the other tables. He had known a few of the other attendees, a pastor from Ft. Lauderdale and another from the town of Jupiter, and they'd exchanged brief greetings as people meandered to and fro between presentations. He guessed his evening had been more – interesting, was that the word? – than theirs.

He looked at the materials he'd picked up at the conclusion of the Grace vs. Works seminar. Scripture, as usual, was ambiguous on the subject of Salvation. Punching one's ticket to Heaven seemed a less than precise procedure. The church always pushed the position that one is saved through Grace alone, the belief in Jesus Christ as Savior. Works had, arguably, no effect. There was an impressive list of Biblical citations to support the argument. Warren had been disappointed that the seminar had seemed a light brush. He scanned the papers without finding any new citations or interpretations. He was familiar with the old references listed, of course, such as Ephesians 2:8-9 which said "for it is by grace you have been saved, through faith . . . not by works." Galatians 2:16 seemed to back the premise up. This was core material, the essence of the Christian message: believe in the divinity of Jesus and you're on your way. The Bible said it many times in many ways by lots of New Testament authors.

Trouble was, though, there appeared to be at least as many references that said the opposite, maybe more. And besides, the concept just didn't seem right. Aspects of the argument troubled him. What if you were a real shitty guy but believed in Jesus? Some had put forth the feeble postulate that if one really believed, he or she would lead an exemplary life. That was crazy. After all, Warren knew, the Crusaders all killed and tortured and burned women at the stake for Him. That wasn't a good thing, and didn't seem to be worth a free pass to the Promised Land. The Inquisition was another clear example. Concentration camp guards had gone home to their wives and kids as loving husbands and fathers who went to church on Sundays, believers all. There were endless illustrations, and he didn't even have to go beyond his own congregation, for that matter. So what sense did it make? None, if you asked James Warren, and few did. Judy had stopped George from discussing this stuff last night, but the preacher knew where the goalkeeper was going. He'd been in the neighborhood himself.

What bothered James Warren, even beyond his innate common sense, was the red print. The red stuff in the Bible was supposed to be the Real Deal: direct quotes from Jesus Christ himself. Even though the whole compilation was billed as the Word of God, the red print was the Big Word, the Straight Scoop, full contact instruction from the Son of Man. And Warren found Jesus was very clear on the subject of Grace v. Works, no matter how hard the minister tried to work around it. In Matthew 19:16-19 he read and reread Christ's words, "If you want eternal life, obey the commandments." Warren found that pretty direct and a hard line to get around. He'd tried, but how could anybody blow that one off? Jesus had even amplified his remarks, specifying which commandments in particular he felt led to automatic disqualification. There were other citations supporting the position, such as Matthew 25: 45-46 – another red ink deal -, Romans 6:23 and James 2:1-26. In fact pretty much all of James 2 said you were toast if you didn't back your faith with deeds.

There were so many conflicting statements and so much tortured logic he had felt discouraged and had hoped the seminar would begin clarify the subject, and with it, perhaps some other thorny theological issues like predestination or what happens to infidels. Especially the Chosen People, the Jews. That one was a real can of worms. But now Warren was as dismayed as ever. The whole thing, the whole Bible, it was like a buffet, really. Take what you want here, grab a handful there. Leave the broccoli and collards and go for the burger and chocolate cream pie. If you challenged a phrase, a sentence, a parable, even a chapter or book, well then the explanation was usually the same: you were taking it out of context. No matter if the offending phrase was clear as a bell.

If you want eternal life, obey the commandments.

You were taking it out of context, missing the overall, reading an ambiguous translation, or told you were using an old argument, as if the age of the question negated its validity. Out went the offending question, the troublesome phrase, the jarring word, baby and bath water. Maybe that was the way it was supposed to be, like modern art, but he didn't think so. It was all a jigsaw puzzle with pieces from different boxes thrown in. You could sort of make it all fit, kind of make it look like the nice cover photo, but not really. You just had to keep pushing the pieces around, turning them this way and that, but you could never finish.

In one narrow sense, James Warren considered himself fortunate in his involuntary exposure to Catholicism, at least during his most formative years at the Oasis Home for Boys. Because the Roman church had the Holy See to interpret God's law, as iffy a proposition as that was, there was no need to rely on the old, perhaps unreliable books of the Bible. He could not remember having seen anything but the four gospels until his twenties, and so was unencumbered by the simple, unquestioning faith in the Bible born in Protestant childhood, dogmatic precepts instilled and nurtured in Sunday School, reinforced by rote and repetition. His father had found his spiritual calling late in his too-short life, studying for the ministry during Warren's early years, and so his son's spiritual upbringing had been bereft of early indoctrination until the stern discipline of the Sisters of the Immaculate Conception. And those who had taken the Veil – Warren's only feminine exposure until Betsy, really – had always been very clear and direct. In a strange way, he thought, it was probably better. He knew they could have had him believing Aesop's Fables if they'd started him early enough.

He felt that early lack of exposure might have given him a better perspective on the Holy Bible, which he believed had many other contradictory and irrelevant parts, if not outright nutty material. Some of the books had pretty much nothing to do with God or religion or anything relevant as far as James Warren could see. He had felt free to question, perhaps freer than those prelates who professed a scholastic approach but who in reality seemed weighted down with the baggage of convention and early indoctrination.

Warren had signed up for a couple of classes in the Old Testament, but he was having second thoughts. Maybe if the convention was in Iowa or Montana or someplace the program would have had more appeal, but he had to admit Las Vegas was the most exciting place he had ever been. He hadn't dreamed a town could be so stimulating, and the mirac– the amazing thing was, there was nobody to shut it all down.

The Old Testament was pretty whacky, anyway, he had decided, like the part in Joshua 6 about marching around the city seven times blowing a horn and the walls falling down. Right. All the king's horses and all the king's men couldn't put Jericho back together. But he could understand the old fables, the myths and legends of the time, and the need to have them, to substantiate faith. It didn't invalidate the overall concept, and James Warren was not about to wipe away thousands of years of poetry and historical record because of some fanciful prose here and there. There were more important things to ponder, like whether Candy Land had infested him or the fact that the God who ruled during the Old Testament times was pretty psycho, murdering and maiming and the like. The only thing James Warren could figure was that having a Son calmed him down. So much for immutable and unchanging. Like others before him, Warren had come to the reluctant conclusion, perhaps without realizing it, that the biggest impediment to Christianity was the Holy Bible itself.

Sidestepping for the moment the subject of Candy and all the baggage that carried, Warren thought about the whole concept of holding the national Presbyterian convention is a city fueled by gambling and – he wasn't that naïve – other vices. He had secretly harbored doubts about the propriety of the entire affair. It was fine for the Baptists, and they'd been doing it since 1989, but these were Presbyterians. Scripture, of course, had been ambiguous. He could relate John 2:13-16, the story of Jesus and the money changers, to their present adventure, for one thing. At least sort of. Warren knew he wasn't a gifted thinker, but he wasn't entirely dim either. The Matthew 20:1-16 parables about the field hands and the single denarius wage for all never had made much sense, although everyone else at seminary had claimed to understand the story, and maybe that had some application here as well. Of course, there was that strange Matthew 19:23-24 business about Heaven, a rich man, a camel and the eye of a needle, but who knew what that could mean? That one bypassed both Grace and Works and seemed pretty whacko. Some clever cleric had invented a story about a Needle's Eye Gate in Jerusalem, so the camel had to get down on its knees. Unfortunately, there was no historical evidence for the idea, and the myth had pretty well been discredited, at least on the scholastic level.

Well, he'd either attend the classes or find Joe and Dexter. George said he left his cell phone in his hotel room when he was working, but Warren could reach the others. He hoped they were attending meetings, but feared they were pursuing their Holy War at the craps tables.

There was some noise in the hallway, some small hubbub outside. Distracted, Warren barely noticed the commotion as Judy Reynolds stumbled past the food court entrance. He looked at his watch. He really should attend the Old Testament stuff, he determined, maybe as a sort of penance for the Candy affair. The Candy deal, he amended. Well, that was behind – that was water over the dam. Betsy's phone call had been a close call, but he hadn't been caught. How could Candy have answered? That was insane. Did she actually have a brain, or just some sort of clever neural lump? Metaphorically, though, maybe it was a wake-up call. Perhaps Candy was really the Lord's instrument. That's why she picked up.

That seemed to make sense, too. It really did. Probably He hadn't meant for Jim Warren to get caught, but rather so he'd take it as a lesson and hopefully, come out the better for it. It had worked with the chocolate cream pie back at the orphanage, if he didn't count the box of glazed doughnuts.

That sounded right, didn't it? He was almost sure.

His cell phone beeped. Pulling it from his pocket, he saw the little message indicator was on. Funny, he hadn't heard it ring.

He pressed the 1 button and heard Katy Lundgren's voice, the part time secretary at Palm Beach Presbyterian.

"Reverend Warren, please call me as soon as you get this. I'm in the office all day today except for lunch. I've gotten a strange phone call from a company called Rainey and James. The man says it's very urgent. He said something about a margin call."

What could that be? The term seemed vaguely familiar. Some construction problem, maybe? Warren called back, but only got the out-of-office message. He'd try again after his ten thirty seminar.

58

As Judy rushed down the hall and James Warren's inwit pondered the theological implications of the dozen missing doughnuts, an important seminar on Ecclesiastes had just begun. Joe Dykes and Dexter Wilcox had enrolled online, back in West Palm Beach, but they would have had a hard time hearing the lecturer from the craps table rail down the strip in Circus Circus. The table was boisterous and unusually crowded for the morning hour. Everyone was intent on the acrylic cubes, oblivious to the high-wire act performing overhead. As the dice passed to a dark-haired Latin woman in her thirties, Joe put two bumblebees on the Pass line.

"Hey!" Dexter yelled. "What the hell are you doing? That's two hundred bucks!"

Dexter reached in to grab back one of the checks when Joe swatted his hand away. Across the table, Father Corr watched the action.

"Relax, Dexter, willya? Look at the shooter. What a tomato."

The woman, in a low-cut, tight red dress, did indeed remind Dexter of a ripe nightshade. Plump and bursting with juice today, likely misshapen and wrinkled tomorrow. But this was today. Dexter formed a vague thought about hot climate, hot peppers, and hot women. Maybe he should've taken that second cruise to the Caribbean.

The object of his reverie shook the dice, blew on them and sent them on their journey to the stars.

She rolled an eleven.

"Hey!" Dexter yelled.

"Hey you're goddamn right, hey! I know what the hell I'm doing!"

The men high-fived each other. The waitress floated by and handed Dexter a Bloody Mary as Joe railed the checks. Father Corr raised his glass in salute. Dexter hoisted his and they silently toasted each other, grinning, and gulped them down in unison. Red juice dribbled down Father Corr's cassock. Immediately, the waitress handed Dexter another drink. He barely noticed her ring, a smaller version of the one worn by the old priest across the craps table, which had disappeared from view as he ran his withered hand up the Latin woman's thigh. At the same time, Dexter ran his along the rows of checks stacked in the rail. Somehow the sensations seemed to melt together. He barely noticed that Joe had let their bet ride. When the vine-ripened Latin rolled a 5-3 with the puck sitting on eight, Dexter almost swooned. Waves of excitement coursed through his body; his heart hammered in his chest. He had not known a human being could have so much adrenaline. Marcy Wilcox knew it, though, and in fact had experienced very similar sensations that same day in her instructor's small office at the Aerobitoreum, back in West Palm.

"Jeez, I never saw anything like this. We got a fortune here."

Joe looked at his partner. "We got maybe three thousand here, is what we got. I'm thinking of calling my bank at home. Pulling my dough out of the savings account. I don't think I need Sally's signature."

Dexter fell to earth. He was aghast. "What? That's a terrible idea!"

"What do you mean? We could be betting thousands instead of hundreds. It's like taking candy from a baby here!"

Across the way, Father Corr was munching on a Peppermint Pattie. A stream of chocolate dribbled down his chin and onto his white collar.

"You're crazy, Joe!" Dexter said.

Joe started to retort, but noticed the empty glass in Dexter's hand. "We just finished breakfast, for Chrissake. It's only ten-thirty."

"Yeah, but the time change?"

59

Davey Cahill closed the folder on his desk, now almost a full inch thick. He leaned back in his chair and stared out the window, unseeing. A continual thread of violence and mayhem ran through the history of 316 Primrose Lane, a thread that wove a pattern going back to the nineteenth century, perhaps further. The detective had used the internet to access old newspaper files, records of the Palm Beach Historical Society and websites of similar organizations. It had taken only a few hours to gather and print the material. With the help of Haley Carradine in the West Palm FBI field office, he'd assembled the pieces and a picture had emerged: fascinating, dark, even sinister. While there had been press coverage for each horror, no newspaper had pieced it all together, no magazine aggregated the overall picture, no television feature accumulated the tragic, violent string of tragedies that had occurred on the site.

In 1901, Westminster Presbyterian Church had occupied the property, possibly the first of several religious entities leasing the land. On August 10 of that year, an unnamed tropical storm made landfall in West Palm Beach and destroyed the sanctuary, killing fourteen members of the congregation who had taken shelter inside. Eerily, the only structure leveled and the only casualties incurred before the storm swirled back out to sea over Stuart, Florida had been at 316 Primrose Lane. The dead included Reverend William Schwarz, his wife Bonnie and their two daughters, Mary Beth and Wendy. As vividly reported in the *Palm Beach County* newspaper, Bonnie had been crushed under the altar while her husband was found impaled by a section of the cross, pinned twelve feet in the air to the only side wall left standing.

Afterward, the property had lain fallow for a year before being leased by the New Testament Anabaptist Church. The pastor was listed as Upton Black. By 1903, a larger sanctuary had been built and services were again being conducted on the property. Five years later, violence revisited Primrose Lane. Upton's brother Jeremy, two years younger and owner of a dreary record of misdemeanors, had languished in the local lockup in the summer of '08 after throwing a Duffy Malt at Carrie Nation. The oversized crusader was visiting West Palm Beach in an ineffective effort to close the whorehouses and gin mills on nearby Clematis Street. With a half dozen Duffy's already inside him, Jeremy's bottle had hit Palm Beach Marshall Wilbur Fredrickson instead. While sweating in the dankness of the Dade County Jail, Jeremy filled the corners of the dark cell with colorful and detailed visions of Lu Ellen, his common-law wife, having an enthusiastic affair with Upton.

On August 10, the day of his release, Jeremy went home to his ramshackle apartment on West Railroad Avenue in a vengeful mood. After slaughtering and dismembering Lu Ellen, he drove his buckboard to his brother's house and raped Upton's wife while his sibling preached the Sunday evening service. Jeremy proceeded to the church, quietly barricaded the door and scattered Lu Ellen's parts around the perimeter of the building in, as reported by the *Palm Beach County*, a "ritualistic manner". He splashed coal oil on the front porch and ignited the building while the long-winded pastor droned on. The ensuing fire destroyed the sanctuary and killed another fourteen people, not counting the additional half dozen souls Jeremy picked off with his new Winchester Self-Loading .22 rifle as they clambered out the windows. He did not shoot those who tumbled out afire. Survivors tore Jeremy apart before he could finish off the congregation.

The land had again been unused for several years before the arrival of Palm Beach Presbyterian, its present lessee, in 1913. Forty one years later, tragedy played a curtain call. On August 10, 1944, a votive candle overturned and ignited a blackout curtain, a mandatory security measure following the torpedoing and sinking of the S.S. *Republic* offshore by U-504 in 1942. The fire killed six people, again destroying the sanctuary and all records of births, deaths, marriages, baptisms, and the identities of those buried in the small graveyard at the back of the property. It was all reported in the *Palm Beach Post Times*. No mention was made of the prior calamities at 316 Primrose Lane.

Davey Cahill munched on a granola bar, thinking. The place had a hell of a history. So why had John Roselli listed the address as his principal residence before migrating to Nevada? It made even less sense than before. Was it some kind of grotesque joke on the part of the casino owner? The detective resolved to soldier on, to try and unlock the key to the mystery and perhaps determine if the strange deaths in Las Vegas were really connected to the Oasis Hotel and Casino.

Cahill's thoughts drifted to Haley Carradine. He'd wanted to ask Tim Moss about the West Palm Beach agent, but couldn't come up with a way to do so without raising Moss' antenna. He needn't have worried. Moss declared right off that Haley was unmarried, attractive, charming and intelligent, and suggested having her fly out for a Las Vegas weekend. He also volunteered to help escort the comely law enforcement officer around town. Davey Cahill reacted noncommittally, but was beginning to like the idea more and more. He had looked forward to his conversations with her, mostly about 316 Primrose Lane, but towards the end they'd chatted about a variety of subjects. Now the research was finished and he had no professional reason to contact her anymore. Davey resolved to call Haley and invite her out to Nevada for the weekend. Of course, he could get tickets to the best shows and put her up in one of the better hotels. Living in Las Vegas had some advantages, after all.

60

George, now playing in earnest, spent the morning circumscribing the corner at Flamingo and Las Vegas Boulevard, working short but profitable sessions at Caesar's Palace, the Bellagio, Bill's Gamblin' Hall and Bally's. Caesar's had been especially benevolent, surrendering twenty four thousand dollars in less than ten minutes at a two deck table. The goalkeeper would have won another twelve hundred but for the bogus 6:5 payout on blackjacks. Around 11:30, George felt a pang of hunger for Mexican food downtown at the old Horseshoe, but instead headed back to the Sacramento for a planned pit stop. He would freshen up, change his appearance, use the bathroom and clear his head for a few minutes before lunch and striking out for the afternoon's sessions. He had found these breaks invaluable in the old days, and he wasn't any younger now.

George opened his hotel room door and walked in. He was startled to find Judy sitting on the bed, staring off.

"Hey, aren't you supposed to be—"

Her eyes were wide, trancelike. She was unmoving.

"What the hell happened to you? You look like you've seen a ghost."

She broke into hysterical sobbing. Her bizarre experience at the convention center tumbled out, and George found himself holding his wife and rocking her until she calmed down. He had no idea what she was talking about.

He took her to lunch at the Bellagio patio restaurant. It was another gorgeous desert day, although becoming uncomfortably hot in the direct sun. Seated at an umbrella table, George heartily ate an enchilada while Judy pushed her taco salad around the plate. He gestured with his fork.

"Eat up, you'll feel better."

Judy formed a wan smile. "You sound like my mother. Food fixes everything."

George shrugged. The cheese and onion enchilada was good and satisfied the craving he'd felt earlier. He spoke between bites.

"There's a name for it. When you're under a big strain you can, you know, see stuff that's not always there."

Judy looked pained. "It wasn't that way, believe me."

Some kind of small bird landed by their feet. George threw it a piece of onion.

"Well, what do you expect me to believe? That chart was really there with my name on it? Maybe it was an attendance chart and it had your name on it or something, I don't know."

The little creature pecked at the offering.

"Look at that," George said, gesturing with his fork. "The dumb thing's eating an onion."

She rearranged her plate and gave a shudder. "Can I tag along with you this afternoon?"

"Maybe it eats onion bulbs in the fields. Except this is the desert," he mused.

"George, please. Can I go with you?"

George nodded as he shoveled in a last mouthful of rice and beans. "Yeah, I guess so. Maybe it wasn't such a good idea for you to come back to Las Vegas." He gestured around with his fork. "Maybe the place triggered some kind of unconscious reaction. You know, from bad memories. "

She looked at him with skepticism.

"Well, what the hell do I know? Listen, we're doing well. Another day or so, that's it. Then we can get the hell out of here." He reached across and patted her hand. He hoped he didn't seem patronizing.

Twenty minutes later, they were riding in a taxi down Las Vegas Boulevard. The traffic was heavy but moving, the sidewalks moderately crowded with pedestrians. The town was beginning to fill. George looked out as they passed the Flamingo, the Imperial Palace, the Mirage. He hadn't yet played most of the casinos on his list. He would have much rather been alone; he had work to do, but Judy was still recovering from the shock of whatever the hell had happened to her at the convention. He really didn't know what to think about what she had told him. She had always been well-grounded, not given to flights of fancy or an overactive imagination.

The taxi pulled up in front of Treasure Island. Judy looked at the marquee. She seemed to brighten a little.

"Look," she pointed. "Are we going to Cirque du Soleil tonight?"

"You can. I'd love to, but I'm working. Maybe you can get Jim to go. Want me to make reservations while we're here?"

Judy nodded. "That would be nice." She seemed subdued now. Maybe she was coming to terms with the hallucination, George thought. An undigested bit of breakfast, the strain of their predicament, who knew what?

In fact, reservations were not available. Cirque was sold out. George was used to being able to see any show, avoid any line, eat anywhere when he was hungry, pass through the crowds as if they were not there. But that was then, and this was now, and there were no available seats to Cirque du Soleil any of the nights during their stay.

He left a disappointed Judy at the roulette table, where she bet distractedly for a few dollars a spin. She said she'd stay there while he went to work. George wandered the floor. He took in the layout of the tables and got a feel for the place. He had never been inside, of course, since the casino had been built long after his last visit to Las Vegas. One thing George knew: each casino had its own personality, and perhaps it was a subjective feel, but distinct nonetheless. Some were comfortable, others less so; this seemed a fair place to play. The floor was moderately crowded, but the higher minimum tables were usually less than half full anyway during daylight hours. The first table he checked was a five hundred dollar game with two players. After a minute's observation, he passed it by. The dealer, a too thin young woman with long, jet black hair, was quick. By itself, that was not a problem but her housekeeping ruled out the game for George. She was not always showing the discards, not turning over and spreading them so they could be seen. She would swiftly gather the dead soldiers and when she turned over the down cards she covered them in one swift motion. Dealers were supposed to show all cards, but some didn't, and that was that.

George wandered the floor. He found a hundred dollar shoe game with a lone player, an Asian woman who appeared in her forties. He watched until the cut card appeared, then took the third spot as the dealer shuffled the cards. He felt comfortable and alert, Judy was safely ensconced across the floor, and it was show time once again.

This would be a fifteen thousand dollar sit-down, which automatically set George's base unit bet at five hundred dollars, or one thirtieth of his session stake. Mathematically, it was accepted that thirty units seemed optimal: a sufficient number of betting packets to ensure the player wasn't wiped out by a streak, and large enough units to maximize return for error-free play. George wouldn't buy in for the fifteen large immediately, though, at least during weekday blackjack. The amount was just too noticeable, and anyone betting a thirtieth of his buy-in invited scrutiny.

George laid his money on the table. The dealer was a pleasant looking woman in her forties who obviously liked her groceries. She smiled at George and counted out his checks. She reminded him of somebody's mom.

"Change five thousand," she called out. Out of the corner of his eye, he saw the floor man nod and wander over to observe the action. He was slim, late thirties, it appeared, and of course chewed his gum as slowly as possible. George felt the man's eyes on him as he checked out the new player.

The first hand he was dealt was a blackjack.

All right, he thought, mentally rubbing his hands together. This was going to be a good session. And so it was, for the first fifteen minutes. George didn't receive many natural winning hands after the blackjack, but the cards ran true to the odds. He won every double down, every split but one, and had gone up eleven thousand dollars. He was rolling with the tide.

Every blackjack player, whether professional card counter or vacation patron, knows the cards run in streaks. The pro plays every hand identically, bets and utilizes the strategy tables as memorized, but nonetheless knows that there are times when the cards seem to defy all logic and bestow their largesse upon the player or give him the bum's rush. That's why all players think of the cards in the feminine gender. This day, George felt the kiss of the queen, the wink of the red lady, and knew he was still safe from detection because he hadn't bet extravagantly or made very many unusual plays. The tide ebbed and flowed, but it was coming in.

Or so he thought.

As he stacked his checks from a winning hand, he felt a tap on his shoulder. In Las Vegas, that meant only one thing. A jolt of electricity and he suddenly knew things weren't going to be well at all in the Treasure Island casino.

61

"Where are you going?" Joe asked Dexter. The pair had returned to the Sacramento and Joe had telephoned his bank. The funds should be in the cashier's office before the close of business, he was told, which would be one p.m. in Nevada. Joe had just over an hour to wait. They were headed for the casino floor when Dexter swerved for the elevator.

"What?" Joe asked, exasperated.

"The bathroom. Big breakfast," Dexter said.

"Just use the one down here," Joe said.

"Are you kidding?"

"Well, come *on*. I'll wait for you here."

"Why don't you grab a paper?" Dexter asked.

"Are you going to be that long? You came all the way here to spend your time in the *can*?"

"Hey, hold your water. They don't close the tables down, you know."

"Aaah, I'll go up with you." Joe wore a disgusted look.

"Suit yourself."

Joe wanted to talk in the elevator. Dexter saw how chummed up he was. "Know what I feel like?" Joe said. They were alone in the car.

"An asshole?"

"Funny, Dexter. James Bond, or somebody like that. I'm all pumped up. Aren't you?"

Dexter already knew Dykes was swimming in adrenaline. "Well, actually, I'd just as soon—"

"Yeah," Joe interrupted, as they exited the elevator. Dexter had been about to say he thought they should go to the convention seminars. "I can't wait to get on that table. It's like a rush or something, like they say about drugs." Joe babbled on. By that time he was two steps ahead of Dexter, heading down the hallway.

"It's exciting, all right," Dexter conceded, "but I can't say that I get that worked up." He looked at his watch. "You know, we signed up for—"

But Joe was out of earshot. He had the door open and was already inside. Dexter went into the bathroom. He heard the television click on. For the entire time, he listened to the channels change every few seconds as Joe flicked from station to station. About every twenty seconds he heard the same thing:

"Hurry up, will ya?"

When they finally entered the gaming pit twenty minutes later, Joe was surprised to find most of the tables closed. Play was light before lunch and there were just two ongoing games in the Sacramento. Joe made a big show out of "feeling the auras" before leading Dexter to the table with the only woman, a middle-aged Hispanic in sweatpants and tennis shoes. Dexter looked at his watch again. Joe took out his wallet.

"Joe, what about if we only stay fifteen minutes? I've got a seminar in less than an hour."

"What, with this streak going?"

"*Joe.*"

The Hispanic lady rolled snake eyes. The table seemed empty of energy. Two people walked away. Joe frowned.

"All right, all right. Actually, I'll tell you what. This place is dead. Let's wander down the arcade until my money gets here. You still got time to make your seminar."

Dexter, relieved, agreed. They strolled around the periphery of the casino and into the shopping arcade. As they perused the windows, it was clear the merchandise was for winners. There wasn't a single sale sign. They found themselves in front of a men's clothing store. There was a variety of expensive apparel in the window. Neither Joe nor Dexter owned anything like the goods on display. Joe eyed a cashmere sweater on a silver, featureless dummy.

At that time of day, there was a single salesman on duty. He introduced himself as Mister Brooks. He had a slight British accent that Dexter thought was real.

Joe was not to be outdone. "This is Mister Wilcox, and I am Mister Dykes."

Dexter tried on the sweater while Joe donned a blue blazer with gold buttons. The blazer was also cashmere. They looked at each other.

"What do you think?" Joe asked.

"Looks great," answered Dexter. "I never saw you look like that, Joe."

Mr. Brooks was checking the sleeves. "We can have it ready for you this afternoon, sir. We'll shorten the sleeves just so." Of necessity, the shop was geared for quick alterations.

"This is on sale?" Joe asked.

"No, sir. However, it is well priced. Cashmere is never on sale."

"It isn't?" asked Joe, seeking reassurance.

Brooks gave it to him. "Oh, no, sir."

"Six hundred and seventy five bucks, eh?"

"Yes sir."

"And no pants come with it." He turned to his gambling partner. "How about that sweater, Dex?"

"Feels great. How does it look?"

"Looks perfect," Joe responded.

"Yes, sir," said Brooks. "It is your size."

Joe nodded his head decisively. "Okay. We'll take both. But we want you to ship them home."

"I can take mine now," said Dexter.

Joe turned to the salesman. "Just a moment, please, Brooks." He took Dexter by the arm and led him a few steps away so that they stood in front of the three-sided mirror.

"What's the matter with you?"

"What do you mean?" asked Dexter.

"What do you mean, what do I mean? We can't take this stuff with us."

"Why not?" It really was annoying Dexter that his conversations with Joe were always in the interrogative.

"We talked about this, remember? Where the hell's your mind?"

"Oh. I didn't think about that."

"It's a good thing I'm doing the thinking for both of us, then."

"I don't like doing this behind their backs, I told you before."

"Well, do you think Reverend Warren would reimburse us if we lost? Even if the church had the dough?"

"I suppose not. Of course not. I'm just not comfortable with this."

Across the store, Mr. Brooks was arranging a new shipment of button down oxfords. Dexter looked down in thought. Joe let him sift things for a little while.

"When you figure it out, let me know, because then I'll know which sleeve to donate next Sunday and you can do the same."

"Well . . ." the little man paused. "This is only a small part of the total so far, anyway, isn't it?"

"That's right. And that's just the total so far."

"Even if we decide to split our winnings with the church somehow, we are buying this out of our half anyway, right?"

"Yep. If that's what we decide."

"Well, then. I guess we probably should just have them sent home. Easier than carrying it. We can always just tell them, anyway."

Dexter thought he heard the rattling of silver.

"That's good thinking, Dex," said Joe. He led Dexter back to Mr. Brooks, who was still busying himself with the oxfords.

"We'll take this stuff. Where are the suits?"

62

"Would you step this way, please?"

As Joe Dykes was admiring the cashmere jacket and luxuriating in its soft feel a few miles away at the Sacramento, George Reynolds was feeling something else: a cold anvil in his stomach. The goalkeeper was absorbing the shock of recognition for the man who had tapped him on the shoulder, who had appeared from nowhere, it seemed, coming up from behind without warning and who now gave George a look that said *I know*. He indicated one of the covered tables in a closed section of the T.I. casino several yards away.

George followed him over, thinking furiously. The man looked in his fifties, which would have made him perhaps thirty five when they had met, wherever that was. The Dunes, where he barely walked out without his picture being taken at the cashier's window? The Sands, maybe, where he had been under observation from three floor men? But then it came to him, and he was certain.

George followed the man to the vacant table and sat down, leaving a seat between them.

"My name is Wolfson. I'm the pit boss here."

"Nice to meet you, I guess," George said, without giving a name.

Wolfson nodded and smiled. "You've played very well," the man said.

"Thanks. I got good cards," George said.

"You got good cards. Yes, you did. But you played better. I thought you looked familiar."

"What do you mean?"

"I'm not certain so I looked through the book. I'm still not sure."

"What book? What do you mean?" George asked. He knew exactly what the man meant, of course.

"I worked at the Oasis for twenty years. I think we met there quite a long time ago. Does that seem right?"

George frowned. "I've never been there."

The man smiled. "Of course not. My mistake, it seems. Well, I'm going to cut you a break, Mister . . . ?"

Out of the corner of his eye, he saw Judy. She'd moved to another roulette wheel and was still playing.

"Given. Shea Given." George had given the name of the Aston Villa goalkeeper.

"That's odd," Wolfson said with a smile.

"What do you mean?" George asked.

The man looked at his watch. "Well, if you're going to get back in time for the match with Liverpool, you've got less than twenty four hours."

George felt his stomach free fall in a supersonic elevator. Who *was* this guy? George opened his mouth, then shut it again. He wasn't winning any of this; his incoming tide had become a tsunami.

"Take your winnings off the table. If I was sure who you are, things wouldn't be so polite right now. If you want to shoot craps, or play roulette, or baccarat, you're welcome to stay. Otherwise, find your lady friend and let's leave it at that."

*   *   *   *   *

In a low voice: "Let's go. Now."

George had tried to look casual as he walked to the roulette layout where Judy had just lost a five dollar bet.

She needed no further prompting. She gathered her checks and went with her husband to the cashier's cage. She asked no questions. George knew what was coming, and knew he had to avoid it. As they approached, he gave her all his checks.

"Cash these in," he said. Judy took the pile and approached the cage as George lagged behind, head down.

She presented his checks to the woman at the cage.

"Ma'am, would you mind bringing those to the window on the end?" She pointed to her right. Judy took their winnings to the last window as the woman moved over. The cashier looked out at George, who already knew the script.

"Sir?" she called out.

"Yes?"

"Would you come here a moment?"

It hadn't worked. George went to the window.

"Where did you win these, please?"

"What?"

"Blackjack, roulette, craps, what?"

"Blackjack," George replied. He rubbed his nose with his hand, then looked down, but it was all to no avail. The woman was fiddling, stalling; she wasn't about to pay him until he faced her. George looked up. The woman stepped out of the way and there was a small flash. He couldn't help it; he smiled for the Griffin book.

63

There were taxis in line and so they got one right away. George leaned forward and said something to the driver and they pulled away from Treasure Island.

"What was all the hurry about?" Judy asked. "And that business at the cashier?"

"I was recognized. A guy from the old days. I couldn't place him right off but he thought he knew me. I don't know if he was sure or not."

"Well, what did he say?" They pulled out onto Las Vegas Boulevard. Traffic had eased.

"He said take my winnings and you and go."

"Well, like you said, you have a whole list of casinos."

"I doubt it now. They took my picture at the cage. That's what that stuff at the cashier was all about, and why I wanted you to cash us out. They weren't having it."

"So now what?"

"I can't tell for sure, but they'll probably email the updated picture all over town. I'm lucky if I have the rest of the day. I'm eighty sixed in the valley now."

Judy had a sharp intake of breath. "What will we do?"

The taxi pulled up in front of their destination. George paid the driver and stood still, looking up at the sign on the marquee.

From somewhere, a hot breeze eddied around the entrance.

Judy followed his gaze. "What."

George took a deep breath, exhaled. "Ever fall off a bike?"

"Hey, isn't this—"

"Yeah."

"Why are we here?"

People walked in and out, past the pair.

"Christ, it looks exactly the same."

"So why are we here?" she repeated.

"I figure this place owes me about four years pay. If I'm already blown, I might as well go out here."

"I really don't like this," Judy said. "Maybe you were lucky, ever think of that?"

"Besides, I'm sure he's not here anymore."

A moment. "You were coming here all along, weren't you?" Judy asked.

George shrugged. "I don't know. Maybe."

Another taxi pulled up and Reverend Warren got out. He hurried up to Judy, a concerned look on his face.

"Judy, I saw you rush out of the convention hall. You looked kind of— distressed. Are you okay?"

She nodded. "I guess so."

"What— how did you get here?" George asked. "How did you know to come here?"

"There was a text message on my cell. I turned it back on after my seminar and it beeped. It said to meet you here."

"A message? From whom?" George asked.

"Well, I assumed it was from you. Who else could have sent it?" Warren asked.

They all looked at each other, standing in front of the casino doors.

"Pull it up, can you?" George asked.

"I guess." Warren fiddled with the buttons on his cell phone. "There. Look." He held out the device. George looked at the little screen.

MEET AT THE OASIS HOTEL 12:15 GEORGE AND JUDY

"I thought the George and Judy part meant the message was *from* you, but I guess it means *to* meet you guys."

George had a small smile. "It's worded exactly as it was meant to be worded," he said. "Click reply and let's see what comes up."

Warren looked oddly at George and pushed the button. Instead of digits, the screen read:

PRIVATE NUMBER

The minister looked perplexed. "Wonder what that means?"

George had a faraway look. He smiled and nodded slightly, as if acknowledging something that had been beyond his comprehension.

Warren snapped his fingers. "Oh, that reminds me. I also had a message from Katy Lundgren at the church office. Something urgent."

He started to punch the buttons.

"What do you mean, something urgent?" George asked. "What did she say?"

"Something about a marginal . . . margin—"

"Margin call?" George asked.

"Yeah, that's it."

Judy paled. "Oh, my God."

George put his hand over Warren's phone. "Hold off for a minute."

He looked around. There was a franchise restaurant half a block away. Not the most private place, but it would have to do.

"Jim, you'd better come with us. We've got a story to tell you."

      *   *   *   *   *

Twenty minutes later, Jim Warren sat in a booth in back of the restaurant, staring off. Judy held her head in her hands. Outside, on the sidewalk, George paced back and forth as he spoke on the minister's cell phone.

Warren sat in stunned silence. The incredible revelation about Judy's malfeasance was almost too gut-wrenching to believe. He was having a hard time processing the horrible story.   Judy Reynolds!

He had to get a grip, had to get past it. The events seemed to cast the minister's former thoughts about money-changing, Las Vegas, the denarius story and the rich man in perhaps a new light. He tried to think it through. It felt like someone was squeezing his brain through the eye of a needle.

Good people sometimes did bad things.

Finally he spoke. "Judy, I just don't know what to say. I guess I'm in shock. I know you didn't mean to lose the church any money – that you were just— that your intentions. . . " He trailed off.

"Please, Reverend Warren," she said, "don't sugarcoat what I've done."

"I wish you'd have told me, I have to say. We'd all have offered our prayers."

"How could I? Theft? Embezzlement?"

"No. It's not that. You didn't take money for yourself."

"I'm just so sorry."

Warren's coffee had grown cold. He looked out the window at George, who had the phone to his ear, listening intently.

"No wonder George hasn't had time for a show or a seminar. My God. He's been under incredible pressure, trying to make the losses good."

"I've been supporting him as best I can."

"You know I'll do the same. What can I do?"

"Pray, Reverend."

Pray, Warren thought. There's an idea. Why hadn't he thought of that? You bet he'd pray. Pray his ass off.

George came back in the restaurant and handed Jim Warren his cell phone as he sat back down in the booth.

"All positions are liquidated, all debts fulfilled. The church no longer holds any open market instruments."

"It's over?" Judy asked.

George nodded. "It's over. With the new margin call, though, Palm Beach Presbyterian is now in hock $297,500."

"Oh, God," Judy said. "I'm so sorry. I thought everything was closed out."

Warren looked at the goalkeeper. "Will we make it?"

George stood up. "We'll see. Anyway, it's time to get back to work."

They left the restaurant. As George crossed the street, he seemed in another world. Once again the pitch had tilted and everything funneled towards his goal. He did not hesitate at the entrance. Judy and Warren looked at each other, then followed. As the glass doors opened and the trio passed through, a momentary electrical short flashed overhead on the marquee sign and sparks cascaded to the ground. The sign dimmed, flickered once and then glowed brightly:

OASIS HOTEL AND CASINO

64

The Oasis casino was exactly as George remembered. It was an uncanny sensation. He could have been twenty four years old again, except that he wasn't, and he had Judy and Jim Warren with him and his leg had started to ache as he walked through the casino, trod across the red and black carpet with the serpentine pattern that was, he was certain, the same as then. He remembered table forty two, where he had won a small fortune those many years ago. It all looked as though time had been suspended. Ancient men in overalls bearing the Oasis logo polished the brass, just as they had almost two decades before. George had wondered if he would have a strong emotional reaction to being inside the place, but was surprised to find he didn't. He avoided thinking about the 23rd floor.

Like Treasure Island, the casino wasn't very crowded on the weekday afternoon. While Reverend Warren and Judy drifted off to the slots, George stood by table forty two until the shuffle; the sign said NO MID-SHOE ENTRY. It was a six deck game, operating at a hundred dollar minimum. The only player, at first base, was an overweight middle-aged man wearing a San Diego Padres ball cap. George bought in for fifteen thousand from the pleasant looking woman whose name tag read DAWN and underneath, Texas. She smiled sweetly as she changed George's money. The goalkeeper put up a five hundred dollar bet and the game began.

Thirty minutes later, George had adjusted his base bet to match his winnings, upping the wager to a thousand dollars a hand. The Padres fan had left after tapping out. Warren and Judy had moved over to a position where they could work the slots and watch

George. From a distance, they could see the stacks of pink, orange and gray checks in front of him.

"Didn't George say he has to get in and get out in a half hour if he's winning? I thought I remembered he said that," Warren said to Judy.

"He did say that. He should've left, or at least changed tables, I think. He got barred at Treasure Island. He thinks it's probably all over town by now. I guess he'll play here as long as they'll let him."

"He was afraid of that, Judy. He told me that back in Palm Beach." Warren nodded toward the table. "Is that his winnings, mostly? Do you think he bought more chips?"

"I think he won them, but I'm not sure," she replied. In fact, as soon as the Padres fan had walked away from the table, the cards had turned.

As George won another hand, he saw in his peripheral vision that the floor man at the podium had picked up the phone and dialed. The goalkeeper's sense of a strange inevitability grew stronger.

Inside the ops center, Jack Richards, seated at a swivel chair, picked up. Richards and Frank Rizzo had been monitoring the closed circuit screens. Richards listened as he slowly chewed his gum.

"How much is he up?" He nodded and hung up, turned to Frank. "Still on forty two, aren't you?"

"Like a hawk. I make it he's into us just over forty grand."

Richards nodded. He had toggled the cameras so six screens were portraying various angles of the action at table forty two.

"What do you think, Frank?"

"He's had real good cards. Could be just a lucky player."

After a particular hand, Richards dialed the podium. The floor man listened for a moment, then moved to forty two. He brought out six new decks of cards.

George waited patiently as Dawn performed the tedious housekeeping tasks. She broke open the new decks and removed the jokers. She spread and showed the backs, flipped the cards over and showed the fronts, making sure every card was present and that none were marked. She began shuffling three hundred and twelve cards. George knew perfectly well what was going on, he knew perfectly well it was time to go. The old decks had been whisked away for analysis of the last hands, and the dealer would be in no hurry.

He didn't go.

The door to the security office opened and a slight, elderly man in a worn, shiny black suit came in with a tray of cards.

"Hey, Frank. Here's the decks from forty two."

"Thanks, Carmine," Frank said. He passed the tray to Richards.

"The son of a bitch stood on sixteen against the jack. Let's lay them out," Richards said. He began to lay the cards out, face up, on a table behind the observation chairs. He spread the cards as Frank peered over his shoulder and play resumed on table forty two.

"Let's see. Okay, here's the hand," Richards said as he reached the jack / ten / six from George's winning hand. Then he went back to the bottom of the deck and began counting the cards using the standard plus-minus system.

"Plus one, even, minus one, even, plus one, plus two, plus three . . ." he mumbled as he tallied the cards. He reached the jack / ten / six combination.

"There it is. Actual count plus eight. True count plus four when he stood against the jack." The true count allowed for the number of half decks remaining; the number became more meaningful as the decks were depleted.

"Then that's a tell," Frank said. "That's Revere and The Grey Knight, standing with that hand and that count."

Richards looked at the cards, thinking. Then he nodded. "That is a tell. You're right. You'd think he'd know it."

He fiddled with the toggles, getting a close-up on George's face. He peered intently at the screen. Despite the HD cameras, the image was grainy and not very clear. Table forty two was unevenly lighted and George was in the seat with minimal illumination and the poorest shooting angles.

"Seen this guy before, maybe?" Frank asked. He wondered if the player had chosen his spot on purpose.

"Hard to say. Get the Griffin book," Richards replied.

Frank pulled out the book containing the pictures of known card counters, cheats, and other unsavory characters. He leafed through the pages.

"Don't see him," he said. "Could be a real old picture, though."

"He reminds me of some guy a while back, maybe fifteen, twenty years ago. He's about the right age. Almost broke this place then."

Frank looked up. "I heard about that guy."

"Before your time. The boss kicked him out personally."

"Look at this picture here. Could that be him that long ago?"

The men peered at the book and puzzled at the old picture of George, taken at the cashier's cage. They looked up at the monitors as the object of their scrutiny won another hand.

Richards turned to Frank Rizzo. "Better call Roselli," he said. He reached for the phone and dialed three digits.

65

Behind a security station in the far corner of the Oasis lobby, away from the mainstream of traffic, Jack Richards and Frank Rizzo stood flanking a solitary bronze elevator door. There was no call button; a sign to the left of the keyhole read PRIVATE USE ONLY. The car went to one stop, the penthouse atop the Oasis. Presently the door slid soundlessly open and John Roselli, impeccably groomed in a dark single breasted Bottega Veneta suit and muted Burberry tie, stepped out. The casino owner looked as he had eighteen years ago. To those seeing him stride by it was evident he was a man of means and power. Jack Richards and Frank Rizzo quickly took up stations on either side, a half step behind. The casino owner glided towards the pit, trailing his pilot fish.

"Sir, he's been here about forty minutes," Richards said. "We notified your office as soon as we suspected who he might be."

"That's about fifty thousand dollars too late, Mister Richards," Roselli said.

"Yessir."

They stopped at the top of the steps to the casino. Jack Richards pointed.

"He's at table forty two, sir."

"Naturally." Roselli made a gesture of dismissal and the two men stepped away. He descended the steps and strode casually over to table forty two. He approached from the side, looked at the profile of the man whose careers he had ended eighteen years ago. He stopped just a foot behind.

He spoke the name slowly. "Mister Reynolds."

George's head did not turn. He smiled slightly, nodded. Beyond, Reverend Warren and Judy stopped playing the slots and watched.

"Hello, Roselli. Long time."

"Finish the hand."

"And . . . ?"

"Just finish it."

"You're still here, I see."

"Whom did you expect? What's interesting is that you're still here. Slow learner, as I recall."

"Yeah, it's a fault. A-D-H-D."

"They say memory's the first thing to go," Roselli said.

George glanced down and flexed his leg. "I remember when it rains."

"Still afraid of heights, eh?" Roselli said. There was a trace of a smile on his lips. The eyes were twin glaciers.

Warren and Judy seemed drawn towards the men, as if by a strange magnetic force. They approached cautiously. Roselli turned and fixed Judy with a stare. Her eyes went wide. She froze, an insect pinned to the cloth.

"Mrs. Reynolds, I presume?"

Roselli nodded slightly, smiled again. Out of the corner of Judy's eye, she thought she saw something small scuttle across the floor.

"I believe you're a home town girl, isn't that so? Welcome back. They say it's like you never left at all, know what I mean?"

Roselli nodded slightly to the dealer, who backed away. He turned to Reverend Warren. The minister eyed the casino owner warily.

"Need a partner these days?"

"He's a friend," George replied.

"Thanks for bringing the Reverend. We're all so glad he could make it," Roselli said. Warren realized with a shock he wasn't wearing any clerical garb.

"Jim, Judy, this is Mr. Roselli, owner of the Oasis Hotel and Casino. This fine establishment here."

The casino owner extended his hand. "This certainly is a pleasure," he said.

Warren gasped; his hand froze in mid-air. "Wha— how did you—??" He stared at Roselli's ring. "Where did you get that ring—?!"

"Maybe one of those arcade machines," George said, "with the little jaws when you put in a quarter—"

"Our mutual friend has quite a sense of humor," Roselli said. "Actually, it's sort of an heirloom. Been in the family forever, so to speak. I'm so pleased you noticed."

Roselli turned his gaze back to Judy. Small game caught in a laser sight, she backed away and bumped into a blackjack stool. She turned to look.

"Looking for something, Mrs. Reynolds? Something you misplaced? Money, perhaps? Think you'll find it here?"

"Leave her out of this," George said evenly.

Roselli cocked an eyebrow. "You can find a lot of things here."

George turned to gather his checks.

"Leave them on the table," Roselli said.

George turned back to see Roselli seated at a closed table, several feet away. The move appeared instantaneous. Warren stared, mouth open in confusion. Judy sat heavily on the blackjack stool, mouth an O. George got up and walked over to the covered table and sat two seats away from Roselli. Warren trailed behind.

"What do you want, Roselli?" George said.

"I'll bet the Reverend would know."

The two stared at each other; the enmity was palpable. Roselli moved to stand. George reached for his arm, but seemed to pass right through it. He was startled for a moment.

"What the—"

Warren, a few feet away, put his head to his head and leaned on the adjacent table.

"Wait," George said. "I've got a proposition for you."

"Not interested," Roselli said.

"George, no! Let's get out of here!" Warren said.

"While you still can, I think he means," Roselli added. "Or can you?"

"One final game. You and me," George said.

Roselli chuckled. "What, showdown at the OK corral?"

"You and me."

"You know, you really are a slow learner."

"I'll buy in for three hundred thousand. That's my stake."

"Are we greedy? Didn't you win enough at T.I. today?"

George felt a shock. Had it gotten around that fast?

"Three hundred grand. Come on."

"Chump change for you, Mister Reynolds, if I remember correctly. Besides, why would I want to do that?"

Roselli leaned in towards George. The look was disturbing, malevolent, menacing.

"You're already here."

66

"Five thousand three hundred, four hundred five hundred fifty. Five thousand five hundred and fifty dollars, Mister Dykes. Please sign here."

Joe signed the form and took his money from the cashier. He pulled out a Louis Vuitton Palladium money clip and inserted the bills.

"Gee, that's nice," Dexter said. "I always wanted one of those. I just never had much to put in it."

"Yeah, well, now we do. I got this while you were taking another dump. What the hell's the matter with your stomach anyway? Cost me— cost us a hundred bucks. I figure we'll split it since it's holding both of our money. What the hell, it's just one lousy chip."

Dexter started to protest, since he hadn't bought it and it wasn't in his pocket, and it wasn't really one lousy chip it was a hundred bucks, but decided to let it go. They were way ahead, after all, and he could always get his own.

"What's our total now, Joe? I've been trying to keep track but I don't know right off."

"We gotta figure that out. Besides, now I've got a lot more money in this than you do. We'll have to figure out the new percentages, right?" Dexter began to wonder if maybe that was why Joe had wanted the extra cash. As long as they stayed on the hot streak, he would now get a much bigger share.

Joe had talked Dexter into charging their store purchases so their playing stake would not be diminished. There had been an embarrassing moment when the credit card company reported Dexter

over the limit, so Joe had put some of Dexter's items on his
MasterCard. In fact, he had put all their purchases on his own card.
Dexter had wanted to pay cash and avoid the embarrassment, but Joe
had insisted.

"What the hell, it's my credit card," he had said. "Don't
worry about it."

Dexter worried about it anyway. "Why do we need all that
dough? If it turns out we need it, we're in real trouble anyway."

"You don't understand," was all Joe said. Dexter thought
Joe liked flashing their wad around, which did not seem too safe an
idea.

They were about to leave the cage when the cashier spoke
up.

"Oh, Mister Dykes? There's a message for you. Pick up a
house phone and dial seven and then your room number." The clerk
pointed to a phone a few steps away. Joe listened to the message and
hung up, a quizzical expression on his face.

"What the hell. You'll never believe who that was." He
didn't wait for an answer. "It was that broad Tom walked away
with. She said her name's Charlotte and she and Tom would meet us
down the strip and then we'll all go to the three o'clock seminar."

"Yeah? Tom? That's a relief. I was pretty worried. Why
didn't he call himself?"

"How the hell should I know? Ask him when we see them.
She said he'll shoot come craps with us. Some place called the
Oasis." He looked at his watch. "He'll be there in a half hour."

"Well, if we have a couple minutes, let's figure out what
we've got," Dexter said. He led Joe to the lounge, deserted at the
lunch hour. They sat down and Joe pulled out his – their – money
clip. Dexter watched, fascinated, as Joe tallied it up.

"Okay. You gave me fifty and I already had three fifty.
That means we take out four hundred." He counted out four hundred
dollar bills and put them in a pile on the table. "My savings here is
five grand, five hundred fifty bucks."

He counted out the sum. It went on top of the pile.

"Okay. The rest is all the dough we've won. I don't guess we need to count tips and crap, although there's a taxi fare in there, I think. I remember I tipped that one dealer five bucks, the place we won about a grand."

Joe began to count. Dexter, for some reason, kept losing track and gave up following along. Joe finished and looked up.

"Well, partner, we're in the clover to the tune of . . . ta da . . ." He made a big musical intro " . . . six thousand two hundred ten – no, twelve – smackers!"

Both were silent for a time as they looked at each other. Neither mentioned that this was the largest amount of cash each had ever seen.

"Joe, how long are we going to be here, do you think? I mean here in town."

"I know what you mean. What do you mean? We've got non-refundable tickets. We fly out of here early Monday morning."

"Do we have to?"

Joe paused. The little man definitely had a point. So what if they were charged a few bucks to change their tickets? They wouldn't stay if their hot streak had cooled. He had a department to run, kind of, but that seemed ridiculous now. Suddenly time wasn't so important anymore. For a nitwit, Dexter had hit it right on the head. And if they continued to win big, maybe some hotel would pick up their tab. It shouldn't be too long before they were in the high roller category, he fantasized. Then you could get everything, sent right up to your suite.

It did not occur to Joe Dykes that perhaps Dexter was angling to leave the convention early, to take their winnings and fly away.

In fact—

"You know, Dexter, that's a good point. We're probably making as much money as George is. Maybe more."

"Should we try to go to a show tonight, do you think?"

The idea of a show struck Joe as a grand idea. In the pictures he'd seen, the women were topless sometimes, and they all had legs that wouldn't quit. Plus he had a big wad to flash around, didn't he?

"That's a great idea, Dex."

"When we meet up with Tom let's put our heads together and figure out what we want to see. I think the concierge guy can get the tickets."

Joe looked at his watch. "Time to roll, partner."

As they rode the short distance in a taxi – both Joe and Dexter had found, like countless others before them, the gigantic signs created the illusion of proximity, and they had already walked several surprising miles between hotels – Dexter thought about Joe's earlier conversation about the phone call from Charlotte.

"What three o'clock seminar was she talking about? I don't remember what I signed up for. I thought I had one at four."

Joe pulled a well-creased program from his back pocket. "Yeah, I don't know what that is. Let's see . . . okay. A Reverend Black's talking. The subject is The Geography of Hell. What the hell's that? I don't remember seeing that. I guess somebody signed us up for it."

"I don't want to be late. I've missed two sessions already." Dexter was growing more squeamish about their winnings, becoming convinced it was time to stop. His suggestion of a show was as much to keep his partner off the tables as it was for the entertainment value. Joe's savings withdrawal had spooked him.

They arrived at the Oasis. Flush with victory, Joe tipped the taxi driver a dollar and thirty cents.

The craps tables in the casino were some distance from the blackjack area. As a result, Joe and Dexter never saw George, Judy or Warren as they looked for Tom and Charlotte. It was clear they hadn't yet arrived. There were fair sized crowds at three of the open tables. Joe drew Dexter aside.

"We've got to come up with a new split. I'll give you credit for your whole two hundred, how's that? And we're splitting the first six thousand two hundred and twelve bucks fifty-fifty. Look, I wrote it down here." Joe showed Dexter his scribbles on the back of the convention program.

"I guess we ought to wait for Tom right here," Dexter said.

Joe was getting antsy again. After all, the high life was right around the corner. He'd heard Las Vegas had been the fastest growing city in America before it tanked in the sub-prime crisis. Lots of bargains around. What the hell, what did he give a crap about Montana anyway? Where had he gotten that stupid idea?

"What the hell, we're just wasting valuable time when we could be making money. Come on, they'll see us when they get here."

They found a spot at the rail just as the puck was flipped to OFF. A young Japanese man, perhaps a student, had made his point. His companions, four or five other young people, buzzed excitedly. One snapped a picture with his cell phone camera and was immediately told by a security guard to put it away.

The croupier was entrancing the newcomers with his steady monotone. "Ten, ten, ten's a winner. Shooter made the point. Six straight passes for the shooter. Hot table here, hot table. Six straight passes, two naturals. Easy money, easy money. Bet the field, bet the field. Lay 'em down . . ."

Joe pulled out the money clip, stuffed with hundred dollar bills. He made a show of peeling off and counting a wad. Across the table, a tall, honey blonde who might once have been a showgirl seemed to notice. She had some mileage, Joe could tell, even in the bum lighting, but what the hey.

"I still can't believe you did that, Joe."

"This clip? Yeah, it's got class."

"Not the clip, the money you wired in. Is that really all your savings?"

"You saw me get it, didn't you? Anyway, I left a couple hundred in for the interest rate. The whole deal was easier than I thought."

"Debbie's going to find out, you know."

"What are you talking about? She won't know anything. I'll have our dough back in next week and what she doesn't know about the rest won't hurt her."

Joe turned to the croupier. "Gimme six thousand here."

Dexter gasped. "Hey! Not all at once, Joe!"

He was horrified to see four thousand in purple five hundred dollar checks and the rest in bumblebees come their way.

"Joe! Get greens! We're not playing these chips!"

"We're too hot to play the greens. We gotta ride Lady Luck, boy." The high roller suite was just a short elevator ride and a few passes of the dice away.

Joe put two hundred dollar bumblebees on the Pass line. An old man with a cane put a red five dollar check on the Don't Pass line. As the stickman corralled the dice, the casino seemed to redden, to darken, and the corners became indistinct. Sound muffled. Underneath, a distant wailing was audible. For an instant, Father Corr appeared to be the croupier pushing the dice to Roselli as the stick writhed and hissed. Something dripped from the ceiling.

The vision passed; no one seemed to have noticed. The dice rolled.

67

Some distance away on the casino floor George and Roselli stared at each other as Warren and Judy looked on.

"Why should I let you play?" Roselli asked. He had a bemused look George had never seen before.

"Because you can shuffle every other hand, and all bets are level," George said.

Roselli shifted in his seat towards the goalkeeper. "Level bets? One hand count? You can't do it."

"Then play me."

Roselli eyed George for a time.

"Come on, what else do you have to do?" George asked. "Shoot some housewife on a ten dollar lucky streak?"

"Maybe."

"Well?"

"You were barred here. I can confiscate your winnings."

"Why not beat me at the tables?"

There was a silence for a time. Roselli cocked his head, thinking.

"Four decks. No double after splitting aces."

"One deck, double after splitting any two cards, double any two cards, full surrender."

"Two decks, no double after splits."

"No double after split aces only."

A pause.

Roselli smiled without warmth. "Just so," he said, finally. He nodded. "Just so."

"Take a check?"

Roselli laughed.

"I thought probably not," George said.

"I prefer Euros or silver. Precious gems or gold, they'll work, too. Dollars, if you must."

Roselli's smile vanished, replaced with a smoldering stare. George was unblinking. It was as each willed the other to waver.

"Tomorrow at noon," the casino owner said.

George was motionless, then nodded. He got up from the table and rejoined Judy and Warren. Roselli watched them head for the exit. A cocktail waitress came up with a shot of whisky and glass of water on her tray.

Still watching the trio as they approached the doors, Roselli downed the shot and picked up the water. The waitress, Sally from Denver, thought it odd that her boss was smiling. She had never seen that before, and she wondered what kinds of things might make John Roselli smile.

68

"Come *on*, Joe, we gotta bet greens," Dexter implored.

"Yeah, okay, Dex. I just want to get a good jump start."

The pair was playing at the Oasis, waiting for Tom Swayne and the mysterious Charlotte. The Japanese student picked up the dice again and shook them furiously as his entourage chattered and gesticulated amongst itself. He threw the dice and they caromed off the rail. They looked up at Joe like a pair of –

Snake eyes.

Joe Dykes stared at the spot his two hundred dollar checks had just vacated. A great anger flashed through him. The change guy next to the head guy sitting down had *taken his chips away, goddamn it!* The crowd groaned and the dice passed to another pair of hands. Joe heard Dexter say something and tug on his sleeve. *If he does that again*, Joe thought, *I'll bash his goddamn head right in right goddamn now.* He put two more hundred dollar checks on the Pass line.

"New shooter coming out, folks. New shooter." It was the honey blonde's turn. Was she alone, Joe wondered? The dice bounced their way to a six.

"Six, six. Six the point. Bet the field. Bet the hard ways. Hot table here, new shooter." The mantra continued; the puck was placed on the six.

The shooter rolled a four. Then she rolled a nine. Then came a seven.

"Seven. Seven out. Pay the—"

"GODDAMN IT!" Dexter looked around, startled. Joe had shouted and banged his fist on the rail. A few nearby people looked at him. He saw the old man with the cane, who was probably poor and lucky to have five bucks to bet, had also lost and was grinning at Joe. Joe stared at him.

"What's so goddamn funny?" he demanded.

The old man kept smiling and shook his head slowly. He looked away. Joe thought he heard "Asshole," but he couldn't be sure.

"What? What did you say?"

Joe became aware Dexter was saying something. "What, Dexter?!"

"Come on, Joe. We gotta go to greens. We lost two hundred bucks."

"Oh, yeah? Maybe not." Dexter watched in horror as Joe put two bumblebees on the Pass line just as the betting closed out. The new shooter was the old man with the cane, to Joe's left. How could that be? he wondered. The dice must have passed him while he was arguing with Dexter. *If we don't win this bet it's all his fault!* was Joe's fleeting thought as the dice hit the rail and bounced to a stop and benignly looked up at him. *Sure are a lot of dots there* and indeed the dice were showing boxcars. Joe felt the blood fall out of his head as gravity finally took over.

Then he saw the old man had *bet against himself the little turd* his stupid nothing red chip was on the Don't Pass line and his stupid worthless little red chip lay there, pathetically alone, not winning and not losing (bar twelve) like for people on welfare and with food stamps in the grocery line, so that Joe could stare at them with contempt as they fumbled through their pitiful little cloth bags for the stamps *you would think they'd have them ready but they never do they fumble and rummage and hold up the line they're never regular white people anyway but lousy little zips and wetbacks and guats and illegals and the schwarzes one had actually tried to join the church but they fixed their tires in the parking lot didn't we* and now Dexter was really going postal next to him.

God, I hate this little shit, he thought. He turned to face him.

"What, Dexter? Are you going to tell me we lost? Do you think maybe I figured that out?"

"We've lost four hundred dollars in about a minute. What the hell is happening? Oh, man, maybe we better quit. We can't bet these hundred dollar chips anymore."

Joe was no longer angry with Dexter. He simply had to explain, as if to a child. "What's the matter with you? We just have to ride this out. I'm going with the house."

He put a black check on the Don't Pass line.

"We shouldn't bet that kind of dough, Joe."

"You ever want to get even? You think we're sitting tall on our wallets right now because we bet chump change?"

"Why are we changing and betting the Don't Pass?"

Joe was a patient person. "Well, what do you think has been happening to us going with the shooter?" Why did he have to explain the obvious?

The new shooter was a forty year old night shift supervisor with Illinois Bell named Mary Maloney, and she had never been to Las Vegas. She was very excited. Mary and her two girlfriends, also Illinois Bell supervisors, had pooled their money for this adventure. Later on, they were going to see Cirque, having bought their tickets eight months ago.

Mary Maloney was so excited she rolled a seven her first roll. She thought she had lost.

"Ooooh," she squealed, as the croupier paid off her ten dollar bet.

"Ooooh," moaned Dexter Wilcox, as their black check was whisked up, like a valet taking away an offensive used cocktail napkin.

"Damn! Goddamn it! Why is this happening to us?!" Joe directed his comments upward.

"This is making me feel crummy, Joe. Let's stop here for awhile." Dexter looked ill. He felt ill.

"Don't you see, Dexter? That's why people lose. They don't have the guts to ride out a bad streak."

"Maybe the bad streak will ride us out. Right out of town."

"You tell me, Dexter. With her or against?"

"I don't know. I don't know. I don't think we should still be here," was all Dexter could manage.

Joe called out to the croupier. "What's the maximum bet here?"

"Five thousand on the Pass and Come lines, sir. Double odds, ten thousand max on the odds. Two thousand on the field and hard ways bets." This was much larger than Joe had thought.

"What the hell are you doing, Joe?"

Joe Dykes put five hundred on the Don't Pass Line. Everyone around the table who saw the bet looked at him. Joe noticed a raised eyebrow of respect from the honey blonde across the rail. He wondered idly if she had worked topless.

"How much did you bet?" Dexter asked. He hadn't seen whose checks were whose on the layout; he thought he'd recognized Tom Swayne on another table. When the guy had turned, Dexter saw he'd been mistaken.

"Five hundred bucks," Joe muttered. "This will put us even." Dexter thought his heart had stopped.

Mary Maloney picked up the dice, closed her eyes, prayed, hopped a little step and threw a nine. She squealed because she hadn't lost yet.

"Nine, nine. Nine's the point. Play the field." Bets were laid. Money went on the Come line. Joe was tempted to place a wager on the Don't Come, but he still did not really understand the bet. The stickman returned the dice to Mary.

Mary Maloney picked up the dice, closed her eyes, prayed, hopped a little step and threw a four. She squealed because she hadn't lost yet.

"Four, four. Pay the hard ways. Hot shooter." Bets were laid. Money went on the come line. Joe was tempted to give the odds, but he still did not really understand the bet. The stickman returned the dice to Mary.

Mary Maloney picked up the dice, closed her eyes, prayed, hopped a little step and threw a nine. She squealed.

"Winner! Winner nine. Pay the Pass line, pay the nine. Hot shooter here."

Mary Maloney hopped and squealed as though she were on fire. The bottom fell out of Joe Dykes' stomach. He wanted to lunge across the table and squeeze the neck of Mary Maloney until his fingers met in the middle and she was dead. Instead, he turned to Dexter. He could think of nothing to say. They had lost a thousand dollars.

"We've lost a thousand dollars," wailed Dexter. He went to church – why would a loving God test his faith? How could Jesus let this happen?

Joe Dykes did not know if he wanted to kill Mary Maloney or Dexter Wilcox more. Or maybe Jesus.

"Okay, Dexter. We've lost a thousand dollars. We're still up over five grand. We were going to shoot craps when we had no winnings at all, weren't we? So let's shoot craps."

Joe decided that betting with Mary Maloney was better than killing her in the long run. He backed off to two hundred, laying two bumblebees on the Pass line. It did not seem quite as daring after the five hundred dollar loss.

Mary Maloney threw boxcars. Joe felt his face get hot. It would have been better to kill her. The world was no longer a devil-may-care place, and they were no longer on top of it.

In five minutes, things were grim and Joe had a sick feeling in his stomach. Dexter pleaded with him to stop. Joe Dykes' vision had shrunk to a tunnel no larger than the layout in front of him. Sound seemed distorted and far away. Even as he grasped them, Joe felt their checks slipping away and was powerless to stop them as they leaked through his fingers.

Joe could not stop. Dexter could not make him stop. The next roll would start them back on their winning ways. God would not let them lose all their money.

In twelve minutes, they were cleaned out. Broke. It was the worst feeling Dexter Wilcox had experienced in his whole life, a feeling like his stomach walls were touching, or that he had eaten stove bolts, or something, much worse than when he was laid off, and even worse than when Mary Anne Werner had turned him down for the senior prom and tried unsuccessfully not to giggle.

The terrible feeling lasted only a few seconds, though, before Dexter became even more nauseated with a sudden realization. They were worse than broke.

"How are we going to pay for all that stuff we bought?" he moaned.

Joe Dykes had also never had a more sickening feeling in his life, until he remembered they had charged all of their purchases on his credit card.

69

As the sun bloated and sank towards the hills around Las Vegas, George Reynolds stood in front of the small steel Halliburton lying open on the bed in front of him. The case was partially filled with stacks of cash, rubber banded in ten thousand dollar packets. Dressed in a sports jacket and open collar dress shirt, he pulled wads of bills from various pockets, counted and banded the money.

Judy came out of the bathroom partially dressed. She'd suggested the two of them enjoy a leisurely supper in the hotel, hoping to drain tension out of her husband. As he placed more stacks inside, she stopped and watched from the chair in the corner. There really was nothing more fascinating than watching money, she realized, especially if it's yours.

"Two sixty five, two seventy, two seventy five, two eighty, two hundred ninety thousand dollars." Three more rubber banded stacks went into the Halliburton.

"Oh, George, you've almost done it!"

"Oh, wait." He pulled out one more stack from an inside jacket pocket and counted. "Okay. Three hundred four thousand, five, no, six hundred dollars." The goalkeeper returned $4,600 to his jacket pocket and snapped the case closed. He turned the lock on three hundred thousand dollars in cash.

"You have done it."

"Not quite. We came with forty thousand, remember? That's all the cash I could get together in two days."

"George, I've still got most of the money my grandmother left me, and we can cover the rest. Let's go home! Tonight!"

George looked down and slowly closed the case.

"Tomorrow," he said.

They looked at each other in silence. Judy turned and gazed out the window. It was growing dark quickly; the lengthening shadows of the casinos were fading into twilight.

"This isn't about the money anymore, is it?" she asked.

"Tomorrow."

"I hope that's not too late," she said, as she walked back into the bathroom.

Twenty minutes later, George stood at the window waiting for Judy to finish dressing. He watched a jet bank on approach to McCarran over the twinkling lights of the city on yet another clear evening. The big jumbos seemed to float so slowly towards the runway, white angels coming home to Paradise Road. *And still they come*, he thought, *another planeload of hopes and dreams, the real currency of Las Vegas*. He recognized the bad cliché. How many loads of people ferried in from the sky over three quarters of a century? He supposed he could Google it and find out. Unconsciously, he reached down and rubbed his leg. He turned as Judy emerged from the bathroom in a smashing black cocktail dress. She gestured toward his leg.

"It hurts again?"

"Only when I laugh. Wow, you look terrific. I think it's swollen."

"Should I take a look at it?"

"I mean the other one."

George and Judy exchanged grins. He really was looking forward to a relaxing, delicious dinner and a quiet evening before the morrow's battle.

70

Davey Cahill stood before his closet, sliding door open, thinking. Before today he hadn't given his wardrobe much thought. It had seemed adequate enough. He had one serviceable suit, a couple of sports jackets and a few favorite shirts. One, given to him by Julie, Lonnie's wif – widow, even had his initials on the cuff. He had several tasteful ties from before the divorce. His pants did not show the ankle holster he occasionally wore.

But that was before Special Agent Haley Carradine accepted his invitation to Las Vegas. Now serviceable wasn't the criterion. Somehow, the whole closet looked tired. The suit was wrinkled and maybe the pants a bit shiny on the backside. It might be a good idea to pop over to Men's Wearhouse, up on North Rainbow. Wilhite said they sometimes had a two for one deal. He really didn't need more than one suit, but maybe for the free threads he'd get the white job he'd always thought would look pretty snazzy if he ever did make it down to South America.

Davey liked seeing the old films, the late night movie stars in their white suits and white hats as they gamboled around places like Rio or Buenos Aires, some hot tamale trailing on their arms. He admired the carefree way they floated through the nightclubs, breezed down the wide avenues in their white convertibles. Of course it was all fake and all, but what the hey, so was Las Vegas. His day-to-day dealings were about the only reality in the town, anyway.

Wilhite had been an inspired choice to escort Sue Flint, Haley's traveling companion. Everybody liked the affable white collar crime detective, who was never at a loss for words and said he'd be glad to help Davey out, provided he saw a picture first. They'd looked up Flint's FBI photo, and were both impressed. What kind of field office was the Bureau running in West Palm, Davey wondered? It looked like a modeling agency. A phone call set things up; the women had gotten a few days off together and it would all come off in three weeks. Wilhite thought the women would like to see *Ka* or *Mystere*, both spectacular productions, he said. Cahill had seen neither, wondering again why he seemed to let life rush by without flagging down most of its pleasures.

Davey kept his ex-wife's closet door shut. It would have made a useful storage area, but somehow he couldn't bring himself to use it. The dance instructor had hung a dress in there one night, and Davey almost said something to her about it. It didn't make any sense though, he supposed, so he'd kept silent. It wasn't something he could express anyway.

He slid his closet door closed and found himself looking at his full length reflection. He squeezed a dime between his buttocks, stood up straight and sucked in. He'd get a haircut and have the guy leave it just a little longer. He'd do it a week before so it wouldn't look too fresh.

He let out his breath. What the hell was he thinking, he thought. He could never use a white suit.

71

James Warren rode the elevator upstairs with a furrowed brow. He had a lot on his mind. The trip was not going as he had thought. He realized he really was not leading his flock, that somehow things had gone awry; their pilgrimage was falling spiritually short. Only George seemed to be on track, steadily winning on his quest. George, who only went to church two times a year. Well, three sometimes, depending on the Christmas cantata. Perhaps he was the Lord's instrument – no, he *was* the Lord's vessel, a vessel to be filled with money that –

He shook his head. How did he think like that? He really wasn't performing. That thing with that woman, what the devil was that? Candy Land – could that possibly be her real name? – how did she happen? He wasn't even sure. As he had speculated in the food court, she was certainly – now he was convinced – a divine message of some sort, a lesson, a call to action. But to do what? Marshal his troops, he guessed.

Anyway, that was all behind him. At least he thought it was, until he had a sudden flash picture of Candy's behind, sticking up in the air on his bed as she slapped it. What was the matter with his mind? He'd missed some of the conference meetings, and he knew Dexter and Joe had been derailed from their purpose. He was not providing guidance, leadership. The news about Judy – sweet, kind Judy Reynolds! – and the church's looming insolvency had stunned him. The minister had beseeched the Almighty for fiscal salvation almost nonstop since learning of the goalkeeper's mission. He had been unnerved by the encounter with that casino owner, that person who went way back with George. He didn't understand what had happened. He needed to think about it, to open his Bible, but first he had to get his flock back on track, re-energize the spiritual. He resolved to—

He suddenly realized the elevator still had not reached his floor. It seemed to be a local. People kept coming on and shuffling backwards towards him. He moved to the rear of the car as a young, attractive couple crowded towards him. The woman was very pretty, another blonde, this time with short hair, wearing a striking chemise type affair, although he didn't really know if that was the proper term, but it was form-fitting and slinky and seemed to be made of a million shiny metallic circles woven together, a million silver scales. The effect was – well, striking, kind of like a serpent. He wondered if the little overlapping circle things were metal or plastic or what. Women like this did not attend Palm Beach Presbyterian, he mused, with some regret.

What was with this elevator? It was still only on the— Where was it? Two of the numbers were lit, six and – sixty six. What? There was no sixty sixth floor. He didn't understand, but no one else on the car seemed perturbed. Something was wrong with the wiring, or something.

Suddenly James Warren felt a huge gas pain, right in his lower gut. It seemed as though a pipeline had burst somewhere and all the high pressure gas was ballooning into his stomach. He almost doubled over in agony. The pain moved lower. He was going to have to let it out, and quickly – a huge, roiling, pressurized hot ball of stomach gas, ready to burst out of his rectum with impossible force, and he knew the explosion would be incredibly loud even in the elevator, and maybe even visible, shimmering its way to the ceiling, but maybe no one would hear, really, because there was laughter and talking and the sound of the moving car. But the air would be unbreathable and unbelievably fetid – as foul, as deadly as marsh gas mixed with Zyklon B, maybe even turn opaque.

Where did he get this stuff? Had Someone miswired his mind?

Of course he couldn't do that, to fart like that would be unthinkable, especially for an ordained minister, but Warren was horrified to realize he was rapidly running out of options. All the gas in the Ukraine had poured into his gut. The car seemed to be moving sideways, or something. He squeezed his sphincter muscle with all his strength, trying to stop the inevitable, squeezed his sphincter and squeezed his eyes shut and the pain increased even more if that were possible as the gas was squeezed back upward and into his –

What? He felt something odd, and there was a strange pressure only now it was in the front of him. He looked down and gasped in horror. His member had swollen to the size of a cucumber, and was bulging, straining against his cotton slacks. Was it the stomach gas? He had never heard of such a thing. His penis seemed to pulsate like some ghastly life-form, an obscene external heart. *Is this my soul?* he wondered. *Am I dying? Don't I get any notice?* He looked around the car wildly, face distorted with dread, but no one seemed to be aware of this new life-form, the writhing vegetable in his pants. Thank God they were all facing front. But now the woman in the metallic chemise, the young slender vibrant woman with the tinkling laugh, she backed up and lurched into him. To his dismay his swollen digit poked the woman right in the cleft of her buttocks, her ass, just as though the engorged crazed zucchini had orchestrated its own attack, using its lone eye to home in on target. Warren recoiled but there was no place to go, and it was as if the elevator car had tilted forward. He could not seem to regain his balance, and only succeeded in wiggling against the woman, who was trying to turn and see with her yellow reptile eyes just what sort of object was spiking her, right through the mail of her dress, and it seemed to Reverend Warren as though his zipper, already bloated and strained, must have caught in one of the metal scales of her infernal armor and stuck them together with a rattling, metallic sound, two mating alloys in the throes of rapture. He pushed in desperation against the sleek exotic metal of her back but actually only succeeded in bending her forward at the waist so that her buttocks were thrust out even more, welding his zipper with the white-hot heat of his uncontrollable passion, the furnace lit and stoked by Candy the previous night, to the round armor plates of her dress.

He thought he heard her scream, but the gas had won out and there was a great gout of an explosion drowning out lesser sounds, an explosion that actually lifted him briefly off the floor of the car. The woman's boyfriend or husband had turned around, looked down at Warren's attacking digit and recoiled in disgust. The air turned murky. James Warren never saw the punch coming but the guy clocked him square on the nose. And then the tilt of the elevator car increased and the floor of the car was zooming up to meet him, and his face bounced off the metal strip at the front of the car, the metal strip with the embossed cryptic message, so that when he bounced up the letters MIAMI ELEV were pressed into his forehead, and he landed on his back and looked up. He looked up and there was a silver halo, high overhead, or maybe it was the hem of her metal dress, the metal dress that must have been magnetized because his moral compass was spinning and spinning out of control, and he was looking up at it, toward Heaven beyond the clouds of her undergarment, seeing indistinctly, through the nylon darkly, and then there was nothing.

72

Joe, carrying a near-empty whiskey bottle, floated down the hallway as his defunct partner trailed behind, glass in hand. Dexter fumbled for the key card with his free hand as he squinted through his coke bottles at the nearest room number. He held up the plastic.

"These numbers don't match," he said.

"What the hell's the matter with you," Joe replied. "There's no numbers on that card. Just find the goddamn room. I gotta puke."

"You shouldn't be drinking so much."

"Look who's talking, Mister A A. Just shut up."

They stumbled on. The corridor seemed as long as forever.

"Nineteen thirty seven, I remember," Dexter said. "Know how I know?"

"Just find the goddamn thing. I gotta lie down."

"They completed the Golden Gate Tunnel and the Lincoln Bri – Lincoln Tunnel in nineteen thirty seven."

"Big whoop."

"The Hindenblimp crashed in nineteen thirty seven."

"Jesus, what are you, the goddamn almanac?"

Dexter's history express was chugging now. "Stalin purged his generals. The Luftwaffe bombed Germany."

Dexter bumped into the wall and dropped the key card. It took him several seconds to pick it up. "No, I mean the Luftwaffe bombed Spain. They came from Germany. China and Japan went to war. Chamberlain became Prime—"

"JESUS CHRIST WILL YOU SHUT THE HELL UP?!?"

Dexter's mental rail yard switched tracks.

"I told you time and time again, Joe – bet the greens."

"Put a lid on it, Dexter." Joe was thinking that one good shot with the bottle would stove in Dexter's skull.

"Six thousand dollars. We lost six thou—"

"I said drop it!"

"Okay, okay. I just can't believe we lost it all. Even my two hundred!"

Joe sighed. "You really are an asshole, you know it? Where's our room? I gotta take a wicked piss too." With his free hand, he fiddled with his pants.

"I think it's the next one down," Dexter said. He stopped and looked around. "Oh, no, wait. We went the wrong way."

Joe thought if he smashed the bottle on something, he could use the jagged neck as a corkscrew on Dexter's face. They passed the elevators and tottered back the other way. As they approached Room 1937, a flickering light emanated from around the door, which stood ajar. Dexter heard voices from inside. He pushed the door open uncertainly and took a hesitant step forward. Joe shoved him aside and lurched into the bathroom. There was no one there; the sound was coming from the television.

A minute later, Joe came out, still holding the whiskey bottle. He sat heavily in the armchair, hand to his head. Dexter, sitting on the bed, was watching a program.

"We must have left it on," he said. "Did you wash your hands?"

Onscreen, the logo LAS VEGAS HOTEL CHANNEL appeared in the lower right corner. Chorus girls danced over the legend:

TWO SHOWS NIGHTLY
DARK MONDAYS

The screen changed to a shot of stage curtains with the logo OASIS HOTEL AND CASINO on them. An off-screen announcer began:

"Good evening, ladies and gentlemen. Tonight, live from The Oasis Hotel and Casino, we are proud to present—"

The curtains parted to reveal giant electrodes connected to an electric chair. Someone was seated in the chair, manacled and wearing a rubber hood. Behind, spotlights played over the flashing sequined curtains. From offstage, Charlotte pranced on in showgirl attire and approached from the side. She bounced and smiled and beamed at the audience. She posed by the apparatus, then ran her hand up and down the electrodes, across the chair back and up and down the side, showing off the wares as if they were a game show prize. Next to the chair was an unlit play clock.

The announcer continued. "— an electrifying floor show! And tonight's mystery guest is—"

Charlotte whipped off the hood with a flourish. Tom Swayne was seated in the chair. His eyes had been gouged out and replaced with a pair of dice showing snake eyes.

"— Tom Swayne of West Palm Beach, Florida!"

Enthusiastic applause.

Dexter leaped to his feet in horror and pointed. "GAAAHH!!!" he yelled.

Joe, startled, looked at Dexter and then followed his finger.

"Jesus Christ!" He lurched backward and dropped the bottle. Onscreen, Tom cocked an ear.

"That you guys? Joe? Dex?"

Tom attempted to peer into the camera.

"You guys have a good season?"

Reddy Killowatt danced onstage, a clever blend of animation and the live stage shot. "See all the power of the Hoover Dam harnessed for your enjoyment!!" he exclaimed.

The program cut to a quick shot of the dam, and then another of the seventeen giant generators humming away inside the bowels of the structure. Cartoon Reddy sat beaming atop the nearest unit. The next shot tracked high tension lines across the desert towards the city, accompanied by the electrical humming sound, as Reddy danced across the wires tracked by the camera. The picture cut back to Tom. Charlotte grinned broadly and backed away from the chair. She scrunched up and squinted in anticipation.

Reddy stood poised before a giant electrical throw switch, both hands on the toggle. The game timer lit up: Five, four three, two, one—

Reddy yanked the handle closed. There was a blinding burst of light, accompanied by a shower of sparks. Tom burst into incandescence. The dice exploded from his eyes and came up boxcars on the floor.

"Craps!" cried Reddy Killowatt, his red lightning body flashing, as Joe and Dexter fled the room.

73

Reverend Warren wobbled unsteadily down the hall. He had felt faint as he left the elevator. He tried to recall his last meal. Was something bad? His gut felt as though the muscles had been strained. Had he lifted something? He couldn't recall. He took out his key card and opened the door to room 1911. There was a soft noise from within.

He turned on the light, and froze, his nightmare revisited. Candy was curled up on the bed, quietly sobbing. She looked up at Warren. Mascara had streaked down her cheeks. The effect was grotesque. Warren was aghast.

"What— what are you doing here, Candy? How did you get in? What's going on?"

"Last night I took one of your key cards. It was there on the night table." She pointed to the piece of furniture as though its existence justified the act. She looked like a poster orphan.

"I don't have any place to go," she said.

"Candy— please. You can't stay here."

"I know you heal people, Father. You talked about your congregation." She held out her hands in supplication. "*Please.*"

"Candy – I'm not a priest. I don't think I can help you." He turned and looked out the window. It was out of the question. She had to go. She was just a child in a woman's body. And that body—

He cut off the thought with difficulty. What was her hold on him? She had simply overwhelmed the minister, like a cosmic bowling ball blasting his pins right off their spots. Was some Divine Pinsetter going to have to reset him? Was he powerless before her erotic juggernaut? Get a grip! he told himself. There had to be someone, anyone, some organization, maybe, able to take her off his hands.

"There must be some people, your parents maybe? I know out here there must be organizations—"

He turned as he spoke, in time to see her run into the bathroom and shut the door.

Oh, damn. Warren stood there, befuddled. Now what?

74

George's hopes for a relaxing evening took a blow when he was startled by a pounding on the door. He opened it and Joe and Dexter tumbled in. They were adrift in a sea of alcohol, frantically drowning. They both talked at once and neither George nor Judy could make any sense out of their babbling.

"Slow down!" George held up his hand. "One at a time." Dexter lurched over and sagged onto the bed. He leaned against the headboard while Joe folded to the floor.

Dexter began. "We went over to this casino. We got a phone message from Tom to meet him at the craps table there."

"So that's a relief," George said. "You found the wayward son."

"No we didn't. It wasn't from Tom," Joe slurred.

George frowned. "He just said—"

"He's right, it wasn't exactly from Tom," Dexter said. "It was from that broad he picked up last night at the Grand. Anyway, he didn't show. Neither of them showed."

"When was this?" George asked.

"I dunno, couple hours ago, maybe less. I don't know."

"So then what?" George asked. Joe had developed the hiccups and was slumped against the chair, staring at the floor. He left the telling of the tale to Dexter.

"Well, we waited a few minutes. They never came. So we shot craps. We lost."

"It happens," George said.

"No, you don't understand. We lost all the money. Not just the money we won, but the money we brought. Plus Joe wired home for some more."

"How much more?"

"All of his money more. About six grand. Plus – well, it's complicated, but we bought some stuff we haven't paid for yet. They got all our dough."

George's eyes narrowed. "Wait a minute. Who got all your dough? What casino were you told to go to?"

"The – what? – the Oasis. Yeah, that was it."

George and Judy exchanged glances. She moved over and sat on the bed next to Dexter. "I'm sorry, Dexter."

"Were you guys drinking when you shot craps?" George asked. "Not that it matters now."

"Not much. Some. Mostly later. What a mess. We should have gone to the convention, period. None of this gambling crap. We had no business gambling."

Joe raised his head. "Shut up, Dexter. For Christ's sake, quit whining."

"Sounds like you learned a valuable lesson," Judy said.

"You both sound like my mother," Dexter said. He paused. "Anyway, that's not all. That's not the b— that's not the worst part. Well, maybe it is. You tell them, Joe."

Joe waved off the invitation. Dexter continued.

"When we got back to our room, the TV was on. We'd turned it off, I'm pretty sure. But it was on."

"Maybe the maid left it on," Judy said. "Sometimes they watch TV from room to room."

"We saw Tom. On the hotel channel. He was murdered on the television! We saw him killed."

"You're goddamn right we did," Joe mumbled from the floor.

George looked at the sad pair. If they'd been sober, he still wouldn't have believed them.

"You saw something, I guess, but I doubt it's what you just said. It's some program probably and the guy reminded you of Tom. I take it, then, you never did link up with him?"

"How could we link up with him when he's dead? He's been murdered," Dexter said.

From the floor: "You're goddamn right he was."

"You boys need some rest, don't you think?"

"Sleep it off, you mean," Dexter said. "Yeah, that's for sure. Come on, Joe." He tugged on Joe and they lurched for the door.

"Let's talk again after you guys have had a chance to rest," George said.

Joe turned. His affect, his voice were flat.

"Think whatever the hell you want to think. I know what we saw. So does Dexter. You wanna know who killed him?"

"Sure – yes," George said. What else was there to say?

"Reddy Killowatt. Reddy Killowatt killed Tom."

And then they were gone.

75

"Please! Come out of the bathroom, Candy," Warren said. It had grown quiet beyond the door. What was he going to do? She couldn't stay in there forever. But then again he couldn't wait forever. She seemed to be the gift that keeps on giving. That wouldn't do at all. He'd think of something. Anxiety was a layer of cheesecloth smothering his brain. He could call downstairs and have them—

Have them what? How could he explain? He could always pray, maybe, as a last resort. God understood when people screwed up, he was pretty sure. This was some other thing, some other level of corporeality, an apex of sensual behavior which had not existed before for James Warren. Was it sinful?

Well, it sure as hell wasn't a new form of prayer, driving one home for the old rugged Cross.

It felt pretty good, which was one indication. On the other hand, it did make him appreciate Betsy even more, though, he was sure of it. Without contrast there is only a weak, washed-out sameness. Sin bequeaths salvation. Candy had provided him with a yardstick, another form of relationship, a backdrop against which to measure and admire Betsy Warren.

Besides, he was certain this was no shock to the Almighty. He'd seen it before, others had succumbed, even men of the cloth. Look at how many—

The bathroom door opened suddenly and Candy Cane came out smiling. The horror show mascara had been cleaned up and her hair combed. Her entire demeanor had changed. The child-woman was gone, replaced by the woman-child. She tugged at her dress.

"You have to help me, Father. Lay your healing hands on me. Like in the Bible," she purred.

Warren backed up, terrified, his gears stripped, engine suddenly racing. He clonked against the closet door. A strap slipped off her shoulder and a breast flopped out, nipple erect. Candy ran her hand over the flesh, squeezing the nipple between her fingers.

"No, please!" he cried. She pressed into him, trapping the minister against the closet door. She looked him straight in the eyes, still with her wicked smile, and kissed his neck. Her tongue flicked over his flesh. Warren's resolve evaporated. He leaned back and closed his eyes. Pleasure washed over like a warm tropical sea.

The sound of groaning metal startled him; his eyelids snapped open. He peered directly into the milk-white eyes of Father Corr, whose tongue writhed like a serpent against his cheek. Warren screamed and pushed the old priest away. Father Corr staggered back into the bathroom.

"Come back to me, boyo. I've waited so long . . ."

Warren slammed the bathroom door and leaned against it, panting. He looked wildly around the room for something to shove against the door, something to defend himself with.

There was a knock.

"George!" Somehow he knew the goalkeeper was behind the door. He flung it open.

"Thank G—!"

Betsy Warren, holding her suitcase, stood in the doorway, perfectly attractive in a plain, sensible dress and sensible shoes. Her jaw and suitcase dropped as she looked at her disheveled husband, lipstick smeared on his face. Each mirrored the other's horror-stricken expression. At that moment Candy came out of the bathroom, one breast exposed. Everyone stood stock-still for, it seemed, all eternity.

Candy giggled. "Oooh! A threesome!"

Betsy shrieked and ran down the hall as Warren swayed, aghast.

"Betsy!" he called. "Oh dear God!"

Warren collapsed on the floor just as Father Corr came out of the bathroom, brushing his teeth with the minister's toothbrush. Foam was flecked around his mouth and on his black shirt.

"Not quite, boyo," he said, sounding mushy. "You always get that wrong."

76

The Sacramento Hotel's California Room was known for its fine dining, having held a four star rating for six straight years. George was looking forward to a lobster dinner with Judy. He recalled wryly the last lobster he had in Las Vegas; it hadn't ended on a tranquil note.

The dining room was moderately crowded as people were arriving in town for the fight weekend. He perused the wine selections. George vaguely remembered the bottle he had enjoyed eighteen years ago, but couldn't recall the name. He handed Judy the wine list and, after some contemplation, she chose the Veuve Clicquot Ponsardin La Grande Dame Rose. If the length of the name had anything to do with the quality, George figured, this would be the top of the line. At least this time he'd get a chance to digest the stuff properly.

Judy was peeling shrimp as George sipped the 1995 vintage champagne. It tasted pretty good, he thought, a little different. He felt himself beginning to relax.

"So it's the trip from Hell," he said.

"Or maybe *to* Hell," she said as she discarded the peel.

"I'm not even going to say I told you so. Religion— Christ." He shook his head as he poured another glass.

"Let's get out of here, George. I know I sound like a broken record."

George decided he liked the somewhat tart, dry flavor of the Clicquot. "Tom Swayne's ditched his fiancé – the one you worked so hard to set him up with – and nobody's seen him since. He's probably shacked up someplace. Joe wired home for more money and lost it all. Dexter's off the wagon big time – I wonder what's next?"

"Like that Mister Roselli said. While we still can. Let's go now."

"We're almost there, Judy. Almost there."

"Almost where, George? I don't understand what's keeping you here. What's really going on?" She'd finished with the appetizer.

"We'll be home by tomorrow night." Home seemed like another planet.

"Will we? It's horrible. I'm so scared."

George swished his champagne around, raised the glass. Tiny bubbles danced to the top on their happy little journey.

He sighed. "I sure can use this."

He sipped just as the background restaurant noise was suddenly broken by a loud wail. He gulped involuntarily and looked toward the sound. Everyone in the place turned toward the commotion. George looked on, astonished, as Betsy Warren stumbled into the restaurant, crying and sobbing, mascara streaking down her cheeks, and lurched straight to their table. He jumped up and caught her she collapsed into an empty chair. He had no idea who she was.

"What-- what--?"

Judy was horror-stricken. "Betsy! Dear God, what's wrong?!"

George realized the woman dissolving in his arms must be Jim Warren's wife. The distraught female continued to sob and gasp without signs of slowing down. George looked around as she wailed.

"We've got to get her out of here." She continued to cry and chug along like a leaky steam engine. He lifted her from the chair and half-carried her past gaping patrons, with Judy a half step behind. He turned.

"I wondered what was coming next, didn't I?" In a small part of George's mind, he realized he wasn't going to get a chance to digest this lobster dinner, either.

77

Warren ran down the nineteenth floor corridor, moaning and gasping and glancing behind, wild-eyed, as Father Corr wobbled after him, still working the toothbrush in his mouth. Toothpaste and spittle ran down his chin and over his black cassock. Warren reached the elevator, sobbing, and jabbed the button repeatedly as the ancient priest neared. The minister spotted a fire axe case nearby. Rushing forward, he yanked on the handle, but the door wouldn't open. He shattered the glass with his fists. Warren reached in and grabbed the axe but it held fast. He yanked again. The priest was almost on him. It was no good. He removed his hands and held them up, bleeding from the wrists and palms.

"The stigmata . . ." he moaned.

"Don't flatter yourself, laddie!" the priest cackled, as more toothpaste dribbled down. "They say it's no good unless you brush three minutes," he said to himself. He removed his teeth and held them in one hand while scrubbing with the other.

"Up and down, up and down," he said, temporarily absorbed in the task.

Warren whirled and yanked with all his strength. The axe came free just as Father Corr reached for him. He turned and swung blindly. The axe thwacked into the priest's outstretched arm. Half-severed, the limb hung at a grotesque angle, spurting bright arterial blood in rhythmic pulses.

Father Corr was clearly annoyed. One of his milk-white eyes turned red.

"Still disrespectful. *Now* look!" He waggled the toothbrush in reproach, then flipped it at Warren, hitting him in the chest. The priest put his good hand on his hip.

The elevator dinged; the doors opened. Warren heaved for the car as Father Corr, temporarily distracted, waved the stricken arm around, blood spurting everywhere.

"I got rhythm, I got music . . ." the priest sang enthusiastically, after replacing his teeth. He tried to snap his fingers but they weren't working correctly.

"Damn," he said, and snapped with his other hand. He found he could stanch the spurting by squeezing his upper arm with his good hand. He squeezed, let go, squeezed let go, aiming his fire in turn at the ash tray, the axe case, the elevator button.

As he reached the car's threshold, James Warren's expression of relief turned to horror. He recoiled and almost backed into the distracted Father Corr. Inside the elevator, two thugs dressed in black had Tom Swayne on his knees. If George had been there, he might have recognized the men from another time. The taller of the two lifted the emergency phone from its cradle and bashed Tom on his head. Tom's shriek was cut off as the burly accomplice wrapped the cord around his neck and yanked.

The two men stopped momentarily and looked at Warren.

"For assistance in English," the first one said," press one." He pressed the die in Tom's eye socket and smashed his skull again with the receiver. The heavy-set man asked Warren a question.

"Is this an emergency? I'm afraid this line's tied up." He guffawed as he yanked the cord harder. There was a strangling noise. "Get it?"

"Going *down*?" his partner asked.

The elevator started down with the doors open. Red, flickering light played up the shaft. Warren backed away and turned in time to elude Father Corr's grasp, then stumbled down the hall to the door of room 1933. He pounded on it as the priest lurched behind him, arm swinging grotesquely. Blood continued to spurt everywhere.

"George! Oh God! Please!" Warren cried as he slid to the floor. His hands left trails of blood down the door.

"We keep telling you. He's not in just now," Father Corr said.

Sensing something, Warren turned and found he was seated next to Candy Land, playing a game of jacks with Tom Swayne. The phone cord was knotted tightly around the young man's throat and the receiver dangled over his chest. He bounced the small ball and missed the jacks clumsily. The ball bounced away as Candy giggled. Tom pointed to the dice jammed in his eye sockets.

"You try it with your eyes gouged out!" His voice sounded hoarse from strangulation.

Tom and Candy looked over at the whimpering minister.

"I thought I heard you, Reverend Warren," Tom said. "How's the missus? Oops, sorry!"

Candy slapped Tom's knee in reproach.

"Get in line, Father. We were here first," Candy said. "Hell, this isn't fair. You're supposed to comfort *me*."

She shrugged and hugged Warren as Father Corr careened to a halt by the door. She looked up at the demonic priest.

"This is so not great," she said to Father Corr. "He's just so weak . . ."

"Hey Father Corr!" Tom exclaimed with a smile. "Nice to see you." He pointed to his eye sockets. "Get it?"

Candy giggled again. She put her hands under Warren's chin, lifted his eyes to hers and blew him a kiss.

Warren moaned and shook his head.

"Please . . ." he said.

Father Corr's expression was one of disgust.

"Have some backbone, boyo," he said as he stood in front of them. His partially severed arm dangled and swung slowly, oozing blood onto the carpet.

Candy formed a curious look. She reached out and grasped the hanging arm and twisted it back and forth.

"Do you *mind*?" the priest asked.

"Just what this town needs!" Tom cried. "Another one-armed bandit. Pull it – maybe you'll win!"

Candy yanked. Blood spurted, showering her hair. Tom applauded.

"A winner!" he said with gusto.

She blinked and swung the arm sideways. She pulled again, with a giggle, spraying Tom this time.

"Takes a licking but keeps on ticking! Hey! You can park in the handicapped space now! Luck-y!" Tom exclaimed.

Candy pursed her lips thoughtfully. "Hard to drive a six speed, though."

Warren jerked back and whimpered again as the dangling arm brushed his knee, leaving a red smear. The fingers clutched clumsily at him. The malevolent ring, Warren saw, was slick with blood.

"Do stop whimpering, you sniveling sod," Father Corr said. "Waited so long to touch you again, boyo. Disrespect is a sin. Remember that."

Tom held up the phone receiver to the minister. "Hey, Reverend! Need to make a call?" He pointed to his eye sockets. "Just press one one for an outside line!"

Candy clasped her hands together in glee. "Oooh. It's going to be so good. You'll see. Just like my *daddy*. He was a preacher, too, you know? Back in Texas."

"Hey, what happens in Texas stays in Texas," Tom said.

"Dear God in Heaven," Warren said.

"Is that where you think He is?" asked Father Corr with a chuckle.

"Gimme that old time religion," Candy sang. Her voice was surprisingly sweet and pure.

Tom sighed. "This town can really get to you."

78

George sat helplessly in the chair while Judy tried to console Betsy Warren. The women were seated on the bed in the Reynolds' hotel room. Betsy's hysterical hurricane had made landfall and disorganized into a quiet, continual sobbing. Judy had just about run through all the tissues in the bathroom and had her arm around her friend. The minister's wife had wound down enough to describe the scene she's found in their hotel room.

"I wanted to surprise him . . . I caught the last flight out today instead of tomorrow. The airline didn't charge me. And then . . . and then . . ."

She fell apart all over again. George shook his head slowly. The degeneration since leaving West Palm Beach seemed complete; the tragic hand that had brushed Judy with its icy fingers was squeezing the life out of the entire delegation. There seemed to be little left for George but to finish what he had started and do what he knew how to do tomorrow. He had no idea what had happened to Jim Warren but he wasn't going to judge the man until he heard his story personally. Of course, it looked pretty bad. Actually, it looked really bad. Maybe the guy—

The message light began to blink. That was odd, George thought, the phone hadn't rung. He picked up and dialed seven. He heard an unfamiliar feminine voice.

"Mister Reynolds, please go to Tom Swayne's room, number nineteen forty two. There's someone waiting for you there." The connection was broken.

He hung up with a frown. He saw Judy's quizzical look.
Was it a trap? Maybe, but Tom Swayne's safety might be at stake.
He had to go.

"A message to go to Tom Swayne's room. Judy, listen.
Stay here. Keep her here. Don't go anywhere."

Judy nodded and watched him leave. George walked down
the corridor and turned the corner towards room 1942. The door was
ajar. He pushed it open and stood in the doorway. John Roselli sat
in the chair, flanked by the two thugs in black. George recognized
the pair from the twenty third floor balcony, even after so many
years. Somehow he wasn't surprised.

"Looking for Mister Swayne? Too late. I don't think he'll
mind us using his room, do you?" Roselli said. He had an amused
look.

George entered warily.   There were bloodstains on the
carpet, the bed.

"You son of a bitch."

"Watch your mouth, dickweed," said the bigger thug.

"You don't even know him."

Roselli shrugged. "Didn't. Past tense. Anyway, you did,
didn't you?"

"He's— dead?"

"So what?"

"Bastard!" George started towards the casino owner but the
first thug stepped forward and slammed him in the stomach with a
savage blow.   George doubled over with a whoosh and reeled
backward. He bounced off the bed to the floor.

"These kickball guys. Not too bright," the assailant said.

"Maybe he needs some air," his partner said, jerking his
head toward the window.

"Déjà vu all over again," Roselli chuckled. "You really
don't learn, do you?"

The first man looked down at George. "Better watch your
language, asshole. You were warned. Show some respect."

"We'll have to charge Mister Swayne an extra night," Roselli said. "Someone used the bathroom, and there's all this mess." He gestured around.

"You own this place, too?" George managed to say. His breath hadn't completely returned. Roselli just shrugged. George got to his feet.

"All right, Roselli. It's me you want. Let the others go."

"What an ego. You sure about that?"

George realized he wasn't sure about that. "Let the others go," he repeated.

"I don't think so. Every chess game has a few pawns, doesn't it?"

"Why'd you kill him?" There was an unpleasant odor in the room, like meat left out overnight.

"Because he's *there*?"

"That's all?"

"Aah, well. He had snake eyes. That's a house winner, isn't it?"

"My God!" George exclaimed.

"Not even close," Roselli said.

"What do you really want?"

"I think maybe you don't know your chess pieces. What if I let you go, goalkeeper, you and Judy, say? First flight out in the morning. First class upgrade and I'll pay the change fee. Leave the others to me."

"Not a chance."

"Suppose I keep her here. I wouldn't tell her it was your decision. What then?" He waggled his hand in a comme ci comme ça gesture. "For better or worse?"

"Everyone or no one."

Roselli laughed. "Where do you get these B movie lines?"

"B movies," the second thug said.

"Everyone or no one."

"How touching. I just might take you up on that. Tomorrow at noon."

79

As George headed back towards his room, he had a terrifying thought. Perhaps Roselli had lured him out to get to Judy and Betsy Warren. The meeting seemed to have made little sense, unless it was just Roselli's way of having fun. He would have known George wouldn't go for his offer, so why extend it? Was he missing something? He rounded the corner and was surprised to see Jim Warren slumped on the floor outside his door. The minister appeared to be unconscious.

"Jim!" he cried, and rushed to his side.

Five minutes later, George, Reverend Warren, Joe and Dexter were all inside George's room. There was a note on the table from Judy. She had taken Betsy to her husband's room and would be there for awhile. George and Dexter sat on the bed, flanking Warren, who was pale and shaking. Joe slumped in the chair, staring off, looking terrified. Dexter patted his preacher on the back awkwardly. Warren lowered his head and held it in his hands.

We're not exactly game ready, George thought.

"Look, Reverend Warren, you're still our pastor. I mean, what the hell, it is Las Vegas," Dexter said.

Warren groaned. George got up and went to the window. He looked out as he spoke. It all looked so serene, except for the flashing cop car lights a couple of blocks down Las Vegas Boulevard.

"Don't worry. We're getting out of here soon. Real soon," George said.

"What are we gonna do?" Dexter asked.

"The game's tomorrow. Until then, we stay cool. No one panics."

"What game?" Dexter asked.

"Maybe the Reverend will fill you in when he's up to it."

"Maybe we should get out of here now," Dexter said.

George shook his head. "No one tries to leave town. I don't think we'd make it."

"What's going on? I don't understand what's going on," Dexter said. "Why couldn't we leave early? I hate this damn place."

"I'll explain in the morning if the Reverend doesn't, okay? It's just too late tonight. I'm exhausted."

The goalkeeper looked over at Joe. He appeared catatonic.

"You hear me, Joe? We stay put one more day."

Joe nodded slowly and continued to stare off. Warren lay down on the bed. He closed his eyes and was instantly asleep. George picked up the phone and dialed the minister's room. Judy picked up.

"We're all here," George said. "I don't know what to do with everybody."

"Well, put Reverend Warren somewhere, anyway. I'll stay here with Betsy, at least until she falls asleep. That seems to make the most sense. Maybe the Reverend can sleep on the chair in Joe and Dexter's room."

George agreed, and hung up. After nudging Warren, he got Dexter to lead him and Joe back to their room. There wasn't much else to do except climb in bed and get as much shuteye as he could, knowing he would need to be at his best tomorrow. Maybe Judy wouldn't wake him when she returned. He sighed. It seemed as thought they'd been in Las Vegas for years.

He was fast asleep in minutes, his body twitching, a tense troubled unconsciousness not at all like the lions sleeping on the beaches of his youth.

80

Las Vegas, Nevada – Day Three

It had been another beautiful desert dawn. Daybreak painted the mountains shades of brown and red as their purple shadows slid to the valley floor and evaporated. High, wispy mare's tails went from gold to white as the sun rose in the crystalline sky. There was no wind in the valley and it was too early for dust devils. All was still.

As though everything was waiting.

Sunlight streamed in the window of room 1933. Judy sat huddled in the chair, warming her hands with a cup of coffee as she watched George get dressed.

"You okay?" he asked.

"I guess."

"You should have gone back with Beth," he said, taking a blue golf shirt off its hanger. The minister's wife – at least for the time being – had left on a six a.m. flight back to West Palm. Judy had loaded the woman, still distraught but only sobbing occasionally, into a taxi. It was all they could do.

"Betsy. No. I couldn't leave you here by yourself. That shirt doesn't go."

George put the shirt back and held up a white one; she nodded.

"How is she?"

"I don't know. Well, she's devastated, but holding together. I'll have to see about her when we get home."

"I don't think you should go with me. At least stay in the hotel."

She sipped from her cup. "The hotel. It wasn't safe enough for Tom Swayne, was it?"

George looked at Judy, then down the Halliburton sitting on the bed. "It's all the ready cash we have, you know. If I lose . . ."

He walked over and put a hand on her shoulder. She hugged him. There was a knock on the door; George disengaged and let Dexter and Reverend Warren in. The minister sat on the bed, staring.

"Did you find Joe?" George asked.

Dexter shook his head. "His bags and stuff are gone." He turned to Judy. "Reverend Warren told me what happened with the money and all. Maybe before yesterday I would have been pretty shocked, Judy. But not now. Not after what's happened out here."

"Thank you, Dexter," Judy said with a warm smile.

George looked at his watch. "Well, we can't wait," he said. "Maybe look around the hotel. Try the restaurant and the casino and then meet us at the Oasis."

"Yeah, sure, but there's no way he's in the casino, unless he hocked his watch. It's just a cheap Timex anyway."

Dexter eyed his minister, who appeared dazed. "Reverend?" Nothing.

"He all right, you think?" Dexter asked.

"I guess so," George replied as he tucked in his shirt. He peered at Warren, who definitely did not look all right. "Hell, I don't know. I'll talk to him."

Dexter nodded and went out the door. George leaned over, close to Warren.

"You okay?"

"No." It really wasn't funny, but George almost laughed.

"Listen, Jim. Judy had a long talk with Betsy. She's good. If anyone can fix things up, Judy can."

"My life's over."

"No it's not. A pretty big bump in the road, though."

Warren looked up at George. "Bump? It's a pothole to Hell."

George thought so too, but tried to buoy the disconsolate clergyman. "Look, Jim. Stuff happens. You're just a human being. Look at all those priests and all. They just transferred them around."

It didn't seem to be what Warren wanted to hear. He groaned.

"Oh, God."

"You got that right," Judy said.

The minister looked at the case next to him. "That the money?"

"Yeah. Three hundred thousand."

"Blood money," Warren said, almost absently.

"Question is, whose blood?" George asked. Maybe Warren meant Jesus.

"Mine," said James Warren.

81

West Palm Beach, Florida

The crack had reappeared, larger than before. It had rained steadily for twenty four hours in the Palm Beaches, and the hasty paint job Mr. Fekete had directed the foreman to put over the patch on the sanctuary's rear wall hadn't worked. Maybe the ground below had shifted in all the rain. They had done the requisite soil sampling prior to obtaining the building permit, but there wasn't much margin in this church job and so the samples may not have been taken in all the representative locations. In fact, the foreman knew they had been taken in only two places, and even that was so they didn't all look the same.

The flaw was probably cosmetic, in any event, because the Florida building code required hurricane clips in the roof and they had already undergone that inspection. Although a couple of cases of Hard Hat beer had persuaded the inspector, a real asshole named Dykes, to look at a few sample trusses rather than clamber over the entire area.

The foreman looked at the reborn crack. It wasn't his fault. He never said they should paint it over, Mr. Fekete did. He debated whether or not to inform the boss. Of course, he had been responsible for the soil samples so maybe it wasn't a good idea. What good would telling Fekete do, in any event? What was he anyway, with that weird name and strange accent? Armenian, maybe?

They certainly weren't going to undo the roof and start all over, so there really wasn't any point. He'd get Carlos and his helper on a scaffold tomorrow and plaster the crack over again. If Carlos came in tomorrow, that is. All those Mexicans were alike, the foreman thought, lazy wetbacks who showed up when they wanted to and half-drunk at that. He recalled that good for nothing hod carrier who had wandered off a couple of days ago, after the rain had started, and hadn't come back. He'd left his rattletrap clunker at the job, for Christ's sake. Well, he wasn't going to have it hauled away – not for forty bucks he'd have to shell out to the tow company. Maybe more, come to think of it.

And to make matters worse, there was that nasty business with a gator and the two boys the other day. The kid was lucky to be alive. The cops and the Fish and Wildlife people had come but hadn't spotted the damn thing. The water was almost up to the edge of the embankment with all the rain. He hoped it was gone. That's all they needed, a nine or ten foot alligator hanging around the job site. What did it find to eat, nails? He hoped the workers hadn't caused the accident, that they hadn't been stupid enough to throw it a taco or pepper or some damn thing. Then it would never leave.

Anyway, something had to be done about the crack. Hell, if Carlos didn't show, he'd do the patch job himself with one of the Haitians. It wouldn't take but an hour or so and it wouldn't do to have someone see the problem and inquire about it. Satisfied with his plan, he packed up his lunchbox and left the jobsite.

It continued to rain, fed by a disorganized system moving up through the Straits of Florida. The soft soil under the rear wall of the new Palm Beach Presbyterian sanctuary continued its slow, microscopic slide to the southwest, toward the left side of the sanctuary. It slid that way because the soft, sandy soil had turned to sludge and was dripping down into the underground chamber that had been the crypt for several of the early members of the church following the hurricane of 1901, unknown and undiscovered and filled with the bones of those who had perished in the storm.

82

Las Vegas, Nevada

The taxi pulled up in front of Concourse D at McCarran International. Joe Dykes tumbled out, disheveled and sweaty. He threw bills at the cabdriver, not caring that he had left an eighty five cent tip, and rushed inside to the Delta ticket counter. He clutched his suitcase in one hand and his carry-on in the other. He almost became unglued as he spied the short line, but managed to wait without coming apart. After about two minutes that seemed like two hours, an attractive attendant of perhaps thirty five finished with a passenger and looked up.

"Sir?," she intoned, and beckoned. Joe careened to the counter.

She smiled a practiced smile at him as he thrust his ticket at her.

"Gotta get outa here now. Gotta use this on the next flight out."

The attendant, whose name tag read JILL, looked at Joe's ticket.

"I think we can do that. Let me check availability for you." She peered at her screen and made keystrokes. "We do have space on the last flight leaving in, let's see, an hour and ten minutes. Connection is through Dallas, arriving in West Palm Beach at 7:33 p.m. Will that be all right?"

"God, yes," Joe said. Relief washed over him; he was getting the hell out of Dodge.

"This should be no problem, sir. There is a seventy five dollar change fee, you know."

"Sev—!" He thought it was twenty five bucks, maybe free if he could have sweet talked her. What a rip-off. Just a little while ago he was betting hundred dollar checks with abandon, and tipping— well, maybe not tipping. But that was then and this was now.

"Yeah, shit. Okay. Just do the goddamn thing."

She frowned at his language. "May I have your credit card?"

He handed her his MasterCard and she processed the transaction. Or tried to. Joe saw her read the screen with disapproval.

"Sir, this charge card won't accept the transaction. Do you have another?" She was no longer smiling at him.

Oh, God, Joe thought. His stomach tightened up. All that crap they'd bought. He must have maxed the thing to the limit. And he didn't have any other credit cards. He pulled out his wallet.

"Lemme just pay cash," he said, and prayed he had enough. Meanwhile, the line behind him was growing longer. People were beginning to peer at him. He counted his bills; he had twenty eight dollars.

"Uh, can you try it for fifty and I'll give you the rest in cash?"

The look she gave him was not sympathetic. "I'll try, sir." She emphasized the "sir" with, Joe was sure, sarcasm. What if it didn't work? Would she take his Timex?

Thank God for small favors, he thought a minute later, as the fifty dollar charge went through. He'd been at the counter all morning, it seemed. He was so agitated he was beyond embarrassment.

A minute later, Joe rushed from the counter with his carry-on and new ticket safely in his pocket. As he headed for the gate area, he suddenly felt a tremendous pressure that almost doubled him over. He felt as though all of Lake Mead was inside his bladder. If he didn't relieve himself immediately, he would—

He looked around wildly. Thank God! The men's room was within ten feet. Joe veered toward the opening just as an attendant in overalls came out of a service door and put a yellow plastic horse in front that read REST ROOM CLOSED.

"What?!" Joe's eyes bugged out. He tried to rush past, but the attendant, a tall black man, blocked his way.

"I gotta go!" Joe cried out.

"It's closed, hey. Cleaning."

"Where can I go!?"

Joe didn't notice the ugly ring with the brown oval stone on the hand that waved vaguely down the concourse.

Joe trotted forward until he came to the security screening line. No men's room. His eyes were watering. He choked back a sob and ran back the other way, past the same men's room that—

The sign was gone. He was beyond wondering, beyond caring. As he rushed inside, the black man came out of the service door and put the yellow plastic horse back in front of the opening.

Joe lurched up to the urinal and dropped his carry-on. He was in such a hurry he failed to notice a flickering red light emanating from underneath one of the stalls. He couldn't find the zipper tab for several seconds; it was stuck up under the fabric. Finally, he grasped it and yanked the zipper down.

"Aaaaah," he said, as he relieved himself for what seemed minutes. What the hell had he drunk this morning?

Behind him, the stall door creaked open very slowly.

Father Corr, dressed in his black cassock, emerged from the glow. He zipped up his fly. The sound it made in the men's room was unnaturally loud and rasping and seemed to echo several times. Joe turned to see two thugs, dressed in black, approach.

"Oh, no. Oh, God," he said.

"He's not in just now," said Father Corr. The priest gestured around the men's room. "Don't you like our little chapel?"

Joe backed up until he bumped the urinal. "Please," he said.

Without warning, the heavier of the two men grabbed Joe around the neck in a half-nelson. He forced his head down and into the urinal.

"The baptismal font," Father Corr intoned as the sensor activated the flushing mechanism.

The man lifted Joe's sopping head out of the water and ran across the room towards the sink. He smashed the head into the soap dispenser at full speed. The heavy plastic shattered and the skin on Joe's head split open. He was instantly covered with green slime mixed with blood mixed with black hair dye.

Joe cried out. His head was still held fast. He was dimly aware of the chanting of many voices in the background. Father Corr approached. With his thumb, he traced an upside down cross in the slime on Joe's forehead.

"In nomine Patris, et Filii, et Spiritus Sancti . . ."

Father Corr caressed Joe's balding head, smearing slime and blood and dye.

"Oh, God. Please . . ." Joe mumbled.

"We keep telling you people," Father Corr said. "He's not in just now. Anyway, it's time for the next sacrament."

The second thug came forward and jammed his fingers into Joe's nostrils. He yanked upward, forcing the mouth open. Father Corr produced a hundred dollar check and inserted it.

"The Communion wafer. Receive thy Host."

The second man slammed Joe's jaw shut. There was a loud, cracking noise.

Joe Dykes passed out.

83

George, Judy, and James Warren stepped out of the taxi in front of the Oasis Hotel and Casino. George looked at his watch; it was six minutes to twelve. High noon in the west. He had a weird vision of Marshal Will Kane awaiting his confrontation with Frank Miller, except that George had his Halliburton case full of money instead of a .45 Peacemaker. He squared his shoulders resolutely, drew a breath and led the trio through the glass doors. As he did so, the Oasis marquee above sparked and shorted out. Letters went dark momentarily, all the letters except the first A and last O.

Once inside, Judy shuddered. It was freezing. The air conditioning seemed to be running amok. George led her and Warren into the pit and towards table forty two.

Roselli stood beside the dealer, a heavyset man in his thirties whose badge read JABEZ and underneath, Nevada. Two decks were ribbon spread across the table and the house tray contained sixty gleaming silver checks as well as a number of smaller bronze pieces, to be used for blackjack payoffs. George walked up.

Roselli looked at his Audemars Piguet Royal Oak Tourbillon. "Mister Reynolds. Right on time."

George recognized one of the world's most expensive watches. It sold for more than he'd brought in the Halliburton. The goalkeeper had been fascinated with elegant watches and their complications since he could remember. His main extravagance after signing with Crystal Palace had been the Breitling Bentley 6.75, still keeping perfect time after twenty years.

"Nice watch." .

Roselli shrugged. "For daytime wear."

Daytime wear? George thought. He wondered the casino owner wore after dark, a Vacheron Constantin?

"Vacheron Constantin Tour de I'lle," Roselli said with a smile.

George put the silver case on the table, snapped it open and turned it around. Roselli looked inside, then ran his hand over the cash. He nodded to Jabez, who removed the stacks and began counting. As they watched, the casino owner reached into his pocket.

"Oh, I almost forgot, Mrs. Reynolds. I think I found what you're looking for." He tossed something small to her; she caught it reflexively.

It was a prescription bottle. The label was typed:

George Reynolds
Hydrocodone
1 2 tablets every four hours for pain

She gasped and dropped the container. As she did so, the dealer finished housekeeping and nodded to Roselli. The casino owner unlocked the drop box and Jabez stacked the cash inside. Once the box was relocked, the dealer counted out thirty silver checks, stacked them in fives and passed them across to George, who had taken the middle seat with Judy and Warren standing behind. George picked up one of the silver pieces and inspected it.

"I can't imagine where you got these," he said.

"Had them for awhile. They were around somewhere," Roselli replied. Warren peered closely at the ducats.

He spoke softly, to himself. "Oh, my God. There they are."

Judy leaned in. "What did you say?"

Warren was dazed. "Matthew twenty six, fourteen fifteen."

George placed a check in the betting square and the game began. He lost the first hand, busting when he drew to a three four against the dealer eight. He pulled a six, a three and another six. He heard an intake of breath from Warren, behind, and almost shot him an annoying glance. Jabez turned over his down card, a deuce. Although George now had a favorable count, he was constrained to a single check bet under the rules he had proposed. The cards ran true the next hand, and George won with a natural twenty.

Jabez shuffled quickly. With only two hands per shuffle, the dealer had to be adept for the game to proceed at a fair pace. Roselli looked on with a steely glare as George's pile grew slowly. Time and the cards flowed as down a river, meandering around the bends in fortune, creating whorls and eddies about the piles of checks, carrying providence in its current. After the first half hour, the goalkeeper had thirty four of the silver checks piled in front of him. George was winning, albeit slowly, and the odds were running true. No potentially ruinous streak had occurred for either side.

Warren suddenly realized he had to go to the bathroom, perhaps thirty yards away on the left side of the casino. He barely noticed the absence of people in the early afternoon. When he came out and began to walk back towards the game, something struck him as odd. The lights seemed to flicker, and dim, and his view of the action some distance way was indistinct. He stopped against a table rail and peered closely, his eyes following along the rug whose serpentine pattern seemed now to writhe slowly, shifting and creeping towards table forty two. His vision of the area was smudged, as through a thumbprint on a pair of glasses, and there was a palpable darkness, an oily murk, and Roselli was at its center with a kind of dark light, and above him fluttered something unimaginable, and Roselli himself seemed to have – what? – perhaps some shaded substance behind him, and Reverend Warren gasped and shut his eyes and shook his head. He reopened them and saw nothing of his vision a moment before. Distressed, he made his way back to the game and his friends, and if he was pale and sweating, no one noticed.

The waitress brought Roselli a drink. He lifted it from the tray, drained the glass quickly and smiled at the player.

"Buy you a drink, goalkeeper?"

"No thanks," George replied. "Got to keep a clear head."

"Your friend Dexter wouldn't agree. Couple of drinks never hurt anybody, isn't that so? You're doing very well. Perhaps your luck will hold out," Roselli said.

"Is that what it is?" George asked.

Warren glanced at the table, and noticed George's pile of silver checks had grown still larger. Perhaps, after all their difficulties in this vale of tears, they were going to be able to save the sanctuary project after all. George was winning! Moses, leading the chosen out of this unholy desert! His spirits brightened and a smile spread across his face until—

Until John Roselli slowly turned and faced the preacher head on. He turned his head and before his eyes locked on Reverend James Warren's a cold dread washed over the cleric, a deliberate terror which froze him to his spot, and he suddenly knew what he had seen across the casino floor. In that moment of absolute realization he knew that what Joe and Dexter had viewed on the hotel television and what he had experienced in the corridors of the Sacramento Hotel and Casino had been real, and true, and what had been in front of him in that elevator was unspeakable and terrifying, a horror risen from some nether kingdom and that there had been no hallucination, no undigested bit of beef, no mistake. Then the eyes of John Roselli did lock upon him and in that instant he saw the purest Evil, Damnation incarnate: not imagined, not represented, but Damnation absolute and real without imagery, without need for reason or excuse, and he knew then what he had not known, what he had perhaps been taught by those veiled constellations but had forgotten or not believed or pushed away, and that was that Evil *was*, and existed, independent of his or anyone's hopes and prayers and behavior and intent, and that whatever protected Man from this great Force had best be worshipped, for Evil was unimaginable terror and infinite destruction, and Heaven was sanctuary from the horror and logic was as grain before the wind. In those eyes he saw fire trapped in ice, flame beyond flame as the ovens sprang up at Belsen and Buchenwald and Treblinka, and beyond the flames, which were the Conflagration, the infinite Darkness, the darkness of a mountainside in India with no moon and clouds of the deadly yellow gas rolling down toward the villages with no sound whatever, and even beyond, the white stillness of the winter at Stalingrad, littered with the frozen bodies and still further, the scorched desert of Iraq and mountains of Afghanistan and the green clouds over the Kurdish settlements and the Gaza wall and the rain of cluster bombs and the circle of Despondency formed by the prisoners, held together by wire through their palms, and deeper and deeper into Darfur and Zimbabwe and Rwanda and Kenya, machetes flashing, further, deeper, crowded together, horror upon horror and he could not look yet he could not look away. And he saw, in his mind's eye, Father Patrick Corr with his eyes completely white, covered with the milk of the goat, as something red darted quickly out of his mouth, still smiling, and slipped back in.

And faintly, in a dank, eddying current of humid air, the aroma of Avon Legacy aftershave: gone in an instant, replaced by freezing cold.

The breath froze in James Warren's breast and he felt the icy talons grip his soul and yank, and he knew that what he had done in Nevada was going to kill him forever and ever because this thing was coming for the soul he had lost, and that only through the Grace of God had he not ridden that elevator back to the depths from which it had risen, through His Infinite Mercy had he not sank into the undergloom with its desolate cargo, and suddenly James Warren found a profound faith, an unshakable belief born of absolute terror, and he saw that God was revealed after all, and that Hell really was eternal fire, and monstrous pain, and that this card game was not a card game at all, George Reynolds the Goalkeeper and the Demon, and he felt the talons seek him again, and he fervently answered his

own questions with the one true prayer of his life as dread froze him
to his spot in front of table forty two:

Yes yes dear God please please I want to go to Heaven.

84

Detective Davey Cahill bounced down the steps from Clark County District Court and eyed the hot dog vendor's pushcart on Lewis Avenue. He looked at his watch, not that it made any difference. He was always starving after a court appearance. Probably a nervous reaction, he figured. As usual, his testimony in the felony burglary case, scheduled for first thing that morning, hadn't occurred until after eleven a.m. and so he'd wasted most of the morning hanging around the courthouse. Cahill ordered a hot dog with mustard, chili sauce, onions and sauerkraut and bent over to protect his white shirt and tie as he shoved most of the gooey mess in, washing it down with a diet soda.

As he walked to the parking garage, he mulled over the Bernie Goldman/John Roselli investigation and the bizarre history of 316 Primrose Lane he'd uncovered. Things got stranger and stranger, but was it progress? Two of the four deaths of the Oasis patrons had occurred on or around I-15. Was there any significance to that?

Before returning to the office, he decided to detour past the sites – first, where Baldanian had taken a swan dive off the overpass at Flamingo Road, and then down the highway to the spot where Henry Wiggins' car jack caved in on him, pinning his chest underneath the rear wheel of his small SUV. The Baldanian site had been treated as a crime scene, the latter an accident. The unanswered question in the Wiggins incident was why no one had seen the guy stuck under his tire for the minute or so it had taken him to die trying to breathe with maybe a couple of thousand pounds crushing his chest. It had been night, true, and I-15 lightly traveled at that hour, but it was a bothersome fact.

He retrieved his car, took Main Street over to Charleston and hopped on I-15. There were few vehicles on the highway and Cahill made good time. Now the Flamingo Road exit was just ahead.

The homicide detective stopped his car by the on-ramp, got out and walked up to the spot where Baldanian had gone over into the windshield of the Whittlesea taxi. He looked around but gained little insight. After a few minutes, he got back inside his sedan and drove onto I-15 South, traveling 3.6 miles and looking for the small fatality marker at the side of the road. It should be—

An old black Ford two door with Nevada plates was stopped on the shoulder, right by the marker. The car looked like maybe a 1966 LTD, a real relic. The hood was up and an elderly man peered inside the engine compartment. Cahill pulled up behind and got out. The old man was a priest, he saw.

"Hi, Father," he said with a smile. The detective knew many of the local priests, but this was an unfamiliar face. Most of the Cahills attended Prince of Peace, over on Charleston. There was something, though, the observant cop couldn't quite place.

"Car trouble?"

"Seems so," the priest said. "I don't know much about automobiles."

Cahill stuck out his hand. "I'm Davey Cahill, Father—?"

"Corr. Father Patrick Corr. My pleasure."

85

Dexter Wilcox rushed down the steps and across the Oasis casino floor to table forty two. He stood there catching his breath for a moment, then leaned in and spoke with a low voice as Judy and Warren huddled around.

"Joe tried to leave town. The cops said he was attacked in the airport bathroom. A couple of big guys in black suits."

The group exchange worried looks.

"Is he okay?" Warren asked.

"He's in the hospital, the trauma center place. They said he'd be okay, physically."

"What's that mean?" George asked.

"I dunno. He's not responding. Like . . . shellshock or something."

"At least he's not— thank God!" Warren exclaimed.

George looked at his ragtag group. He spoke with finality. "This time— we've got to end this. Roselli's not letting us out of this town alive."

"What can we do?" Judy whispered, looking over at the casino owner, who was leaning again the podium a few feet away.

"Don't mind me," Roselli called out. "I've got all the time in the world, don't I? All the time in the world." He inspected his nails and began to whistle.

George looked at his watch, then up at Roselli. "Get rid of the dealer."

The casino owner straightened up. "Beg your pardon?"

"This is between the two of us," George said.

Roselli chuckled. "Oh, no, there's more than the two of us. You could say it's legion. Plus all of you— all the leaders of Palm Beach Presbyterian."

Roselli formed a benign smile and gestured with his head. Jabez clapped his hands, showed his palms and backed away. Roselli moved behind the table.

"Cocktails for Mister Wilcox, there."

George noticed the casino was no longer freezing. The waitress handed Dexter a seven and seven. He gulped it down and she handed him another from her tray.

George pushed all his silver forward, into the betting position.

"Deal the cards," he said.

"What's this?" Roselli asked. "Maximum bet is—"

"Screw the maximum bet. Let's end this."

Roselli appeared shocked for a moment, then smiled again.

"What did you have in mind?"

"I'm playing for all of us."

"Hmmm. Well, it's a little too late for Tom Swayne, isn't it?"

"You—"

George shot up in his chair. Warren jumped forward and placed his hand on his shoulder, pushing him downward.

"No, George! That's what he wants, don't you see?" Judy said.

"Did you drop something, Mrs. Reynolds?" Roselli asked.

"I told you before, leave her out of this!" George said.

Roselli looked George square in the eye. *"You brought her here though, didn't you?"*

All was still. The words seemed to travel around the casino floor, around the pillars, over the tables, under the observation domes.

"Or is it the other way around, I'm thinking?" Roselli mused.

No one spoke. George noticed it had gotten cold again. The air seemed to swirl, slowly, as if it had a presence. It wasn't just the atmosphere, he realized. Roselli's last statements were chilling, ominous. He began to see a larger design, and it scared the hell out of him.

Roselli broke the silence. "So. I assume you want to get out of here alive, as well as with the money. Am I correct?"

He looked around for confirmation. Everyone was still, everyone looked fearful except George, who was expressionless.

"Well, what's in it for me?" Roselli asked. George eyed him suspiciously. He waited for the man to answer his own question.

The casino owner continued. "If I'm going to give you the chance to walk away scot-free, cancel your debts, then I should have the chance to win something. Don't you agree?"

Roselli wagged his finger between them, as though taking a poll. "No? Yes? Come on, now. You've accumulated quite a lot of debt, haven't you? Financial, spiritual, moral, you're all in my service. Fair's fair. What do you have that I could possibly want?"

Warren and Dexter looked at George with panic in their eyes. The goalkeeper was perfectly calm. He thought he could almost see his breath in the frigid air.

"Something the minister here might place a high value on," Roselli continued. "Well?"

He nodded toward the silver checks. No one said anything for a time.

"Oh, come on," cajoled Roselli. "You're not getting into this. How about some more religious instruction, Reverend? I know a good teacher. He has a winning way. He might help you with a certain lady."

Warren paled. "My God."

"Wrong guess. Candy from a baby. Or was that the other way around?"

"She's a friend of yours, eh, Roselli?" George asked.

Roselli smiled, lifted an eyebrow. "My compliments to the Reverend."

"Bastard," George said.

"Nobody unzipped his fly for him."

Roselli stared. There was a hunger in his eyes as he brought out a new deck of cards. He unwrapped the cellophane, extracted and inspected the deck, ribbon spreading them on the table, front and back. He picked them up and shuffled effortlessly. The leathery sound was unnaturally loud.

Speak of the devil and hear the rustle of his wings, Warren thought.

Rites of the Nevada church.

"It's game time, goalkeeper."

86

As Roselli shuffled the cards on the Oasis floor, Davey Cahill peered under the hood of the priest's LTD on the I-15 shoulder. "You local, Father?"

"Shrine of the Unholy Demon."

"I'm sorry?"

"Shrine of the Holy Redeemer."

"Oh, sure. Over on Reno."

"Yes."

"Boy, this is a classic, isn't it?"

"Nineteen sixty six."

"I think I see the trouble here. One of your distributor wires came loose." He reached in farther, trying to keep his white shirt clear of the old, greasy engine and connected the spark plug wire to the—

Ow! The damn spark plug shocked him, somehow. He yanked his finger back, reflexively, and smacked his elbow on the oil pump. Damn! And now his shirt was caught, the cuff had come undone, and it was stuck in between the distributor and – what was that in the black grease?

"You can blame your nephew for this, boyo," the old priest said.

"What?" What was the old man saying? He was stuck. He didn't want to rip the shirt; he'd just bought it.

"He's a good cop, isn't he? He smelled something fishy right off. That James kid crashed out of there ninety to nothing. Wonder what terrified the lad?"

"WHAT?" What the hell was this? What was this old priest saying? How did—

The hell with his shirt. He put his other hand on the radiator to yank free and screamed in pain. The radiator was red-hot. He jerked his hand off. Suddenly the radiator hose let go, spraying scalding steam right in Detective Davey Cahill's face. He screamed again, and managed to deflect the rubber with his free hand. His other hand was still stuck fast, somehow, between the distributor and—

"And you. Big deal investigator. Couldn't let well enough alone, hey? Poking around, stirring stuff up. Say, know what I did with the jack? The jack on that Wiggins kid's car?"

He felt the skin hang from his cheeks, scalded away. The pain was incredible. Somehow the spark plug was shocking him rhythmically.

"I collapsed it. Like this!" The old priest smacked the hood rod with the heel of his hand. The hood slammed down, trapping Cahill's left arm and breaking the fingers of his right hand. He screamed again as the Father Corr, surprisingly agile, jumped up and sat on the hood, breaking the detective's left arm.

"He couldn't breathe, you know? His face turned red, purple, black. So pretty. A rainbow of death, kind of. I jumped up and down on the hood and heard his ribs crack like a lobster."

All the agonies from the cop's various injuries melted together. He was losing consciousness, sliding into shock.

"Right over there! Not ten feet from this very spot!"

Cahill slumped, arms still caught under the hood. He couldn't fall to the ground.

"Nice job, Mister Goodwrench! You really know your automotive, hey? We met before, you know. Twice. The second time when you desecrated that senile old pastor's grave, turning the cross around like that. Couldn't let well enough alone, could you? I fixed his ass too, right on this road, not ten miles from here."

Through his agony, Detective Davey Cahill wondered briefly if Special Agent Haley Carradine had bought a non-refundable airline ticket.

Seconds up the road, the driver of an eighteen wheeler drifted off to the side as he gaped down at the stunning redhead passing him in a black Mercedes SL-Class convertible roadster. Her low-cut black dress had come up to her hips and she gave a smile and a wave going by.

Father Corr leaned in close, spoke the last words Detective Davey Cahill would ever hear.

"Well, you're going to get a bang out of this one, boyo. You just had to save his life, didn't you? *I was there! You should not have interfered!*"

And somehow, without knowing why, Davey Cahill's fading thoughts were not of his ex-wife, or his nephew Wade, or even Special Agent Haley Carradine, but rather flashed back to a young man at the intersection of West Harmon and Aldebaran some eighteen years prior, when as a rookie traffic officer he'd drawn his weapon for the first time and saved a brave goalkeeper who had tried to stop a mugging.

Father Corr stepped back as the semi veered off the road and plowed into both cars, destroying the vehicles and Detective Davey Cahill. The LTD, loaded with gasoline in its old-style non-crash resistant tank, burst into flames trapping the truck driver, who had thought the redhead was waving to him.

87

Roselli spoke as he mixed the cards.

"One deck, Mister Reynolds. Just as you like it. Five hands, played at once."

George beckoned for Roselli to proceed. The casino owner extended the deck and George inserted the red plastic cut marker. Roselli burned the top card and began to deal, laying a card down on the first spot face up.

"For Joe's life," he said. George realized the floor was deserted, somehow. He hadn't noticed people leaving.

The casino owner dealt another. "For Dexter's."

"For Tom." Roselli made as if to deal to the third spot, then pulled back in an exaggerated manner.

"Oh, I forgot—" He paused, holding the card momentarily in mid-air. He smirked as he looked at George, seated before him. There was no reaction. The goalkeeper would not take the bait again.

"Who's the missing link? The raison d'être, so to speak?" Roselli asked.

He cocked an inquiring eyebrow. "Oh, come on now, goalkeeper. Who misplaced the missing funds? *How did this all happen?*"

Dexter wore a puzzled expression.

"Anyway, it's only fair that Judy should participate. Hey, for better or worse."

George rocked back, stunned. Warren gasped and Dexter's eyes went wide.

Roselli parodied the song. "Judy Green Eyes. Will you come see me? Hey. *What have you got to lose?"*

George recovered his voice. "What? You bastard! You – you can't—"

Roselli's sudden intensity was terrifying. His eyes shone and something appeared to be moving behind the pupils. He seemed to grow taller; the casino darker and suddenly much warmer. There was an odd smell, as though a match had been lit. A sharp, stabbing pain knifed into George's leg.

"Can't I? *Can't I?* Do you not remember? *You should have listened!"*

His mood, his demeanor changed in an instant. He straightened up with a smile, gave a nonchalant shrug. "Besides, what did you expect, really? This is an equal opportunity casino. She's a prize, isn't she? And please, your language. This is a holy place, kind of."

He turned slightly. "Now the Reverend."

A blast of arctic air made Judy and Warren shiver; no one else seemed to notice. A fourth card went to the next spot.

"And, last but certainly not least, your life, goalkeeper."

George looked on grimly as Roselli dealt his card to the third base spot and followed with his own down card, completing the first round. When the deal was completed, George saw:

- Joe's up cards were 8,7
- Dexter's were 5,5
- Judy had Q, 8
- Warren had 6,6
- George had K, 3
- The house up card was a jack, the jack of spades.

George had an opening count of plus two, throwing him on the positive side of the strategy table.

"Oh, look," Roselli said. "I seem to have the black jack, don't I? Let's see . . . did I win already?"

Roselli slid his cards over the small table mirror. Feigning the blackjack, he hesitated, cocked an eyebrow and looked at the group with a sly smile. He made an exaggerated movement, as if to turn over the ace.

But then he simply shrugged and continued play. Warren and Dexter had been holding their breaths; now they exhaled with relief. They huddled around George as he stared at the cards. He signaled for a hit on Joe's hand. Roselli obliged by dealing a five. Joe had a total of twenty, and the count had moved to plus three. Since Roselli's down card had not been the ace, there was an additional slight advantage. The odds were the count was really plus four.

"Well, things are looking good for Joe, aren't they? Well, that's a change. Religion didn't seem to agree with him. They tell me his brain's working like a turnip right now."

Roselli made a gesture. The waitress handed Dexter a drink from her tray. The little man didn't even appear to notice as he drained the glass.

"Of course I could still wind up with a total of twenty one. That would be a real shame, wouldn't it?"

"No tricks, right, Roselli?" George asked.

"Maybe we'll push. A tie goes to the runner, don't they say?"

"Roselli! No tricks, right?"

George turned his attention to Dexter's pair of fives.

"Want to split them?" asked Roselli, who couldn't conceal a smile at his own joke.

"Just hit the hand."

Roselli shrugged. "Worth a try. Not much point in doubling down, is there, goalkeeper? We can't kill Dexter twice. Or can we?" He gestured to the waitress. "Let's get the man another drink. His glass is empty."

Dexter whimpered fearfully as he was handed another seven and seven. He gulped it down as Roselli dealt the next card.

A seven, for a seventeen total. George waved off. The count remained where it was and no one had busted. Roselli inquired about Judy's eighteen. George gave Roselli a pained look and waved off.

"Are you sure?" Roselli asked. "Some men I know would take a hit on their wife's eighteen in a game like this. She'd never know, I promise."

George ignored the remark and shifted his attention to Warren's pair of sixes. He beckoned for a hit. Roselli readied a card and paused for a moment.

"Sure you don't want to split them?"

"I'm sure," George replied. Under normal game conditions, with a single deck, the sixes wouldn't be split against a ten value card no matter what the count. Doing so would require doubling the bet, and both hands would be likely losers. In this game, though, the increased wager wasn't a factor, but the math still told George to keep the sixes together and take a card.

"Nervous, Reverend? Let's see what's under the hood, so to speak." Roselli made a gesture miming removing a cassock hood from over his head.

"Oh, I guess maybe I shouldn't have said that." Roselli jerked his thumb at George while he fixed Warren with a look.

"If you bust, it's his fault. Then you'll be staying here with me. And I know a deceased priest – defrocked priest – whatever – who's anxiously awaiting your company."

Roselli smiled as Warren steeled himself.

"Just deal the damn card!" the minister said.

Still smiling, Roselli cocked his head. "The damn card? Just so, Reverend. Just so."

Warren winced in anticipation of disaster, but Roselli turned over another six. At least he was still alive.

Roselli gazed at the hand. "Well, would you look at that? Six, six, six. Mean anything to you? Yes? No? I seem to recall something. Isn't that in that book of fairy tales we leave in every hotel room?"

Roselli paused and looked over the table. "Well, this is interesting. Your wife and the Reverend here, both with eighteen. I guess they come as a matched set, you think? A prize pair for me. Quite a rush playing with other people's lives, isn't it, goalkeeper? I know. But now the life's yours. Different story, eh?"

George was concentrating hard, not really listening to Roselli's chatter. With the last six showing up, the count had moved to a plus four with a slightly better than even chance it was really plus five. A high advantage for a single deck game. He looked at his thirteen total against Roselli's jack. Despite the high count, there was no logic, no decision table, no system that called for a player to stand with thirteen against a dealer jack.

Roselli formed a quizzical expression as George stared at the cards. What was there to wait for? Finally, George nodded slightly and waved off.

"Beg pardon? You don't want a card?"

"No. I stand. Hold. Stay."

For the first time George could ever remember, Roselli seemed agitated.

"What do you mean? That's nuts, that's the wrong play. That's completely the wrong play. You know that. You can't do that. It's completely wrong."

George took a breath, resolute. Roselli cocked his head and stared at the goalkeeper with narrowed eyes, appraising, thinking. George realized even the slot machines had become silent.

Roselli regained his composure; the bemused smile reappeared.

"Last chance to beat the other players," he said, mimicking a television game show.

"You heard me. I stand."

Roselli leaned in. He spoke quite slowly. *"The devil you say . . ."*

He turned up his down card. A two, showing a total of twelve.

"Shall we see, then? Shall we see what you turned down?"

Roselli slowly turned over the next card. The three of clubs flopped on the felt. Now his total was fifteen, and the count had risen to an impossible plus six, with a likely plus seven. He had to take another card. He looked around the table.

"What's behind door number three?" he asked. He hesitated, then turned over a queen.

And busted.

88

"Yes!" George exclaimed as his fist punched the air.

"You did it!" Warren shouted.

"George!" Judy hollered.

"Thank God!" Dexter yelled.

Warren and Dexter exhaled loudly with relief. Judy leaped forward and squeezed her husband, who almost fell off the stool. Warren and Dexter embraced the pair; tears streamed down the minister's cheeks. Roselli frowned as he stared at the cards, then gave George an odd smile. He nodded his head towards Dexter.

"He might be right."

"What? What do you mean?" George asked, grinning from ear to ear.

"About thanking God."

"What?" George asked.

"So that's what it feels like. I've never lost to luck before. A bad jury, once."

"If it was luck, everyone would do it," George said. "Go on, turn it over."

Roselli stood motionless.

"Turn it over. The nine."

"You know the rules," Roselli said.

The two stared at each other, old foes at the end of a great battle. The casino owner scribbled on a voucher and handed it to George.

"Take this to the cage," he said. "Leave the silver. They're my souvenirs. Congratulations, Mister Reynolds. Enjoy your trip home. We won't be meeting again, will we? Not for awhile."

George nodded and stood up. He took the voucher and started for the cage, Warren, Judy and Dexter a step behind.

"Not here, anyway," Roselli said to himself.

George had gotten maybe fifteen feet.

"Goalkeeper!"

They all stopped dead and turned around. No one moved as George walked back towards the casino owner.

"What is it, Roselli?"

Roselli looked George dead in the eye. He wore a sardonic expression.

"I think you'll find you made enough money here to save your little church project."

"How did I know you knew that?"

"Yes. The Oasis Hotel and Casino has paid for your folly. We have bought our stake in your church."

George eyed Roselli carefully.

"Not my church, Roselli. What does that mean?"

"And in you. The thing is, goalkeeper, you have to know what team you're really playing for. Whose goal you're really guarding."

George leaned across the blackjack table and lowered his voice. He nodded back towards his group and spoke with intensity.

"What about the missing money, Roselli? You know about that, don't you? You knew about all of it, didn't you?"

"Why did you really come back here, goalkeeper?"

"And who's we? Whose goal was I guarding?"

Roselli straightened and spoke with an air of finality.

"The Unholy Trinity. It is complete."

"Is it? Is it complete?"

A hint of a smile from Roselli. The two stared at each other for long seconds. George turned and walked towards his friends and the casino cage.

It was over.

Wasn't it?

89

A quiet afterglow surrounded the Palm Beach Presbyterian delegation as they rode the taxi back to the Sacramento. Every mile away from the Oasis was a mile closer to the world of sanity. No one spoke for a time; each celebrated and pondered the climactic events quietly in his or her own way. It was another beautiful desert day, the heat almost benign after the frozen chill of the Oasis. It was as though a gray veil had lifted. The air seemed cleaner, somehow, the mountains sharpened in the distance, colors more vibrant, the crowds on the Las Vegas Boulevard sidewalks more animated. It was good to be alive.

It was good to be alive, especially when the possibility – perhaps the likelihood – of not being alive had loomed a short time ago. Each knew the euphoric feeling would evaporate soon, and so they hugged it close. Tragedy had dogged them almost since the moment they got off the plane. One of their number, young and foolish Tom Swayne, was dead and another, Joe Dykes, incapacitated, broke and possibly catatonic in University Medical Center. Dexter Wilcox had fallen off the wagon, lost money and was going to have to explain to Marcy a package of expensive clothing that would show up at their door. James Warren's marriage was on the ropes, and Judy wondered how many of the horrors had been triggered by her actions. They all had seen things they did not understand and would not understand completely, but they knew the threat of death had been very real and had left the sharp metallic battlefield taste in their mouths.

But for now, for a little while, they were together, a band of warrior victors, rag-tag and alive and comrades-in-arms, having triumphed on a battlefield they still did not fully comprehend, and likely never would, but one they knew was as real as the sands of Iraq, the jungles of Vietnam, the forest of the Ardennes, the snowy endless plains to Stalingrad.

James Warren broke the silence.

"That last conversation – what was that about, George?"

"Nothing. He just wanted to know why I didn't draw to the thirteen."

Dexter leaned forward to look at George. "Why didn't you? How'd you know you'd have busted?"

"I didn't, at first. Then suddenly, it all fit. All those cards, how they played out. I had a hunch – he just couldn't leave it to chance."

"You mean skill," Judy said.

"Well, he just had to rig the hands. If I had made the right move, we'd all go down. He wanted me to lose by my own choice."

Warren turned in from the window. "It fits, I guess."

"Yep," George said. "When I stood, he got the poison queen. There's no doubt the next card in the deck was a nine. He'd have had twenty one, and we'd all have been toast."

"Maybe literally," Warren said.

"I was just lucky I guessed right."

"That wasn't luck. And it wasn't a guess. You outsmarted him," Judy said.

George looked out the window. "Did I? We'll see . . . "

Not for awhile.

The trio looked at George with puzzled expressions.

"I feel like I've been here five years. I think I've aged that much," Dexter said.

"Let's get Joe and go home," George said.

Not here, anyway.

Judy leaned forward and nodded. "Amen."

90

A week after the funeral of his friend Davey Cahill, FBI Special Agent Tim Moss sat in his office in the John Bailey Memorial Building and pondered the contents of Cahill's Oasis/John Roselli file. He'd asked Davey's nephew Wade to retrieve it from the detective's townhouse. Moss had met the young officer twice and had found him earnest and likeable. He wondered if he might bring the rookie cop into the picture and tell him what his uncle had been doing.

Moss had added two more ghastly deaths to the documentation: that of his friend, killed in yet another mishap on I-15, and the homicide of Tom Swayne, a young man who'd checked into the Oasis' sister hotel, the Sacramento, and who had been slain in an alleged bar argument downtown. Perhaps coincidentally, Swayne was from West Palm Beach, the city John Roselli had listed on his gaming license application. He had been traveling with a religious group, several of whom had gambled at the Oasis. One of them had been barred from blackjack play around the time of Swayne's death.

The body had been found behind a downtown strip club, horribly mutilated. The Las Vegas police were withholding details, except to say his wallet and watch were missing. The violation of the young man's corpse fit into the pattern Davey Cahill had unearthed. If for no other reason than loyalty to his dead friend, Moss had decided to continue the investigation into the Oasis and its owner. And there did appear to be additional reasons now. Davey Cahill hadn't believed in coincidence, and that was before the latest round of tragic deaths with possible ties to the Oasis.

Moss was monitoring the Swayne investigation. Las Vegas police had tentatively concluded Swayne had gone downtown alone and had been the victim of a mugging gone awry, probably triggered by a dispute in the club. Fare records for both Whittlesea Blue Cab and Union Cab showed trips from the Sacramento to downtown destinations near Ogden and Sixth, within walking distance of the homicide, during the time window indicated by the Clark County Coroner.

Moss interviewed one of the strippers, a stunning redhead named Charlotte Gehenna, in a back booth at the club. He tried to ignore her outfit, and what was partially inside it. Moss had to shout over the music.

"Like I told the police, I believe I did see him that night, Agent Moss," she said as she looked at the picture of Tom Swayne, lit by Moss' flashlight. "I remember because he's – he was – such a handsome guy."

"What do you recall?" asked Moss.

"Kind of like you," she said, with a dazzling smile.

Moss remained professional, although with some difficulty. He pressed on. "What do you recall?"

"There was an argument with another patron. It got pretty loud. The fellow in the picture seemed nice enough, but the other guy was really belligerent. I think they maybe took it outside."

"Why do you say that?"

"Happens a lot."

"But you're not sure."

Charlotte shook her head. "I had to dance. When I finished, they weren't there anymore." Moss pushed aside the vision of Charlotte Gehenna dancing onstage, pole or no pole.

"What did this other guy look like? Do you know him? Had you seen him before or since?"

She shrugged. "I see a million guys. He wasn't a regular, I can tell you that. Average height, maybe thirty, dark hair. Trucker type, you know? He was wearing some kind of rock band t-shirt. I didn't notice what band."

Moss told her he might have to show her some photos, and Charlotte suggested someplace quieter. Based on her vague description, he was definitely going to put together a mug shot package of local criminals. In Las Vegas, he'd have a lot to choose from.

Interviewing the redhead again would be tough duty, but someone had to do it.

91

West Palm Beach, Florida – Five Weeks Later

The affair had been hastily organized. When Reverend James Warren had announced he would be taking an indefinite leave of absence, Judy Reynolds had put together the farewell event, a barbecue on the church grounds. There were a few whispered questions, a raised eyebrow or two especially since Betsy Warren was absent due to a "family situation up north."

The party was well attended. It was a raw and windy evening, with the temperature in the sixties. George was cooking burgers and hot dogs on the large grill, made from a 55 gallon drum sawn in half. A pot of chili simmered away. When Dexter arrived, he waved and walked over to Judy and Warren, standing together on the lawn. The preacher's hair was slightly longer than it had been and he wore jeans and a windbreaker. They exchanged greetings.

"Hi, Reverend," Dexter said.

"Where's Marcy?" Judy asked.

"A little under the weather. Might be the flu."

"Sorry, Dexter," Judy said. "Need anything?" Dexter shook his head.

"Have you visited Joe lately, Dex?" Warren asked.

"Last Saturday. They say he's making real progress. That's what they tell me too, at the clinic."

"That's great, Dexter," Judy said.

"Every day without a drink . . . well, you know the saying. One step at a time," Dexter said.

Warren gave the little man a pat on the back. "I know you're trying, Dexter. You'll make it. I'd really like Joe to see how the new sanctuary turned out. I know he'd really be proud to see it at Sunday service."

"It's nice to have some elbow room," Dexter said.

"The new organ is wonderful," Judy said.

"Do you think the screen thing is . . . tacky? Is it too intrusive?" Warren asked. The words to the hymns now flashed on a screen that descended from the ceiling, off to the side.

"Not at all," Judy said. "It's an improvement, not having to always flip the hymnal pages."

"They're all doing it now," Dexter said. "That's what I heard."

They watched George flip burgers. One bounced off the spatula onto the grass. George looked around, scooped it up and put it back on the grille. Warren chuckled.

"So you're really leaving?" Judy finally said.

Warren nodded. "I need some time to sort things out. I couldn't lead the congregation right now. Besides, I need some time alone with Betsy. I don't know what you said to her after we got back, but she's hanging in there. Barely, but . . ."

"George will miss you, too," Judy said.

"Thanks for saying that. He means a lot to me. I talked to him a couple of minutes ago. We wished each other well."

Judy kissed him on the cheek and the minister smiled again warmly.

"Don't worry. I'll be back to check up on you guys from time to time. I'll miss you. I'll miss everybody." He looked toward the grill. "Especially George. Especially our goalkeeper."

George was looking over. Dexter and Warren waved; George wiggled the spatula.

"Please come back soon, Reverend."

Warren's eyes welled up. He pressed his lips together and nodded. "I'd best say goodbye to everyone."

Judy and Dexter watched him shake hands, mingle with the congregation. Later that evening, when she climbed into bed, she told George she thought it was about the saddest thing.

92

Eight weeks after Las Vegas, the memory of those tragic events had gradually receded to somewhere between dream and reality. George and Judy were back in familiar surroundings, almost a continent apart from the Oasis Hotel and Casino. The money was real enough – the new sanctuary had been completed, albeit four weeks late, with the replaced funds, and no one the wiser except George, Judy, Warren and Dexter. Joe Dykes, if he was aware, wasn't talking, but then again he wasn't talking at all.

Judy spent time consoling Tom's former fiancée, Jane Pont, who could not understand why Tom would have gone off by himself to a questionable neighborhood.

As the water receded from the drainage ditch alongside the new church, the half-eaten body of Erubiel Sanchez had been exposed. Fish and Wildlife located and killed the alligator, which hadn't strayed far from its food source. Palm Beach Presbyterian sent flowers to the family in Oaxaca. Erubiel's remains – all eighty pounds – were sent home in a metal coffin.

With Joe, Tom and Reverend Warren gone, there really was no one for George and Judy to talk to about the trip except each other. Dexter Wilcox had not been in their circle of friends before the pilgrimage, and except for the farewell barbecue George hadn't seen the little man since they left him at Baggage Claim at PB International. Judy had been to Palm Beach Presbyterian deacon meetings with Dexter, and they'd carefully avoided the subject of Las Vegas.

Sunday breakfast at the Reynolds residence was a routine scrambled eggs and toast affair. Judy was dressed in church clothes while George wore a Manchester United shirt and white shorts. He read the sports section as they drank coffee. She looked up at the clock.

"Time to go." She stood and brushed invisible crumbs off her dress as George looked out the window.

"Better take an umbrella. It's pretty cloudy."

"Sure you won't come? Meet the new pastor?"

George shook his head. "Naah, I've had enough of that stuff for awhile. Besides, I've got some things to do this morning."

"He's going to dedicate the new sanctuary. You should see it, George; it's beautiful."

"Yeah, one of these days."

"After all, you paid for a lot of it."

George lowered the paper. "Yeah, maybe I'll go next Sunday."

Judy had a wistful look. "Maybe next Sunday . . ."

*   *   *   *   *

The church lawn had been dressed for the happy occasion. Ribbons, bunting, balloons, and a chocolate egg hunt for the toddlers. The south Florida weather was threatening; the forecast called for rain showers. The sun still shone weakly on the scene. A banner was strung across two temporary poles:

WELCOME REVEREND BLACK

Judy held a plastic water bottle and waited, along with most of the congregation, for the arrival of the new minister. She found herself next to Dexter.

"Hello, Judy," he said.

"Good morning, Dexter. How are you?"

"Oh, I'm okay."

Judy looked around the crowd. "How's Marcy? I don't see her this morning." Perhaps she was sick.

Dexter's eyes were downcast. "Oh, well, I don't suppose she comes anymore."

"What do you mean?"

"She moved out. It looks like our marriage is over."

"Oh, I didn't know. I'm sorry to hear that, Dexter. Are you sure?"

"Well, if moving in with her aerobics instructor is any clue, I'd say so."

At that moment, a black sedan with tinted windows pulled into the church driveway and proceeded slowly towards the gathering as the sun disappeared behind a low, heavy cumulus bank.

"Oh, that must be the new minister now," Judy said, standing on tiptoe. "I understand his wife is really sweet. Can't wait to meet them."

93

Las Vegas, Nevada

Tim Moss sipped his coffee and looked at his watch. He'd gotten the message to meet Wade Cahill at the IHOP on Las Vegas Boulevard, just north of West Sahara. Since Mary had moved out, he'd been getting up way too early, and so he'd arrived at 6:30 a.m. and was on his second cup. Surprisingly, the place was fairly busy despite the hour.

Moss thought that if they were going to meet on occasion, he'd need to upgrade the kid on his choice of restaurants. Nothing against the IHOP, but he did prefer the buffets, especially since he was now on his own for meals. The Main Street Buffet was his favorite; he hadn't wanted to go back to the Excalibur since Davey Cahill's death. Although, now that he was taking the stunning stripper Charlotte Gehenna to dinner Friday night, it might do to lay off the eggs and bacon and hash browns and doughnut for awhile.

Well, at least the doughnut.

Wade, in uniform, arrived promptly at 6:45. They shook hands, exchanged greetings. Cahill waved for the waitress. "I didn't want to get you up too early, but I'm on a four ten schedule. Sorry."

"That's all right. I got here early anyway. What've you got?"

"I don't know how I missed it. It's about the strip club homicide, Tom Swayne."

"Okay."

The waitress arrived. Cahill ordered o.j. and the breakfast sampler. Moss looked at the menu. He saw that the sampler could feed everyone in the place, with bacon, eggs, sausage, hash browns and two fluffy buttermilk pancakes.

The FBI agent wavered. Maybe he'd work out later and call it even. He ordered the same thing.

Cahill leaned forward. "Well, remember Swayne was with a church group, and they'd been to the Oasis and the one guy was a counter?"

"Sure."

"I didn't think to check out the church."

Moss hadn't either. Why would he?

"They were from West Palm Beach, remember?"

West Palm Beach. Something light seemed be crawling up the back of Moss' neck.

"They were from Palm Beach Presbyterian Church."

"Wait – that's—"

"Yeah. On Primrose Lane. 316 Primrose Lane."

94

West Palm Beach, Florida

As the sedan rolled to a stop in the Palm Beach Presbyterian driveway, a few miles away George wandered into the well-appointed, spacious master bathroom and picked up his toothbrush. He turned on the water and squeezed the tube, but nothing came out. He squeezed again, from the bottom this time, walking his fingers towards the opening, but the tube was empty. He opened the mirrored cabinet and a couple of drawers without finding a new one. He went over to Judy's half of the bathroom, where the marble counter continued to a vanity with chair underneath. He couldn't recall actually being on her side before. He slid open the medicine cabinet part way. A partially used toothpaste tube lay on the shelf. As he lifted it out, something fell to the counter and rolled into the sink. George picked it up. It was an empty prescription vial.

It had grown quite overcast outside; George saw a dim flash followed by distant thunder. He turned on the light over the vanity to read the label:

Hydrocodone 1 2 tablet(s) every 4 hours for pain

George slowly slid the medicine cabinet fully open. Dozens of vials rested on the shelves. He turned a few around to look at the labels. They all read the same. He picked up and shook a few; they were empty. Rapidly, he opened the other drawers and rummaged through the contents, lipstick and cotton balls and mascara and bottles of women stuff and—

Nothing else. He closed the drawers, replaced the vial and slid shut the medicine cabinet.

For a reason he didn't fully understand, George went back into the master bedroom and over to the sitting alcove where Judy wrote letters on her small, light blue Louis XIV desk. It was another place he never visited. He sat behind the desk looking out at the water. Veils of gray rain hid the Intracoastal both north and south, perhaps a mile or two away in either direction. They would arrive soon.

George sat for a moment, took a breath and slowly pulled out the center drawer. Inside, there was only an unmarked manila envelope. He removed it carefully, undid the clasp and took out the piece of paper. It was a legal document entitled

OASIS HOLDINGS
Boston, MA

LEASE In perpetuity

George scanned the single page. The contract was between Oasis Holdings and the Reformed Calvinist Church for the property at 316 Primrose Lane. The signatures at the bottom were Judy Reynolds, Treasurer and Rev. William Black. The shaky, childlike signature on the Oasis Holdings line read Father Patrick Corr.

The document was dated today.

George became aware that all background sound had become muffled. He could no longer hear the water in his sink. Slowly, he walked back in the bathroom and looked at his faucet.

It wasn't running.

Not for awhile.

Not here, anyway.

95

In the church driveway, the passenger door opened and a striking redhead emerged. The knot of well-wishers pressed forward, Judy in front. She was the first to greet the new minister's wife.

"Welcome to Palm Beach Presbyterian, Mrs. Black. I'm Judy Reynolds."

The redhead smiled a warm, dazzling smile. "Why thank you, Judy. It's a pleasure to be here. Please, just call me . . . *Charlotte*."

For a brief instant, her features morphed into those of Tom Swayne, silently screaming. The driver's window slid down. A hand appeared on the top of the door, pushing it open. Visible in the rapidly fading light was a large, ugly ring with an oval brown stone. The door opened fully and a tall, handsome man dressed in black emerged. He flashed a winning smile, not unlike the smile of Upton Black, or perhaps that of Francisco Negron, or maybe a bit like that of William Schwarz, but not at all like the grin of James Warren in happier times.

Dexter moved forward, extended his hand. "Welcome, Reverend Black!"

The minister turned to Dexter. "Thank you. You're very kind. I feel like I've been here forever."

As Dexter shook the hand of his new pastor, the skies, which had rapidly grown more leaden, opened suddenly and it began to pour. Everyone scattered and ran inside the new sanctuary.

Everyone except Reverend Black, Charlotte and Judy.

The three stood there in the downpour, still, not moving as the rain, driven by the frontal boundary wind, whipped at their clothing. A few of the congregation, safe inside the sanctuary, peered through the windows at the strange sight. Weren't they coming in out of the rain? They'd catch the death out there, it seemed. It was almost as if they were waiting for something.

A rear door to the black sedan opened slightly. Had there been someone else in the car? The door extended fully. An arm encased in black appeared, holding the armrest. The strange ring was visible on a withered hand. Slowly, a leg in black pants emerged, and then the ancient priest unfolded and stood looking at the new sanctuary, expressionless. Father Corr walked slowly over and stood next to the others. He reached into his pocket and came out with a vial as Judy Reynolds knelt on one knee. Had she dropped something? The priest opened the vial, withdrew a pill and made the sign of the cross before placing it on her tongue. She crossed herself, rose, turned and walked into the sanctuary and took a place at the window, gazing out toward the driveway.

Still unmoving, the Unholy Trinity smiled at each other with milk white, dead white eyes and chilling, knowing smiles as the rain poured down and cascaded through the channel in the sandy soil underneath the altar of Palm Beach Presbyterian, dislodging Erubio Sanchez's box of dynamite and causing the rear wall to move the last two inches.

END

www.ingramcontent.com/pod-product-compliance
Lightning Source LLC
Chambersburg PA
CBHW072055020726
47501CB00003B/596